PRAISE FOR SIMON BRETT
AND THE FETHERING MYSTERIES

'A new Simon Brett is an event for mystery fans'
P. D. James

'Murder most enjoyable . . . An author who
never takes himself that seriously, and for whom
any fictional murder can frequently form
part of the entertainment industry'
Colin Dexter, *Oldie*

'A crime novel in the traditional style, with
delightful little touches of humour and vignettes
of a small town and its bitchy inhabitants'
Sunday Telegraph

'With a smidge of adultery thrown in,
some wise observations about stagnant marriages,
disillusioned lovers and the importance of friendship,
and, of course, plenty of whiffy red herrings, it all
makes for a highly enjoyable read'
Daily Mail

'This is lovely stuff, as comforting – and
as unputdownable – as a Sussex cream tea.
More please'
Brighton Evening Argus

'Crime writing just like in the good old days,
and perfect entertainment'

DEATH ON THE DOWNS

Simon Brett worked as a producer in radio and television before taking up writing full time. As well as the Mrs Pargeter novels and the Charles Paris detective series, he is the author of the radio and television series *After Henry*, the radio series *No Commitments* and *Smelling of Roses* and the bestselling *How to Be a Little Sod*. His novel *A Shock to the System* was filmed starring Michael Caine.

Married with three grown-up children, Simon lives in an Agatha Christie-style village on the South Downs.

Death on the Downs is the second novel in the Fethering Mysteries series. Simon Brett's most recent novel, *Death Under the Dryer*, is out now in Macmillan hardback.

Also by Simon Brett

A Shock to the System   Dead Romantic   Singled Out

The Fethering Mysteries
The Body on the Beach   The Torso in the Town
Murder in the Museum   The Hanging in the Hotel
The Witness at the Wedding   The Stabbing in the Stables
Death Under the Dryer

Mrs Pargeter novels
A Nice Class of Corpse   Mrs, Presumed Dead
Mrs Pargeter's Package   Mrs Pargeter's Pound of Flesh
Mrs Pargeter's Plot   Mrs Pargeter's Point of Honour

Charles Paris novels
Cast, In Order of Disappearance   So Much Blood
Star Trap   An Amateur Corpse   A Comedian Dies
The Dead Side of Mike   Situation Tragedy
Murder Unprompted   Murder in the Title
Not Dead, Only Resting   Dead Giveaway
What Bloody Man Is That?   A Series of Murders
Corporate Bodies   A Reconstructed Corpse
Sicken and So Die   Dead Room Farce

Short stories
A Box of Tricks   Crime Writers and Other Animals

SIMON
BRETT

DEATH ON THE DOWNS

A FETHERING MYSTERY

PAN BOOKS

First published 2001 by Macmillan

First published in paperback 2002 by Pan Books

This edition published 2007 by Pan Books
an imprint of Pan Macmillan Ltd
Pan Macmillan, 20 New Wharf Road, London N1 9RR
Basingstoke and Oxford
Associated companies throughout the world
www.panmacmillan.com

ISBN 978-0-330-44526-9

Copyright © Simon Brett 2001

1 3 5 7 9 8 6 4 2

A CIP catalogue record for this book is available from
the British Library.

Typeset by Intype Libra Ltd
Printed and bound in Great Britain by
Mackays of Chatham plc, Chatham, Kent

To Priscilla

Chapter One

The bones didn't look old, but then what did Carole Seddon know about bones? Her work at the Home Office had brought her into contact with forensic pathologists from time to time, but she didn't lay claim to any of their arcane knowledge. She was just an ordinary member of the public – in retirement an even more ordinary member of the public.

But any member of the public who'd done the rudiments of anatomy at school, who'd watched television or been to the cinema, would have recognized that the bones were human.

Carole saw them as she picked herself up off the floor of the barn. When she had realized the rain showed no immediate signs of relenting, she had tried to make herself comfortable on a pile of roughly cut planks. They were dark green with the slime of ages, but her trousers and Burberry raincoat were already so mud-spattered and wet that more dirt would make little difference. She planned to spread out a newspaper over the immaculate upholstery of her Renault when she got back to the road where it was parked.

Maybe it was the slime, maybe it was the fact that they had recently been moved, but the planks proved an unstable seat. When Carole had put her full weight on them, they had tipped forward, spilling her unceremoniously on to the hard earth floor of the barn. Their collapse revealed the bright blue fertilizer bags, out of one of which protruded the unmistakable ball-joint of a human femur.

The barn was not on one of Carole Seddon's regular walking routes. Indeed, she rarely went on to the Downs. Gulliver, her dog, was too easily distracted up there, over-excited by the smells of cattle, rabbits and other smaller but infinitely intriguing species of wildlife. Given the luxury of all that space, it would have been cruel to keep the dog on a lead, but she didn't trust him to return from his manic forays into the Downs. Despite impeccable Labrador breeding, Gulliver wasn't a natural country dog. He was at home on Fethering Beach; he knew it well, and always returned safely to his mistress from quixotic tilts at seagulls, breakwaters or the fascinating detritus that the tide brought in. Carole even reckoned he could, if necessary, find his own way back from the beach to her cottage, High Tor, in Fethering High Street.

But a sortie on the beach was the reason why Gulliver wasn't with his mistress that February afternoon on the Downs. The week before, with customary bravado, he'd attacked a seaweed-shrouded potential enemy, only to back off limping from a gash to his forepaw. His quarry had proved to be a rusty can with a jagged edge. An immediate visit to the vet, injections and bandaging had left Gulliver a mournful, housebound creature who snuffled piteously by the Aga, pressing his nose and teeth against the intransigent dressing on his leg. The bandages were swaddled in polythene to keep out the damp when he hobbled off with Carole on the essential toilet outings, which were the only social life the vet's instructions allowed him for a fortnight.

That was why Carole was up on the Downs. Without Gulliver's curiosity to worry about, she told herself positively, she had the freedom to roam. But in her heart she knew another reason for her choice of walking route. She was likely to meet fewer people on the Downs. In Fethering Gulliver was her prop. If she was seen walking alone on the beach, she might look as if she was lonely.

She had parked the Renault on the outskirts of Weldisham, a village on the foothills of the South Downs that looked from the outside as though it hadn't changed much since the days when Agatha Christie might have set a murder there.

The squat tower of a Saxon church rose above the naked trees. There presumably the aristocracy, the gentry and the commonalty might meet, casting suspicious glances from pew to pew after the dirty deed had been done. In the village pub, the Hare and Hounds, old men with rough-hewn accents might become indiscreet over foaming pints of ale, letting drop conveniently vital clues.

Weldisham offered a couple of homes substantial enough to host house-parties at which crimes could be committed. A scattering of smaller dwellings might accommodate those local professionals – the doctor, the solicitor, the vicar – who didn't quite cut the social mustard, but who could prove invaluable as suspects and witnesses.

There were two old barns in the village whose agricultural purpose was unspecified, but which would provide ideal venues for the discovery of the second murder victim, probably impaled by a pitchfork. And then there were small, flint-faced cottages to house the peasantry – the farm workers, the gardeners and the wheelwright – one of whose quaint dialect testimony would provide the final piece of the jigsaw, allowing the visiting sleuth to bring another malefactor to the unforgiving justice of the scaffold.

Though that was how Weldisham may still have looked to the uninformed observer, at the turn of the new millennium it housed a very different set of characters. The church looked no different, though its congregation could usually be counted without recourse to a third hand. And the Hare and Hounds, after many and varied refurbishments, was now owned by a chain whose corporate mission was 'to maintain the authenticity and individuality of idiosyncratic country local hostelries'.

A few Estate cottages remained as Estate cottages, though the farm workers who lived in them these days drove in closed tractors with heaters and music systems. Manual workers not employed by the Estate couldn't begin to afford Weldisham prices. The other cottages had been made over into bijou residences for the retired or for London-based weekenders. Solicitors and doctors, now rather higher up the social pecking order than they had been in Christie's day, still inhabited the middle-range houses, from which they made their short commute to local offices and surgeries. Some hardened souls resolutely travelled up to London on a daily basis, their constant assertions that they had found 'quality of life' undermined by the fact that for half the year they left and arrived back at their country idylls in pitch blackness.

One of the barns in the village had been tastefully converted into a dwelling with large rooms, high ceiling and horrendous heating bills. The other, whose mangy thatch slid slowly from broken-backed rafters, remained unconverted and was the subject of continual planning applications. But each approach ended the same way.

4

The Village Committee pointed out that the building was inaccessible behind other houses, and its residential use would necessitate the construction of a new road in Weldisham, which was bound to cause disruption to existing home owners. The barn was also too close to other dwellings; its use as a residential property could only cause a nuisance. So, despite the repeated efforts of the Estate and a sequence of developers who recognized its huge financial potential, the Village Committee stood firm. The planners, hyper-sensitive about press criticism of other blunders and eyesores in West Sussex, paid heed to their arguments and the barn continued its quiet decay.

Had it had a more visible profile in Weldisham, local people might have felt differently, but the barn had been built in a dip behind a row of houses and visitors to the perfect Downland village were completely unaware of its dilapidated existence.

And of the two seriously big properties, one remained in private ownership, while the other had been titivated into a 'country house hotel'.

Carole Seddon didn't know Weldisham well. She had been to the Hare and Hounds once, when her son, Stephen, had made one of his rare visits to the South Coast. The pub hadn't made much impression. It was too like every other idiosyncratic country hostelry whose authenticity and individuality had been maintained by a pub chain.

But she had no friends in Weldisham and that afternoon, after parking the Renault, she'd set off very firmly in the opposite direction from the village. There was a track rippling upwards over the swell of the Downs. On summer weekends it would be dotted with family groups and serious walkers with waterproofed rectangles of map hanging about their necks. On a damp Friday afternoon in late February there was no one but Carole on the track.

With the village behind her, she could see no sign of human habitation ahead. Man had been there, fencing up the curves of the Downs into huge rectangular fields, but man did not live there. The horizon seemed infinite, as though the undulations rolled into each other for ever. Carole felt that she could walk for days before she saw another human being.

The prospect did not worry her. Carole Seddon had trained herself to be on her own, certainly after the collapse of her marriage and, according to the uncharitable view of her former husband, David, for a long time before that. Loneliness, like dependence on other people, was a luxury she did not allow herself.

But she couldn't deny that she was missing her next-door neighbour. Jude had been away for nearly two weeks, having departed suddenly with characteristic lack of specificity as to where she was going, who she was going with or what she would be doing there. Only in Jude's absence did Carole realize how much she had come to rely on their occasional contact, the spontaneous knocks on her door inviting her to share a bottle of wine. Though their views differed on many subjects – indeed, on most subjects – it was comforting to have someone to talk to.

Still, Jude was away from Fethering for an undefined length of time. No point in brooding about it. Carole had been brought up with the philosophy that one just got on with things. She pulled her knitted hat down over short steel-grey hair. Through rimless glasses her pale blue eyes looked determinedly at the track ahead of her. She was a thin woman, as spare in outline as a piece of cutlery, and, in her early fifties, the age when women can start to become invisible. But for the fact that she was the only person on the Downs that afternoon, no one would have given her a second glance. And that was the way Carole Seddon liked it, and the way she wanted things to stay.

The weather was sullen and threatening, truculent clouds ready to unburden themselves of more rain. Their efforts over the last week had left the ground heavy and clinging. On the higher parts of the track, strips of exposed chalk offered firmness underfoot, but in the wheel-troughs of its hollows coffee-coloured water lurked between banks of slimy mud. The sensible walking shoes Carole had bought when she took early retirement to West Sussex were quickly covered, and small commas of beige mud spattered up her Marks & Spencer's trousers and even to the hem of her precious Burberry. She realized – too late – that, though the raincoat was eminently sensible for walking on the beach, it wasn't suitable for the Downs. Never mind, she'd just have to take it to the dry-cleaner's.

She walked determinedly on. Like housework in the morning and the *Times* crossword after lunch, a walk was a necessary division in Carole Seddon's day. Without such disciplines and rituals, the time stretched ahead of her, unbounded and threatening. Gulliver's injury had broken the continuity of early-morning walks on the beach; a substitute needed to be found. Not just a walk, but a walk with a goal. And the goal Carole had prescribed for herself that afternoon was a high point of the Downs from which she could look down to the sea. Once that had been achieved, she could return to her car and drive back to Fethering, to Gulliver's enthusiastic but melancholy welcome.

The Downs, lacking the steep gradients of mountain

ranges, still performed the same kind of trickery, not peaks hiding higher peaks, but mounds hiding higher mounds. Carole, after some half-hour's walk, had reached what she thought to be a summit, from which she would be able to look down over the flat coastal plain, with its shining threads of glasshouses, to the sulky gleam of the English Channel.

But when she got there, another level shut off her sea view. In front of her, the track rolled downwards to a declivity in which trees clustered like hair in a body crevice. At the bottom stood an old flint-faced tiled barn, structurally sound but with an air of disuse. One of its doors was gone, the other hung dislocated from a single hinge. Outside an old cart lay shipwrecked in waves of grass.

Past the barn the track climbed up again to the top of the new level, from which the sea might perhaps be visible. Or from which only another prehistoric hump of Downs might be revealed.

Carole decided she'd walked enough. Forget the sea. She could see it from Fethering, if she was that desperate. When she got back to the car, she'd have been out an hour. That was quite long enough. Anything that needed to be proved would by then have been proved. She could get back to the comfort of her central heating.

Even as she made the decision and turned on her muddy heel, it began to rain. Not a rain of individual drops, but a deluge as if, in a fit of pique, some god had upturned a celestial tin bath.

Within seconds water was dripping off her woollen hat, insidiously finding a route inside the collar of her Burberry to trickle down her neck. It cascaded off the bottom of the coat, quickly seeping through the thick fabric of her trousers.

She was in the middle of the Downs, half an hour from the car. The barn offered the only possible shelter in the bleak winter landscape. She ran for it.

The inside of the building was fairly empty, though tidemarks of discoloration up the high walls bore witness to the crops that had once been housed there. And, though the roof looked in need of maintenance, it was surprisingly watertight. Here and there the shingles had slipped and water splashed down vertically into hollows made by previous rain. These irregular spatterings provided a rough melody to ride above the insistent drumming on the roof.

The thought struck Carole that she had put herself into a West Sussex minority. She was one of the few who'd actually been inside a barn, as opposed to the many who'd been inside barn conversions. The idea amused her.

She waited ten minutes before looking for somewhere to sit. But the deluge showed no signs of abating. The relentlessly sheeting water had made the day dark before its time. She checked her watch. Only quarter past three. She could give the rain half an hour to stop and still in theory get back to the Renault in daylight. Assuming of course that daylight ever returned.

So Carole sat on the pile of planks. And the pile collapsed. And the blue fertilizer bags were revealed.

Once she had identified the human femur, taking a large swallow of air and holding her breath, she leaned forward to look inside the sacks.

The bones were free of flesh, a greyish white and, when Carole did have to take another gulp of air, appeared not to smell at all. A cursory glance suggested that she was looking at the remains of one complete human body.

Inside the two stridently blue sacks, the bones had been neatly stacked and aligned like a self-assembly furniture kit.

Chapter Two

It was when she got back to the car that Carole realized she couldn't just drive straight home and phone the police from there. Human bones were not like other bones, particularly when they had so clearly been moved by another human agency. There could not be an entirely innocent explanation for their presence in the barn. At the very least, sacrilege had been committed. And at the worst . . . Carole didn't like to pursue that thought. All she knew was that the police had to be informed as soon as possible.

Pity she didn't have a mobile phone like Jude. Pity Jude wasn't there. Carole wanted to talk to her, throw at Jude some of the ideas jostling for prominence in her mind.

She was briefly tempted to delay contacting the police. The famed waterproofing of her Burberry had proved inadequate to the deluge and she was soaked to the skin. Also they looked to her like old bones. The fact that they had lain uninvestigated for years meant that another twenty minutes was not going to make a great difference in the cosmic scheme of things.

But Carole couldn't allow herself to be persuaded by such casuistical reasoning. She'd had a previous run-in with an unsympathetic policeman about delaying the provision of information.

Stronger than that, though, was an unease that her grisly discovery had started in here. Not fully defined, and she didn't yet want to probe into it too deeply, but she knew there was something wrong.

The bones had not been in the barn for long. The fertilizer bags were relatively unsoiled, and little dust or moss had accumulated inside them. Whoever had found that makeshift hiding place beneath the planks had been taking a temporary measure – perhaps a panic measure. It happened to be Carole Seddon who had found the bones, but someone else would have got to them very soon. The barn was remote, but not that remote. Someone owned the land it stood on, and that someone might well still use the space to house machinery, or have a system of regularly checking in case of vandalism.

So Carole knew that whoever had left the bones in the barn must have intended to return fairly soon to move them on. Indeed, she might have met the person. That thought sent down her spine a trickle much colder than rainwater.

She drove into the centre of Weldisham, though in a village of some thirty houses she didn't have far to go. There was a small grassy area, surrounded by a low railing, which she felt sure would be called 'The Green'. A noticeboard displayed a few dampish posters behind glass. There was a map for walkers, a reminder that Weldisham was a Neighbourhood Watch Area, a faded orange flyer for line-dancing on Wednesday evenings in the Village Hall.

And, sure enough, beside the board, was a public phone box. One of the old red ones – no doubt the Village Committee had rejected as unsightly any plans to replace it with a modern glass booth.

Carole dialled 999 and was very calm when asked which Emergency Service she required. The police voice at the other end was a woman's, solicitous, motherly. She took down the details Carole gave her, asked where she was and said how much it would help if she could stay there until her colleagues arrived.

'I'm sorry it's so wet,' the woman said. 'Is there somewhere you could go to wait out of the rain? The church perhaps.'

'I've got my car. And actually the rain's stopped for the moment. I'll stay parked by the phone box.'

'Very well. If you're sure you don't mind. It would help enormously if you could wait for our officers.'

Carole gave a grim inward smile. Her last encounter with the police had been with the Bad Cop. Now she'd got the Good Cop. It was disorienting.

The car was cold, so with a mental apology to the environment Carole switched on the engine to try and get some heat into her sodden body. The windows soon steamed up and, though she couldn't be said to be comfortable, she felt strangely peaceful. There was an inevitability about what was happening now. Carole had no decisions to make. Everything was in the hands of the police.

At one point she became aware of someone close by the car window. She swept a little circle in the condensation to reveal the face of an elderly woman with a beaky nose and a purple woolly hat pulled too far down her face. Carole smiled. The old woman continued to look at her with undisguised hostility. So much for the myth of everyone in the country being friendly.

Doing her bit for the Neighbourhood Watch, Carole decided. A strange car parked, engine running, in the

13

middle of Weldisham. It must belong to some burglar planning his or her next incursion. She tried another smile, her most unburglar-like one, and was about to wind down the window for reassurance when the woman abruptly walked away, dragging an unwilling black and white spaniel in her wake.

Soon after, the police arrived. A liveried Range Rover with two uniformed officers in the front and a plain-clothes man in the back. Carole felt obscurely disappointed. She'd expected more. A full Scene of Crime team with all their paraphernalia. And yet why? No one knew that a crime had been committed. Even she couldn't be sure. All the police had to go on was a call from a middle-aged woman who claimed to have found some human bones in a barn. She'd probably got it wrong, they got enough calls from cranks and the confused. Turn out to be sheep bones, cow bones, possibly even chicken bones left from someone's picnic.

The plain-clothes man got out of the Range Rover to greet Carole, profuse in his apologies for keeping her waiting on such a disgusting day. He introduced himself as Detective Sergeant Baylis. A thick-set man with short brown hair and a nose surprisingly small in his broad face, he had an avuncular manner beyond his thirty-five years. It should have been patronizing, but to Carole it felt immensely reassuring.

After her Bad Cop experience, she now felt like the subject of a Good Cop charm offensive. Was it just down to individual officers, or had one of those Home Office directives about the police becoming more user-friendly really had an effect?

DS Baylis checked the location of her find. 'Sounds

like South Welling Barn, Hooper. Go and see what you can find.'

As the Range Rover set off towards the barn, Baylis squinted up at the louring sky. It wouldn't be long before more rain fell. 'I'm sorry, Mrs Seddon, but I would like to check a few details with you.'

'Of course. Would you like to come and sit in my car?'

'Very kind, but I think I can do better than that.' He looked at his watch. 'Ten to five.' He produced a mobile phone from his pocket. 'Will Maples from the Hare and Hounds owes me the odd favour. I'm sure he can find us a warm room.'

In case any visitor did not know what the small alcove by the bar was called, the word 'Snug', carved on an authentically rustic shingle, hung over the doorway. Will Maples, an efficient slender young man in a sharp suit, ushered them in and switched on the log-effect gas fire. Though its initial flare was blue and cold, it soon emanated a rosy flickering glow, rendered suspect only by the fact that the logs never changed their outline or diminished in size. Carole knew about fires like that; she had a similar, smaller one at home in Fethering.

'Anything I can get for you?' asked the manager. He seemed over-anxious about their welfare, almost subservient, as if DS Baylis had some hold over him.

The nature of that hold was quickly revealed. 'Mrs Seddon's soaked to the skin,' said the sergeant. 'I'm sure she could probably do with a nice warming brandy. That is, Will, if you could see your way to bending the law a little and serving drink out of your licensing hours?'

Even without the sergeant's wink and the young man's blush, the implication would have been unmistakable. The Hare and Hounds had indulged some out-of-hours –

probably after-hours – drinking and DS Baylis had turned a blind eye to it.

'Certainly.' Will Maples bustled behind the bar. 'Is brandy what you'd like, madam?'

It was a drink she rarely touched but, lagged in dampness, Carole couldn't think of anything she'd like more. 'Yes, please.'

'Just on its own?'

'Thank you.'

'And will you take something, Sergeant?'

'Not while I'm on duty – that's the line the coppers always use on the telly, isn't it?' Baylis chuckled. 'I'll have a large Grouse, thank you, Will. Same amount of water.'

The manager placed a large brandy and the whisky on the table in front of them. 'Leave you to it then,' he said, and discreetly left the room.

DS Baylis took a gratifying sip from his whisky and nestled back into the settle. 'So, Mrs Seddon, if you wouldn't mind just taking me through precisely what you saw . . .'

It didn't take Carole long. At the end of her account there was a silence. She waited, anticipating further questions, or even disbelief. Like most people, from schooldays onwards she had always felt absurdly guilty in the presence of an authority figure, even one nearly twenty years her junior. She felt ready to confess to all kinds of things she hadn't done.

'Well, that's fine,' said DS Baylis easily. 'Let's wait and hear if Hooper and Jenks have found anything else on the site. Must've been a nasty shock for you, Mrs Seddon.'

And that was it. No further probing, no suspicion, no recrimination. Baylis moved on seamlessly to talk about his former ambitions as a footballer and how he still turned out, shift patterns permitting, every Sunday morning for his old school side. 'I was brought up round here and there's a bunch of us've kept the football up. Waddling old men now, though, I'm afraid. I used to be quite fast. Now I've got all these younger kids running circles round me. They still let me in the team. Don't know for how much longer, though.'

Carole realized that DS Baylis was rather good at his job. His apparently inconsequential chat was a kind of counselling. She was, as he had said, in shock, and his easy conversation masked an acute observation of her state. He was deliberately relaxing her, distancing her from the horror in the barn.

It was nearly six when his mobile rang. 'Yes, Hooper? Really think it needs a SOCO? OK, call them.' He listened to a little more from his junior, then switched off the phone and turned apologetically to Carole. 'Sorry, Mrs Seddon. I'll have to go. Ring me on the number I gave you if there's anything else.'

'There's hardly likely to be anything else, is there?'

'I meant if you had any adverse reactions to what you saw, Mrs Seddon. We could put you in touch with a counsellor if you like.'

'I'm sure I'll be fine, thank you very much.'

'Well, you just take it easy.' Good Cop had become Extremely Caring Compassionate Cop. What was happening to the police force?

There was a tap on the door behind the bar and Will Maples appeared with a tentative cough. 'Sorry, Lennie. I'm afraid we're going to have to open up.'

'Of course, Will. Can't keep the good people of Weldisham from their pints, can we? Could you do the lady another large brandy, please?'

'Certainly.'

'On my tab.'

There was another unmistakable wink from Baylis. And an embarrassed look from the manager. Whatever the hold Baylis had over him, Will Maples would rather it didn't exist. Carole felt certain that the tab which had been alluded to did not exist. But she did not feel the righteous anger such an arrangement might normally have fired in her. DS Baylis was a kind man, a good policeman. A few free drinks to ease relations with the public couldn't do much harm.

'You just relax, OK, Mrs Seddon.' He stopped at the door. 'Let's hope we meet again one day . . . in more pleasant circumstances.'

'Yes, I'd like that,' said Carole, as the latched door clattered shut behind him.

But she didn't relax. All she could think was that a SOCO was being called up to the barn. She knew 'SOCO' stood for 'Scene of Crime Officer'.

Which meant that the police thought there was a crime to investigate.

Chapter Three

Left on her own, Carole had an opportunity to look around the interior of the Hare and Hounds. Another carved shingle over a doorway the far side from the Snug announced that that way lay the restaurant. More rustic notices over doors beside the bar identified the toilets.

The atmosphere being sought after in the pub was that of a comfortable country house. There were pairs of riding boots and the odd crop, metal jelly moulds, blue and white striped milk jugs and cat-gut tennis racquets in wooden presses. Wooden-shafted golf clubs and antiquated carpenters' tools leaned artlessly against walls. Books were randomly scattered, without dust-jackets, their covers faded reds, blues and greens. Names like John Galsworthy, Warwick Deeping and E. R. Punshon gleamed in dull gold on their spines. To the wall of the Snug an ox yoke and an eel trap had been fixed. Behind the bar loomed a stuffed pike in a glass case.

All of these artefacts were genuine, but bore the same relationship to reality as the log-effect gas fire did to real flames. They had no natural affinity with their environment; they had been carefully selected to create an instant ambience.

Some of them also raised logical anomalies. For a start, everything that wasn't firmly screwed to the wall was in a glass-fronted cupboard or on a shelf out of reach. Suppose someone came into the pub and fancied reading a chapter of E. R. Punshon? They couldn't do much about it while the volume remained three feet above their head.

The piscatorial exhibits prompted the same kind of questions. The Hare and Hounds was a good five miles from the nearest river, the Fether, which reached the sea at Fethering. So it couldn't really be counted as a fisherman's pub. The eel trap looked quaint and out of place. There probably were eels in the Fether, but Carole wondered whether they had ever, at any stage in history, been caught by the contraption fixed on the wall. And, though she didn't know much about fish, she thought it unlikely that a pike would ever have lived in such a fast-flowing tidal river.

On the dot of six, Will Maples unlocked the pub's one exterior door, and was only just back behind the bar before his first customer of the evening arrived. Red-faced, in his fifties, ginger hair turning the colour of sand. Everything about the man seemed self-consciously to breathe the words 'pub regular', from his bottle-green corduroy trousers, deceptively clumsy shiny brown brogues, Guernsey sweater and over-new-looking Barbour to his cheery, 'Evening, Will, old man. Pint of the usual.' It was a voice that had been to the right schools, or learned to sound as if it had been to the right schools.

The man shook himself like a dog, as if to remove stray raindrops, though in fact there were none on the waxed shoulders of his jacket. He gave a quick nod to Carole through in the Snug, though with an air of puzzlement, almost of affront. How did she come to be there? He had the look of a man who prided himself on being first into the Hare and Hounds at six every evening.

'Evening, Freddie,' said Will Maples with automatic bonhomie. 'How's your week been?'

Carole corrected her surmise. It wasn't *every* evening that the regular made his appearance. Perhaps just Friday evenings.

'Bloody awful,' the man called Freddie replied. 'Up in the Smoke, dealing with bloody idiots all the time. Wonderful to be back down here. Minute I get off the train at Barnham, I feel my lungs opening up for the first time in a week. Bloody great to be back in Weldisham.'

On a day like this, thought Carole, in pitch darkness?

'Oh, it's a beautiful village,' the manager agreed, in a tone that made not even the smallest attempt at sincerity. 'There you are.' He placed the pint on the counter. 'In a jug, as per usual.' But his next words went even further to undermine his customer's status as a genuine 'regular'. 'Settling in all right then, are you?'

The man called Freddie raised his hand dramatically to freeze the conversation and took a long swallow from his tankard. He smacked his lips in a cartoon manner and licked the little line of froth from the upper one. 'Sorry, old man. Best moment of the week. Can't talk till I've done that, eh?'

He chuckled fruitily. Will Maples joined in, a meaningless echo.

'Oh, we're getting there,' Freddie went on. 'Pam has the worst of it, of course. She's been up and down from town like a bloody yo-yo this week. Trying to stop the builders treading wet footprints all over the bloody kitchen. Waiting in for deliveries of fridges and what have you from men who never bloody turn up when they say they're going to.'

'Still, early days.'

21

Carole was beginning to wonder whether Will Maples had a stock of bland responses to every kind of customer's remark and moved a mental dial round to the right one as required. Maybe it was a skill all landlords had to develop. She wondered whether Ted Crisp, owner of the Crown and Anchor in Fethering, had a similar range of programmed responses. Not for use with her, of course, but with the general run of his customers. Though she wasn't by nature a 'pub person', Carole Seddon tentatively liked to think of Ted Crisp as a friend.

'Oh yes,' Freddie agreed. 'Less than a month since we moved in. Rome wasn't built in a day, eh?' Once again the 'eh?' cued a fruity laugh, and a dutiful echo from the landlord.

The duologue was then opened up by the arrival of another regular, though this one's credentials seemed more authentic than Freddie's. Dressed in jeans and a thick plaid workshirt, the newcomer had a thin face, scoured red by exposure to the elements, over which hung a hank of tobacco-like hair. The fingernails of his large hands were rimmed with black. His mouth was a lipless line that didn't look as if it opened more than it had to. His age could have been anything between thirty and fifty.

'Evening, Will.' The words were the minimum politeness required, and were delivered with a nasal West Sussex twang.

'Nick, hi.' No order was given, but the landlord reached instinctively to a tall glass which he started to fill with Heineken lager.

'Hello, Nick.' Freddie's voice was full of common touch. 'Now let me get you that drink.'

'I buy my own, thanks.'

Freddie's face got even redder in the silence that continued until the pint of lager was placed on the counter. The man called Nick put down the right money, picked up his drink and moved to a stool as far away from Freddie as possible, at the end of the bar nearest to the Snug. He showed no signs of having seen Carole.

She looked across at Will Maples as Freddie embarked on a monologue about how careful you had to be with companies who did fitted kitchens. 'Always offer you special offers and discounts, but when you come down to it, you end up paying through the bloody nose for all kinds of extras, things they never actually thought to mention until it's too late for you to tell them to get packing.'

On the manager's face, too thin to be quite handsome, Carole could identify an expression of deep boredom. That, coupled with the young man's smart suit and metropolitan manner, suggested that he didn't see the future of his career in pulling pints. The Hare and Hounds was a temporary measure, a stopgap, or perhaps an essential staging post to the next promotion.

The disguised gas fire and the brandy were having their effect. Carole still felt sodden, but it was now a warm dampness. Though she could see no sign of it, she felt as though she were quietly steaming. Drowsy, but more as though she were drugged than about to fall asleep. Sleep, she knew, would not come easily that night. She would keep waking to the image of bones in fertilizer bags, a picture made more disturbing by its simplicity and anonymity. She would be haunted not by what she had seen, but by the implications of what she had seen. Detective Sergeant Baylis had been right. Carole Seddon was in shock.

The pub door clattered open again. The new arrival was thin and so tall that he had to stoop under the low entrance. He wore a three-piece suit in greenish tweed. It had cost a lot when collected from the tailor's. But that had been many years before. The elbows and the cuffs were protected with leather patches.

'Evening, young Will.' It was the patrician, slightly lazy voice of someone who didn't think he had anything to prove. But there was also tension in the voice, even a kind of suppressed excitement. Ungainly as a giraffe, the man propped himself on a tall bar stool and pulled a pipe out of his jacket pocket.

'Evening, Graham. Large Grouse, is it?'

'With a splash of soda, that's right. Hello, Nick.'

This latest arrival had received a nod of acknowledgement from the lager drinker by the Snug. Carole got the feeling that, had the offer been made, Nick might have accepted a drink from the man called Graham, whose manner was easily superior and didn't carry the patronizing overtones of Freddie's. The newcomer to Weldisham was too eager to please, too eager to be thought generous. Someone like Nick would take his time before accepting charity from such a source.

As he looked across to the Snug, Graham caught Carole's eye. He smiled courteously. The eyes had been brown but were now faded in his lined face. He was quite old, probably well into his seventies.

'Graham Forbes, isn't it? We met in here last week.' Freddie seemed anxious to receive his own acknowledgement. There was an air of power about the older man, something that, as a new boy in Weldisham, Freddie needed to tap into.

'Did we?' It wasn't said rudely, but without a great deal of interest.

'Yes. Freddie Pointon. I was in last Friday with my wife, Pam. Had dinner in the restaurant.' This did not seem to be a sufficient *aide-mémoire*. The old eyes concentrated on tamping down tobacco in the pipe bowl. 'We've recently moved into Hunter's Cottage.'

'Oh yes, of course.' Graham flashed a smile of professional charm. 'The Pointons. Irene and I were only just talking about you. You must come to dinner with us at Warren Lodge.'

'We'd enjoy that very much.'

'I'll get Irene to give a call to . . . er . . .'

'Pam.'

'Pam, yes, of course. So are you settling in all right?'

'Not bad. Having problems with the people who're putting in our bloody kitchen, mind.'

'Ah.'

The older man did not feign interest in the problems of kitchen-fitting. Carole suddenly identified the strange tension in his manner. It was excitement. Graham had news to impart. And he was waiting his moment, timing the revelation for when it would have maximum impact.

He took a long sip from his drink, made sure that Will had turned back from putting his money in the till and decided that the moment had come. 'Anyone see the police cars?' he began casually.

'I've been in here all day,' the manager replied. 'Bloody paperwork.'

Graham looked at Nick, who gave a curt shake of his head.

'I saw one at the end of the lane,' said Freddie, 'when I was on my way back from the station. Presumably they wait there to catch the poor buggers who've had a skinful in London and shouldn't be driving home.'

'That's not why they're there today.'

'Oh?'

'A rather nasty discovery has been made on Phil Ayling's land.'

Carole tensed. Surely he couldn't be talking about what she had found. It was too soon after the event. And the police wouldn't be volunteering information on the subject.

Graham Forbes played the scene at his own pace. He waited for a prompt of 'What?' from Will Maples before continuing. 'In South Welling Barn it was.'

Nick had his back to her and she couldn't see any reaction from him, but Carole was quick enough to catch a momentary narrowing of the manager's eyes. He seemed over-casual as he asked, 'What's been found then, Graham?'

'Bones. Human bones.' There was silence in the pub. Graham Forbes didn't need any prompts now. He had their full attention. 'A complete set,' he said lightly. 'That's why the police are here. Any number of them over at the barn. Lights, photographers, the whole shooting match.'

'But . . .' Will Maples licked his lips as if to moisten them. 'Have they any idea whose bones they are?'

Graham Forbes let out a dry laugh. 'Give them time. I know your chum Lennie Baylis is a bright boy, but I don't think even he could provide a complete life history from one look at a skeleton.'

'No.' The landlord chuckled, but he didn't sound amused. 'I wonder where they'll start their investigations . . .'

'You don't have to be Sherlock Holmes to work that out. Presumably they'll start right here in Weldisham.

Check out whether anyone's gone missing from the village recently.'

Will Maples was thoughtful for a moment. Then he hazarded, 'The Lutteridge girl?'

'That's a thought, Will.' The old head nodded insecurely on its thin neck. 'The Lutteridge girl.'

Chapter Four

'Oh, I've met the Lutteridges,' said Freddie, eager to be part of things. 'Met them at a drinks party we were invited to first weekend we arrived. Miles and Gillie, isn't it?'

'That's right.' Graham Forbes's manner towards the newcomer was diplomatically balanced. He was polite, but kept his distance.

'So this is their daughter you're talking about?'

'Tamsin, yes.'

'They didn't mention her when we met.'

'Probably wouldn't have done. She's hardly covered the family name with glory.'

'Oh?'

'Had a perfectly good job in London, working on some magazine or other, then chucked it just like that and came back to sponge off her parents.'

'I heard she was ill,' Will Maples interceded cautiously.

'Ill?'

'Some allergy or something.'

'Allergic to hard work, if you ask me.' Graham Forbes was clearly saddling up a hobbyhorse. 'Trouble with kids these days, they're cosseted. Cotton-woolled through school, subsidized by the state to laze around for three years at university. They don't even read, you know, just waste their time on videos and computer games. Then after university they come out into the real world, and is it any wonder they can't cope?

'I think drugs have a lot to do with it too. In my young day, everyone drank themselves silly, but drugs were for the really depraved. Nowadays, the kids seem to think no more of taking drugs than blowing their noses. And it's all over the place, you know, not just in the inner cities. Police stopped some kids in a car on the Weldisham Lane only a couple of weeks ago and found they were under the influence of drugs. God knows where they got them from.'

There was a silence. Will Maples looked studiously at the counter. If Graham Forbes was suggesting anyone had got drugs in the Hare and Hounds, it wasn't an accusation he wished to discuss.

'This is the Excuse Generation, you know. Whatever happens, whatever weaknesses of character kids show, there's always some excuse, some psychological reason for it. Father didn't show enough affection to them, mother showed too much affection to them, they've got an *allergy*.' The word was marinated in contempt. 'In my young day, we just got on with things.'

This statement, delivered with finality, seemed to require some endorsement. Carole couldn't say anything, Nick clearly never said more than he had to. Will Maples still seemed to be working round his mental dial, finding the right cliché rejoinder, when Freddie came in with the necessary response.

'Yes, you're right, Graham. They've had it easy.'

'You got children, Freddie?'

'No. Pam and I . . . No, we haven't . .' He seemed about to add something. 'Sadly . .' Carole wondered. Or 'Thank God'? It was hard to tell from Freddie's manner.

Will Maples seemed over-casual as he asked, 'You haven't heard definitely that it was Tamsin's body they found?'

'Not body, Will. Bones.'

'Comes to the same thing, doesn't it? Either way, the person in question's dead.'

'True enough. No, no, obviously not been confirmed it's anyone. Police have to do all their forensic stuff, off to the labs, what have you. But since you've mentioned Tamsin, I wonder . . . Could be right. She's the only person in the village who's gone missing recently.'

'How long's she been missing?' asked Freddie, eager to make up lost ground on village gossip.

'She disappeared round the end of October. The parents haven't a clue where she went. But she'd been funny for a while. Gave up a perfectly good job in publishing . . . Couldn't cope, like I said.'

'No, I think this discovery's pretty ominous. Tamsin was always a bit loopy, wasn't she? Quite capable of wandering off, high on drugs, falling asleep in the barn and dying of hypothermia. That's what I reckon happened.' Graham Forbes spoke with the manner of someone whose opinions were rarely contradicted.

'Do you actually know she was into drugs?' the landlord asked cautiously. 'Hasn't been any mention of it from the police, has there?'

'Hasn't been time for that. But I'm sure Tamsin was. Dressed like a hippie, didn't she? And she was certainly into all kinds of alternative therapies and what have you. Only one step from herbal remedies to herbal cigarettes. And only one step from them to the hard stuff, in my view.' Again, his view was presented as incontestable.

Carole was having difficulty keeping her mouth shut.

She knew more about the subject under discussion than anyone else present. She knew Graham Forbes was wrong. Whether or not the remains belonged to Tamsin Lutteridge, his theory of how she'd died was way off beam. The girl hadn't just curled up in the corner of South Welling Barn. Somebody had left her bones there in two fertilizer bags.

For a moment Carole was tempted to speak, to share her knowledge. But she stopped herself, surprised that she'd even contemplated the idea. It would have been out of character for her to have put her oar in. And she realized the reason why her inhibitions had been relaxed. She was drunk. The two large brandies, reacting with her state of shock, had gone straight to her head. She felt distinctly woozy. There was no way she could drive back to Fethering, particularly given the heavy police presence along the Weldisham Lane.

She had a sudden mental image of Gulliver by the Aga, feeling sorry for himself and his wounded paw. She looked at her watch. After six-thirty. She must get back.

Catching Will's eyes in a conversational lull at the bar, she asked, 'Is there a phone I could use?'

He pointed to a payphone by the entrance to the toilets. On a board above it were pinned cards from three local taxi firms. Carole tried them all. None could do anything for an hour. Friday evening was a busy time. The trains at Barnham were full not only of the usual daily commuters but also of second-home owners making the weekly journey to their country retreats.

Carole stood by the phone, undecided. She had a thought that wouldn't have come into her mind without the brandy. Making a quick decision, she dialled the number of the Crown and Anchor.

Ted Crisp answered. He seemed unsurprised by her request. Yes, he'd pick her up. He'd got two bar staff in. They could manage for half an hour. Friday nights didn't get busy in Fethering until after seven-thirty.

Carole put the phone down, slightly stunned by her audacity, but also pleased at what she'd done. Throughout her life she'd hated being dependent on other people, hated asking for favours. The fact that she'd asked Ted Crisp to help gave her a feeling of a slight mellowing in her character.

And, since the driving was sorted out, she felt like another drink. On her way back past the bar, she asked Will Maples for a large brandy. As she reached for her handbag, he said, 'No. It's on Lennie's tab.'

'Are you sure?' But then why not? If it was ever charged, it'd be on police expenses. Carole accepted graciously.

Her movement across the pub had made her aware again of how soaked through she was. It would be good to get home and into a hot bath.

Little more was said at the bar about the bones. Graham Forbes left soon after Carole had made her phone call. He downed the remainder of his whisky in a gulp and, pipe clenched between his teeth, announced, 'Better get back. People for dinner. Irene no doubt needs help with the seating plan.'

He gave courteous farewells to Will and the two men, a polite nod to Carole, and left. She took in his lack of overcoat, which must mean that he lived very close to the Hare and Hounds.

Conversation at the bar trickled away to nothing. Two girls arrived to start their seven o'clock shift at the bar and, since it was the first day for one of them, Will Maples was kept busy giving her instructions. Freddie made a couple of attempts to engage Nick in conversation, but met with no success.

Carole snuggled into her damp cocoon, brandy balloon reassuringly in her hand, and pondered what she had just heard.

Did the remains she'd found really belong to Tamsin Lutteridge?

But the more puzzling question was how on earth Graham Forbes had found out so quickly about the discovery of the bones at South Welling Barn.

Chapter Five

'Not my idea of a pub, that Hare and Hounds,' Ted Crisp grouched.

His presence seemed to fill the car. He'd arrived in the pub, looking as ever, hair and beard both in need of trimming, paunch in need of slimming. The usual grubby jeans, trainers and sweatshirt, with a zip-up hooded sweater over the top in deference to the February weather.

He'd nodded to Will Maples, but refused Carole's offer of a drink. 'No. Got to pace myself. Be drinking later at the Crown. Friday nights get frenetic. All the old farts and their doxies in, the air heavy with the scent of Germolene.'

At seven the Hare and Hounds had suddenly become busy. The 'Reserved' tables in the bar were quickly filled with people who were going to eat bar snacks, and diners started going through to the restaurant. Will Maples and his newly arrived staff had not a moment to turn round. But, Carole observed, it was an efficient operation. Will was a good manager.

He was too busy for her to catch his eye when she left. Never mind. It was Lennie Baylis she had to thank for the drinks, after all. With unexpected chivalry, Ted Crisp had picked up her Burberry. 'What you been doing?' he asked as he felt its sodden fabric. 'Auditions for *Singing in the Rain*?'

Carole had never been in his car before, but it was in character. An old Nissan Bluebird estate, its back seat and luggage space piled up with boxes. There was a stale whiff of beer and smoke. In fact, Carole realized as she got in, the car smelled exactly like the Crown and Anchor. So did Ted. He was a non-smoker, but he always smelled of cigarette smoke. An occupational hazard. His customers' smoke clung to his clothes, to his hair and to his beard.

'No, not my idea of a pub,' he repeated. 'Everything too neat, too calculated. No real character.'

This chimed in exactly with what Carole had thought. 'But you know Will, do you? I saw you nod at him.'

'In this job, you know most of the opposition, to talk to anyway. He used to manage clubs in Brighton, only recently moved into the pub trade. He's a bright boy, though. He'll go far.'

'How long has he been landlord there?'

'He's not the landlord, Carole. Just the manager. Works for the chain. Home Hostelries, they're called.'

'But they're just a small chain, aren't they?'

'Yes, but owned by one of the big breweries. Like everything else these days. I don't like places like that. A pub should have its own identity, not be part of a bloody olde English drinkers' theme park.'

'And what do you reckon gives a pub its identity?'

Ted Crisp chuckled wryly. 'Got to be your landlord, hasn't it? Reason, I'm afraid, why the Crown and Anchor is like it is. A reflection of me – a bloody-minded, cussed ex-stand-up comic. And people who don't like that can bloody well lump it.' He sighed. 'Trouble is, I don't know how much longer the independent landlord can keep going. What did I read in the paper the other day? Six village pubs closing every week. It's like the supermarkets killing off the village shops a few years back, isn't it? Only the big boys can afford the investment to keep a pub going.'

'Have you had approaches from some of the chains?'

'Oh yes, plenty.'

'From Home Hostelries?'

'Not yet. The Crown and Anchor's not quaint enough for them. They prefer something a bit older, more rustic. But other groups have been sniffing around. Not a great building architecturally, but the Crown's got a good position in Fethering. Someone with half a million could turn it into something *extremely bijou*.' He shuddered at the thought and was silent. Then he asked, 'What's the matter, Carole?'

'Matter? What do you mean?'

'You're upset. Something's upset you.'

Not for the first time, she was surprised at his perception. Ted Crisp's aggressive manner masked an unexpected sensitivity to the people around him.

Carole's instinctive reaction would normally have been to deny there was anything wrong, but the brandy had lowered her guard. Besides, she did want to talk about what she'd seen. Ideally, she wanted to talk about it to Jude, but Ted's large bulk felt reassuringly trustworthy.

'I found some human bones in a barn,' she said. The rest of her narrative didn't take long. There wasn't really much to say. Indeed, the smallness of the initial incident seemed disproportionate to the shock she was feeling. She included what she had heard from Graham Forbes in the pub and his potential identification of the victim. 'Do you know anyone in Weldisham, Ted?'

He shook his head. 'Hardly ever go up there. I think Jude's got some friends in the village, though . . .'

'Has she? Did she mention any names?'

Another shake of the head. 'When is it she's back?'

'Early next week? I'm not sure.' Suddenly Carole couldn't wait to see Jude. There was so much she needed to discuss. 'Did she tell you where she was going, Ted?'

She'd felt a sudden pang of jealousy at the thought Ted might have received confidences denied to her. But it was quickly dissipated by his reply. 'No. Never gives away much about what she's up to, does she?'

'Do you think that's deliberate?'

'What do you mean?'

'Do you think Jude deliberately withholds information? That she's secretive?'

In the oncoming headlights Carole could see his face screw up as he tried to get the right words for his answer. 'No, it's not deliberate. It's not devious, certainly. I'm sure if you asked a direct question, she'd give you a direct answer. I think it's more that Jude has a lot of different parts of her life and she doesn't really see the necessity for them to overlap.'

Ted's answer had the effect of making Carole feel even more jealous. Not jealous of him, just jealous of the rare serenity that surrounded Jude. They'd been next-door neighbours for nearly four months. Carole felt cautiously that she could describe Jude as a friend; and she was confident Jude would have no hesitation in describing Carole as her friend. But she still knew distressingly little about the new arrival in Fethering. She didn't even know whether Jude had ever been married, for God's sake. Was she divorced? Did she have a permanent boyfriend? Somehow the cues for such basic questions never seemed to arise. Jude wasn't evasive, she was very honest; but an air of mystery still clung around her. Mystery and serenity.

Carole would have given a fortune to know the source of Jude's inner peace.

They'd arrived outside Carole's house, High Tor, in Fethering High Street. 'I'd invite you in for a drink or . . .'

'No. No. Got to get back to the Crown. Before the brawls break out. Doesn't take much to get the old geezers hitting out with their crutches, strangling each other with the cords of their hearing aids . . .'

Carole chuckled. 'Can't thank you enough for picking me up.'

'No problem. You going to be all right to get up there for your car in the morning?'

She was tempted to see if he'd actually offer to take her. But no, she'd already presumed too much on his goodwill. 'Yes, I've got that sorted, thank you,' she lied. Organize a cab in the morning.

He was silent. 'And you're sure you're all right?'

'Absolutely fine, thanks. Hot bath, early night, be as good as new.'

'Great.' Another silence. 'Well, it's been very good to see you again, Carole.'

Surely she was wrong to detect a reluctance in Ted to let her go. No, that'd be ridiculous. She reached for the door handle. 'Good to see you too. And I can't thank you enough.'

'Keep me up to date,' he called out, as she stepped into the cold February night. 'When you find out who owns dem bones, dem bones, dem dry bones . . .'

'Course I will,' said Carole.

She waved as his car drew away. Gulliver, alerted by the click of the garden gate, set up a reproachful barking from the hall. He only did that for her. She never knew how he recognized her step. He never barked for anyone

else. Burglars could come and go into High Tor unser-
enaded.

But as Carole walked up the path to her front door,
she felt strangely elated.

Chapter Six

On the Saturday morning, the village of Weldisham looked apologetically picturesque, shamefaced about the bad weather of the day before. The sky was a clear pale blue, rinsed clean by the recent rains. Thin winter sunlight glinted off the stone facings of cottages, warmed the green of lichen-covered clay tiles and gilded the outlines of the naked trees.

As her cab drove up the lane from the main A27, Carole could see no evidence of police presence. She looked along the track up which she had walked the afternoon before, but again could see nothing. South Welling Barn itself was out of sight, tucked away in the folds of the Downs. They must still be investigating there, she thought, wondering whether the bones remained where she had found them, or whether they had been spirited off to reveal their secrets under the intense interrogation of a forensic laboratory.

It was half past nine when she arrived, but already the area in front of the Hare and Hounds had been neatly swept. In summer, like the garden adjacent to the car park behind, this space would be full of wooden table and bench units of the kind that can't easily be removed by the unscrupulous in search of garden furniture. Now there was just one low bench in front, on which customers could sit to obey the printed injunction 'Please remove all muddy boots and shoes.' By the locked pub door was a row of metal rings to which leads could be attached, and on the ground, also for the dogs, stood a green bowl of clean drinking water.

After paying off the cab, Carole squinted up at the pub's sign, which in the confusion of the day before she had failed to register. The painted animals had almost a cartoon quality, the hare close-up, bright-eyed and mischievous, looking over its shoulder at a straggling pack of black and white hounds, whose tongues lolled with the effort of pursuit. Their hunt was doomed to failure; there was no chance they were going to catch the hare.

Like so much about the Hare and Hounds, the sign was out of keeping in its rural setting. Its archness seemed to be saying, Yes, you really are in the country, but don't worry, there's nothing threatening or remote about it. You're still safely in the hands of a slick metropolitan marketing operation.

Carole crossed to her Renault, neatly parked opposite the pub, where she had left it the afternoon before, and was surprised to see that a piece of cardboard had been shoved under the windscreen wiper. On it, written in shaky but forceful capitals, she read: 'THIS IS PRIVATE PROPERTY. IF YOU'RE INTENDING TO DRINK TOO MUCH AND NEED A LIFT HOME, DON'T BRING YOUR CAR IN THE FIRST PLACE!!! OR IF YOU DO, LEAVE IT IN THE CAR PARK!!! THE NOISE FROM THE PUB IS BAD ENOUGH – PARKING HERE IS AN INSULT!!!'

Carole looked at the side of the road where she'd parked. There were no yellow lines, single or double. Nor were there any 'NO PARKING' signs in evidence. She hadn't left the car obstructing a garage or gateway.

She decided that she'd come in in the middle of a

long-standing argument between the Hare and Hounds and the owner of the cottage opposite. She looked for the name. An iron plaque with a white heron across the top identified it as Heron Cottage.

But of its resident, the writer of the note, there was no evidence. The windows, double-glazed leaded units, looked blindly out at the pub.

Carole wondered for a moment whether the owner might be the old lady who had looked so suspiciously into her car the afternoon before. The woman with the purple hat and the black and white spaniel. The note under the windscreen wiper would have been in character. But it needn't have been the same person. Perhaps, thought Carole wryly, everyone in Weldisham is equally unwelcoming to visitors.

She got into the car and immediately felt the dampness of the seat beneath her. Have to dry out the upholstery when she got back to Fethering.

And then a rather unpleasant thought struck her. Whoever wrote the note may have been generalizing, knowing that a car left overnight outside Heron Cottage meant someone had drunk too much to get home safely. But a much likelier explanation was that Carole had been seen parking the car and going into the Hare and Hounds. And she'd been seen being driven away in Ted Crisp's Bluebird.

In other words, someone had been watching her every movement.

She shivered, and not just from the dampness of her seat. She knew that not much went unobserved in Fethering, but that constant surveillance must be even worse in a tiny village. Everyone knew everyone else's business.

In spite of the beauty of the day, Weldisham suddenly felt claustrophobic.

The rest of Carole's Saturday passed uneventfully. She gave the car a thorough cleaning, inside and out. She took her Burberry to the dry-cleaner's. Gulliver's foot seemed to be giving him less pain, so she took him for the most extended walk he'd had since the accident. She didn't dare let him off the lead, which he thought to be a gross breach of canine rights, but his foot seemed to cope. His recovery was on track, according to the time-scale given by the vet.

At around six in the evening, Carole for a moment contemplated going to the Crown and Anchor for a quick drink. But that was madness. She was Carole Seddon, for heaven's sake. Fair enough to go out for a drink with Jude once in a while, but she wasn't the kind of woman who went to a pub on her own.

She put the idea from her mind and settled down to an evening of watching serious, historical things on BBC2.

As well as being vague about where she was going and why, Jude had also been vague about when she was coming back, so Carole was totally surprised to see her friend on the doorstep early evening on the Sunday. Jude wasn't dressed for outdoors. She wore a drifty cream shirt over a drifty long burgundy skirt, and had a sand-coloured drifty scarf around her neck. Her blonde hair had been piled up into a cottage loaf on top of her head. Her face had more colour than when she'd left, though whether that was from wind or sun was hard to say.

Above all, she looked welcome. There was something reassuring, calming, about her ample feminine contours. Her wide brown eyes prompted trust. Jude always seemed rooted, wherever she was, in touch with some unseen source of energy. In her right hand, characteristically, she held the neck of a wine bottle.

'Carole, hi. I just got back.'

'How are you, Jude?'

'Great.' She waved the wine bottle. 'Wondered if you fancied sharing this?'

'Well . . .'

'Or we could go down the Crown and Anchor, if you'd prefer.'

It was tempting. But no, that sounded rather unhospitable. 'Come in, Jude. Are you sure about the wine, because I've got some . . .'

'No, no, let's have this. It was given to me.'

'Where you were staying?'

'Yes.'

In the kitchen Carole busied herself finding corkscrew and glasses. Gulliver was winsomely pleased to see Jude. He slobbered all over her outstretched hand. 'You're in the wars, aren't you? What's he been doing to himself?'

'Cut his paw on a tin can on the beach.'

'Poor old boy. All right now?'

'He's on the mend. Come through to the fire.'

When they were sitting in the warm, with glasses in their hands, Carole decided it was time to elicit a few basic facts. 'Now, you never told me why you were going away. Was it business or pleasure?'

Jude grinned, but there was a hint of pain in her voice as she replied, 'Bit of each, I suppose.'

Carole pressed on. 'So where is it you've been? Abroad?'

'Mostly,' said Jude with an air of finality. 'What's been going on round here? Or is it the usual old "Nothing ever happens in Fethering"?'

'I haven't been aware of much happening in Fethering, certainly. Though, according to the *Fethering Observer*, plans for a new entertainment complex on the seafront have just been turned down. That's about the biggest news, I think.'

'What does an "entertainment complex" mean? Slot machines, arcade games, that kind of stuff?'

'Probably. Very *un-Fethering*, anyway. The residents here don't want anything to change, ever. Most of them moved to Fethering because they were looking for a place where time stood still.'

Jude tossed her loose bundle of blonde hair. 'That's not why I moved here. And surely it's not why you moved here?'

'Well . . .' Carole thought about it. 'I think it probably is why I moved here in the first place. That illusion people who live in London have that values in the country have more permanence, more validity perhaps. And, after David left me, it's maybe why I stayed here. I didn't want any more change then, I didn't want an environment that threatened any more surprises. Mind you, I don't think it's why I'm still in Fethering now.'

Jude grinned. 'I'm sure it isn't. Becoming a bit of a tearaway these days, aren't you, Carole?'

'Hardly.' But she was flattered by the idea. Jude seemed so different, so unconventional, so alien in the all-enveloping conformity of Fethering, that to be described by her as a 'tearaway' was rather flattering. Even if, as Carole feared, it wasn't really true.

'Anyway, that's it, is it? Planning permission for an entertainment complex turned down. Nothing more exotic? No New Age travellers' convention at the Yacht Club? No ramraiders emptying all the stock out of Allinstore – assuming, of course, that they could find any? Nothing else to set the weak hearts of Fethering aflutter?'

'Nothing in *Fethering*, no,' said Carole.

Inside, she felt a little bubble of excitement. It was the feeling she had identified in Graham Forbes in the Hare and Hounds on the Friday evening – the knowledge that she had sensational news to impart. The same news as he had had, in fact. And, like Graham Forbes, Carole was going to deliver it at her own pace.

'So where?' asked Jude, on cue.

'Weldisham.'

'Ah.'

'Ted Crisp said you'd got friends up there.'

'I know some people, yes.' But before Carole had time for the automatic supplementary question, Jude had pressed on, 'What, though? What's been happening up there?'

'A lot of police round Weldisham on Friday,' said Carole, deliberately enigmatic.

'What brought them there?'

'I did,' she replied proudly.

'How?'

Carole realized she'd strung out her revelation long enough. To continue the teasing would be merely tiresome. 'I found some human bones,' she said, 'in a barn on the Downs.'

The rest was quickly told – how she'd called the

46

police, her conversation with Detective Sergeant Baylis in the Hare and Hounds.

'Have you heard from the police since?' asked Jude.

'No. Sergeant Baylis has got my number, so presumably he'll be in touch when he needs to be.'

'And you're sure they were human bones?'

'I'm not a pathologist, but they looked like it to me. And, as I said, a SOCO team was called for. They're not going to do that if the victim is an animal, are they?'

Jude looked thoughtful. 'Nor if they're dealing with a natural death . . .'

'However natural the death might have been, you'd be hard pushed to explain away what was done to the bones *post mortem* as a natural phenomenon.'

'True.' There was a sparkle in her eye as Jude took a large swallow of wine. 'This is potentially rather exciting, isn't it?'

'Who knows? It depends rather on what the police come up with.'

'I'd have thought it depends on what we come up with.'

'Jude, we don't know for sure there's been a crime. We haven't even got a definite identification of the victim.'

'Your tone of voice suggests you do have some kind of identification, even if not a definite one.'

'Well, only pub gossip. I stayed in the Hare and Hounds after Sergeant Baylis had gone, and the manager and an old bloke in there said they reckoned they knew who it was.'

'Who?'

'Apparently there was a girl in the village who'd gone missing.'

The sparkle in Jude's eye was quickly extinguished.

Her voice was tense as she asked, 'Did the man say the girl's name?'

'Yes,' Carole replied. 'It was Tamsin Lutteridge.'

All the colour drained out of Jude's face.

Chapter Seven

It turned out that she had known the girl. 'Her mother, Gillie, brought her to me.'

'Why?'

'To see if I could help.'

'Help with what?'

Deliberately using the present tense, Jude said, 'Tamsin is suffering from ME.'

'Should I know what that is?'

'Myalgic encephalomyelitis. Though it's not called that now. I just thought you were more likely to have heard of ME than anything else.'

'Though, as you see, I hadn't.'

'No. Was known for a while as "malingerer's disease" or "yuppie flu".'

Graham Forbes's comments about Tamsin Lutteridge giving up her job and 'coming back to sponge off her parents' suddenly made sense. 'Oh yes, I've heard of that,' said Carole.

She had been brought up in the 'snap out of it' school of mental health treatment, and too much of that attitude must have come across in her voice, because Jude said firmly, 'It's a real illness, no question. Also called "post-viral syndrome". Most recent name I heard for it was "chronic fatigue syndrome", but there's probably something new by now. Doctors – those who believe it exists, and there are still some, I'm afraid, who don't – are divided on the proper treatment, anyway. All kinds of therapies are recommended, though the results are very variable.'

'But why did Tamsin and her mother come to see you about it?'

'Because I do some healing.'

Carole could not have been more surprised if Jude had said she did bungee-jumping. '*Healing*? You mean all that laying-on-of-hands nonsense?'

'Call it nonsense if you like. It sometimes works.'

'Yes, I'm sure it does, but . . . but . . .'

Carole tried not to think about illness. She knew what could be treated by aspirin, and she knew what needed a visit to the doctor for a prescription of antibiotics. Certain conditions required surgical procedures, and she devoutly hoped she would never experience any of them. Her attitude to alternative or complementary medicine was that it was all 'mumbo-jumbo'.

'Anyway, Gillie brought Tamsin to me, because she thought I might be able to help.'

'By "help" you mean *cure* her?'

'Maybe get her closer to a cure, yes.'

'And did it work?'

Jude grinned. Carole had failed dismally to eradicate the scepticism from her tone. 'Work? What does work mean? A complex illness like that, you're not going to get an instant result after one session. Healers aren't miracle workers.'

'That's the image of them that's projected in the press.'

'The image projected in the press of civil servants is that they're all boring and unimaginative . . .' It was rare for Jude to make such a pointed remark, and the fact that she did so showed that Carole had strayed into an area of strong belief. Jude eased the situation by smiling. 'But I'm sure that's just another mistaken popular stereotype.' Carole opened her mouth to say something, but Jude went on, 'So . . . my attempts to *heal* Tamsin didn't have time to have much effect. Whether they would have done, given that time, I don't know. But I do know they did no more harm to her than the various treatments traditional doctors had prescribed. As I said, we're dealing with a very complex illness. The mind and the body are deeply interinvolved in what happens to sufferers like poor Tamsin. Anything that might help is worth trying.'

Jude looked up suddenly, and Carole was surprised to see tears glinting in her friend's eyes. 'Poor Tamsin . . . What basis did this man you heard have for saying the bones belonged to her?'

'Very little, I imagine. Except that the girl was known to be missing from Weldisham. Simply putting two and two together, I suppose.'

'I must ring Gillie!' Jude reached into a pocket for her mobile phone. 'She'll be desperate.'

'Use my phone.'

But Jude had already got through. The tension she heard in Gillie Lutteridge's voice communicated itself as she made arrangements to go up to Weldisham the following morning.

After she switched off the mobile, Jude was still clearly upset, more upset in fact than Carole had ever seen her. The atmosphere of the evening was broken. Jude accepted Carole's offer of a lift up to the Lutteridges' the following morning, but seemed distracted. She finished her glass of wine and said, 'Better get back and sort out my unpacking.'

After Jude had gone, Carole realized with annoyance that she had no idea where the luggage that required unpacking had travelled from. She hadn't found out anything about where her friend had been for the past two weeks.

And by the next morning the moment for such questions seemed to have passed. Jude lived in the present and the future, always much more concerned with what she was about to do than with what she had done. Carole could only piece together her friend's history from the occasional irritatingly incomplete allusion.

The weather wasn't quite as perfect as it had been on the Saturday, but Weldisham was still doing a pretty good impression of an archetypal English village. The houses, mostly built before such concepts as planning existed, clustered round the spire of the church, as if theirs was the only configuration possible. Weldisham was meant to look as it did. There was no alternative. That air of permanence was comforting, reassuring, but to Carole in some strange way threatening.

She dropped Jude outside the Lutteridges' house. It was called Conyers, and Carole noticed that the name of the house next door was Warren Lodge. That must be where the Forbeses lived. The Lutteridges' was one of the village's middle-sized houses, late nineteenth or early twentieth century. Four bedrooms perhaps. Not grand, but still requiring a pretty high income in a property hot-spot like Weldisham. The privet hedge either side of the farm-style front gate was neatly squared off, the gravel inside raked and unmarked by leaves. On the drive sat a large BMW with the latest registration letter. The space either side of the house gave the impression of a large garden behind, dipping down over the curves of the Downs. Through the gap could be seen the top of an old barn's collapsing roof, a discordant note of untidiness that couldn't be part of the Lutteridges' property. Everything about their house breathed well-ordered middle-class affluence.

'OK,' said Jude. 'I'll be about an hour, then join you up at the Hare and Hounds. You be all right?'

'Of course. I'll have a walk. I've got the *Times* crossword, if all else fails.'

Carole took the Renault the hundred yards up to the pub and, just out of interest, drew it to a halt outside Heron Cottage in exactly the place where she had parked it on the Friday. And she sat there. Occasionally she glanced at the downstairs window. Through the leaded windows she could see a plaster shepherdess figurine on the sill and a faded silk pin-cushion in the form of a fat Chinaman.

Carole didn't have to wait long. Within two minutes, a face had appeared behind the shepherdess. The long sharp nose left Carole in no doubt that the author of the aggrieved note on her windscreen had been the old woman she'd seen walking the black and white spaniel.

Carole restarted the engine of the Renault and drove it round behind the pub to the Hare and Hounds car park. She tucked her folded *Times* inside her padded green Marks & Spencer anorak. (She still didn't feel right without her Burberry – she must remember to pick it up from the dry-cleaner's when she got back to Fethering.) Then she set off for a walk through the village.

The circuit didn't take long. Weldisham was really just one street, along which were placed all its houses, except for the peripheral farms with their clusters of outbuildings. The village seemed to be exclusively residential. One house with a disproportionately large bay window must once have been the village shop, but that had long since had the life choked out of it by the building of local superstores. Though no doubt they had complained bitterly about the erosion of country lifestyle when it closed, the well-heeled of Weldisham were soon happy to fill up their four-wheel-drive pantechnicons from the sumptuous choice available in the local Sainsbury's or Tesco's (mostly Sainsbury's, actually – in spite of its remarketing makeovers, Tesco's still carried a resonance of being 'common').

And that was it. Houses, the village green, the pub, the church. St Michael and All Angels. Carole decided she'd have a look inside.

She walked under the lych-gate, rustic but of recent construction. It was topped by a pointed lid of new thatch, still too light in colour, looking like a particularly indigestible wholefood breakfast bar. With a *frisson*, Carole remembered the derivation of the word 'lych-gate'. From 'lich', meaning a body. A place where the pall-bearers could rest the bier on the way to a funeral.

She wondered whether the bones she had found at South Welling Barn had received the benefit of any kind of religious committal. Somehow she doubted it.

The graveyard was full of green-stained stones, uneven like an old man's teeth. For one or two more recent arrivals the marble still gleamed, and fresh flowers – expensive in February – paid homage in glass vases. The grass between the graves was meticulously short.

In a corner of the portico of St Michael and All Angels, Carole noted with surprise there was a discreet CCTV camera. Security, presumably. A deterrent to the vandals for whom the holiness of the church had no meaning. The old wooden church door had a modern keyplate on it. Carole would have put money on the fact that it was locked at night.

She pushed the door and moved into the interior, which smelt of damp fabric. The air inside the church felt colder than outside. It took Carole's eyes a moment to adjust to the gloom. No lights were on and the February sun was too feeble to spread much through the stained-glass windows.

St Michael and All Angels was pretty and neat, well looked after. The wooden pews glowed from regular polishing. The brasswork of the hanging chandeliers had also been recently cleaned. Whoever was on the flower rota that week had invested a lot of pride in the displays down near the altar. On the wall a carved Christ twisted in frozen agony.

And there was someone kneeling in a pew near the front. Carole could see the outline of a fur hat on a head bent in prayer. And she could hear the sound of sobbing.

Her arrival had disturbed the supplicant. The sobbing instantly stopped. The figure, now recognizable as a woman, rose to her feet, brushed a hand across her face, gave a quick nod of respect to the altar and came up the aisle towards Carole.

As the woman passed, she flashed a quick shy smile at the intruder and left the church.

Carole had a fleeting impression of a tear glinting on a face of extraordinary beauty.

But, perhaps remarkably in Weldisham, the face was Chinese.

Carole had a desultory look around the church and paid a dutiful fifty pence into the honesty box for *A Brief History of St Michael and All Angels*. Then she set off for the Hare and Hounds to address the *Times* crossword.

Chapter Eight

It was only just after twelve, but already there were people having lunch in the Hare and Hounds. Their average age was probably round seventy, but they looked well groomed in their leisurewear and prosperous, enjoying their well-endowed pension plans.

For a moment Carole luxuriated in the boldness of walking into a pub on her own. She wasn't by nature a 'pub person' and a year ago she wouldn't have done it. The new boldness was a symptom of the changes that had come over her. Until she met Jude, Carole had expected – indeed courted – a predictability in her life in Fethering. Jude had shown her that change was possible, and even desirable.

Carole ordered a Coca-Cola. She was sure she'd have a glass of wine when Jude arrived, but she needed to pace herself. Mustn't forget she was driving. She was served by a girl she hadn't seen before. There was no sign of Will Maples.

All the seats in the Snug were taken, so she found a table for two by a front window that looked out at Heron Cottage. But after a brief glance across the road, she turned her attention to the crossword. Usually easy on Mondays. She had a suspicion the compilers did that deliberately, to make their addicts feel intellectually on top of things, put them in a good mood at the beginning of the week.

But, to her annoyance, that day's clues read like a foreign language. Carole's approach to the crossword was very linear. She always started with the first Across clue; if she couldn't get that, she moved to the second Across clue. Only when she'd got one correct solution did she investigate the possibilities opened up by its letters. And if she got stuck again, she'd move on to the next Across clue.

That Monday, the clues seemed particularly intransigent. She knew it was her attitude that was wrong. Solving crosswords required a kind of mental relaxation, a willingness to think laterally, to let ideas flow. But Carole's mind wasn't feeling relaxed. It floated over the words of the clues, not concentrating, not breaking them down into components to tease out their solutions.

She knew that her mind was really with Jude and what was happening in the Lutteridges' house. To her annoyance, she found herself at the end of all the Across clues without having got a single answer. She couldn't remember that ever happening before. With a ferocious effort of concentration, she focused on 1 Down.

'Tricky today, isn't it?'

She looked up to see the tall figure of Graham Forbes stooping over her. He was wearing the same three-piece tweed suit and holding a whisky glass. His unlit pipe was clenched in his teeth. He must have just arrived. He certainly hadn't been in the pub when she came in.

'Yes. Yes, it is,' she agreed.

'And one always thinks Mondays' are going to be easy.'

He so exactly reflected her own views that she grinned.

'Took me ages to get started today,' said Graham Forbes. 'Had to stay at the breakfast table much longer than I'd intended. Then I got a couple and it all fell into place.'

'Well, please don't tell me any of the answers.'

He raised a hand histrionically, appalled by her suggestion. 'My dear lady, what do you take me for? There is honour among crossword solvers, you know.'

'I do know. And I apologize humbly for my careless imputation.'

He chuckled. 'Didn't I see you in here on Friday?'

'Yes.'

'Have you just moved to Weldisham?'

'No, I live in Fethering, actually.'

'Ah. Different country.' He chuckled and indicated the chair opposite her. 'Mind if I join you?'

'I've got a friend coming . . .'

'Oh, well, I'll . . .' He made to move away.

'No, please.' Carole glanced at her watch. 'She won't be here for another twenty minutes.'

'I'll be gone by then.' He sat down and raised his whisky glass. 'Just always come in for my pre-lunch tincture, you know. Are you an every day *Times* crossword person?'

'Oh yes, part of my ritual.'

'Me too. Get in a very bad mood when I can't finish it. Wife knows to keep out of the way on those days.' Another chuckle.

Carole couldn't help being charmed by this man with his old-fashioned urbane courtesy. He seemed entirely different from the pontificator she'd heard talking on the Friday. Maybe she had misjudged his character. What had sounded right-wing might just have been nostalgia for a simpler time.

'Don't like a lot of things about *The Times* these days,' he went on, confirming her conjecture. 'Going very tabloid, all those colour photographs and what have you. Any excuse to get a pretty girl on the front page. And the Diary is an absolute disgrace. I'm afraid I'm of a generation that looks back fondly to the days when *The Times* didn't have any news on the front page.'

'I can remember that too.'

'Well, all I can say is you must've been very young at the time.'

Graham Forbes's gallantry was of another time, but it was comforting. Carole regretted that political correctness had rendered modern men wary of making that kind of remark.

'Tell you the favourite *Times* crossword clue I can remember . . . It was a Down clue, and it was just two words. "Bats do." Five letters.'

He looked interrogatively at Carole. ' "Bats do" . . .' she repeated slowly, trying to take the words apart.

'Not fair to throw it at you like that. You have to see it written to make sense of it. I'll tell you, because I don't want to prolong the agony. PEELS.'

'Right.' Carole nodded her appreciation. 'SLEEP upside-down. Bats sleep upside-down.'

'Exactly. Damned clever, I thought.'

'It is, yes.'

'Sorry, should have introduced myself.' He stretched a thin freckled hand across the table. 'Graham Forbes.'

'Carole Seddon.'

'Pleased to meet you. I live just a couple of doors from the pub, so I keep turning up here like a bad penny.'

He took a sip of his whisky. 'Lovely stuff. I swear my innards are pickled in it, you know. So what do you do, Carole?'

'I'm retired.'

'Really? Must've been an extremely early retirement.' Again the automatic chivalry contrived not to be offensive.

'Well, it was early, yes.' And that earliness still rankled with Carole. She hadn't wanted to stay till she was sixty, but she'd have preferred to have made her own decision about her leaving date, rather than being informed of it.

'What did you do before you retired?'

'I worked at the Home Office.'

'Fascinating. What part of the Home Office?'

'Moved around. A lot of the time dealing with the Prison Service one way or the other.'

'Hm. Travel much?'

'Only round this country.'

'I think maybe you were fortunate. Now I'm permanently settled here, I realize how much I missed about England.'

'You worked abroad?'

'Yes. British Council.'

'Oh, I had a friend at university who went into the British Council.'

Carole hadn't thought about him for years. She wondered whether he still kept up the front he'd maintained at Durham that he wasn't gay. Or maybe more tolerant times had allowed him to relax into his own nature. 'His name was Trevor Malcolm.'

Graham Forbes shrugged his thin shoulders. 'It's a big organization.'

'Of course.'

'Anyway, I worked for them all over the shop. Had

the place here in Weldisham for a long time, but only used to come back for leave and breaks between postings. Often wonder if I wouldn't have been happier staying here all the time.'

'I never think there's much point in talking about might-have-beens.'

'And you're absolutely right. What a sensible woman you are, Carole. No, I can't really complain. Seen some fascinating places, met some fascinating people. Real characters, you know, the locals, librarians, drivers we had . . . And yet . . . Oh well, it's human nature not to be content, isn't it? Always remember a line of Hazlitt's . . . "I should like to spend the whole of my life in travelling abroad, if I could anywhere borrow another life to spend afterwards at home." '

'That's good. I think it sums up what most of us feel.'

'Yes, grass is greener, all that stuff. No, can't complain. Had an interesting life, still with the woman I love at age seventy-five . . . What more can you ask, eh?'

'Not a lot.'

'No.' There was a silence. 'Incidentally . . . when you were in here on Friday . . . did you hear what I was talking about with that chap at the bar?'

Carole blushed, though there was no real reason why she should have felt guilty. Short of putting in earplugs, there was no way she *couldn't* have heard what was being said at the bar.

'About the discovery of the bones at South Welling Barn?'

'Yes. Well, putting two and two together, I reckon you must have been the person who found them.'

'Where did you get your two and two from?'

'Lennie. Sorry, Detective Sergeant Baylis. The policeman who you talked to.' In response to her look of surprise, he explained. 'Lennie talked to me on Saturday. I'm Chairman of the Village Committee here, you see. He wanted us to keep an eye out for press, snoopers, ghouls . . . You know, the people who turn up when something nasty's happened, the kind who queue up on motorways to look at pile-ups. Anyway, Lennie said he'd been talking to you in the pub, I saw you in the pub, I put two and two together.'

'Right. But was it Detective Sergeant Baylis who told you about my finding the bones in the first place?'

'Sorry?'

'Well, what struck me last Friday was how quickly you knew about what'd happened. I'd found the bones at . . . what . . .? Round four o'clock? And by six-fifteen you were in here, talking about them.'

'Ah, with you, see what you mean. Yes, it was Lennie. He was brought up here in Weldisham. He knows how the gossip-mill works in a village like this. So he gave me a quick call the Friday afternoon. Thought it better someone heard officially about what'd happened, rather than letting rumours run riot. Dangerous things, rumours.' Suddenly, he was into quotation.

> *'Rumour is a pipe*
> *Blown by surmises, jealousies, conjectures,*
> *And of so easy and so plain a stop*
> *That the blunt monster with uncounted heads,*
> *The still-discordant wavering multitude,*
> *Can play upon it.'*

'I'm sorry. I don't know the reference.'

'No reason why you should. I think it's probably too

obscure to crop up in the *Times* crossword. The Bard, inevitably. *Henry IV, Part 2*. The Induction. "Enter RUMOUR, painted full of tongues." I'm not sure that any of the good folk of Weldisham are actually "painted full of tongues", but they're nonetheless very skilled in the dissemination of vile rumour.'

'Ah.' There was a silence. Graham Forbes took another swig of whisky, before Carole asked, 'So was there something you wanted to say about the bones?'

'Sorry?'

'Well, you raised the subject.'

'Yes. Of course I did. No, I only wanted to say, so sorry, you have my sympathy. It must have been a horrible experience for you.'

'It has been . . . surprisingly unsettling.'

'I don't think you should be surprised at all that you've been unsettled. Ghastly for you, coming upon that little cache by pure chance. Or at least I assume it was by pure chance . . .'

'Hm?'

'Well, you hadn't set out looking for bones, had you?'

'Hardly.' She gave him a strange look, until she realized he was joking.

'I'm sorry, Carole,' he chuckled. 'You get plenty of odd types walking on the Downs. Archaeologists, people with metal detectors . . . Some of them probably are looking for bones.'

'Well, I can assure you I wasn't.'

'No. I'm sure you weren't.' Graham Forbes looked at his watch, swilled down the remains of his whisky and said, 'Must be off. Lunchtime. It's been such a pleasure to meet you, Carole.'

'You too.' She meant it.

'I'd love you to come and meet my wife, Irene, at some point. As I say, we're just down the lane. Warren Lodge. We always give a little dinner party Friday nights. Maybe we could inveigle you along to one of them?'

'I'd like that very much.' Carole was slightly surprised by the offer, but certainly not averse to the idea. Her Fethering social circle was narrow and not wildly interesting. It would be a pleasure to meet some new people, particularly if they were all as charming and cultured as Graham Forbes.

They exchanged phone numbers and he left for his lunch. Carole readdressed her crossword. Instantly she got her first solution.

The clue was: 'A sailor's in brass, for example, and bony (10).'

She wrote in METATARSAL.

Chapter Nine

Jude had been to the Lutteridges' house before, and the first time she had seen its interior she had been impressed by how 'finished' everything was. All the paintwork gleamed like new, the carpets might have been laid the day before, the furniture just delivered from the show-room. Jude, whose own style of décor was 'junk-shop casual', was amazed how anyone could keep a home looking like that. She could understand that a museum might maintain such standards, but couldn't equate it to an environment in which people actually lived. When she first went there, the fantasy grew within her that somewhere in the house was a glory hole, a haven of dusty squalor into which were tumbled all those miscellaneous objects which lend character to the average dwelling. But the more time she spent with the Lutteridges, the more that fantasy dwindled. There was no glory hole; the house was perfect throughout.

Gillie Lutteridge also looked as if she had stepped straight out of a brochure. Jude had worked out, from hints and date references in conversation, that Tamsin's mother must be in her late forties, but the smoothness of her made-up face and the immaculate shaping of her blonded hair could have placed her anywhere between thirty and fifty.

She didn't seem to possess any ordinary clothes, like most people did. Her garments came straight out of the brochure too – and a pretty up-market brochure at that. She wore them in a way that defied creasing. If she hadn't seen it happening with her own eyes, Jude would have sworn Gillie Lutteridge never sat down.

That morning, she was wearing a loose ash-grey cashmere sweater, black and white tweed trousers with ruler-edge creases and gleaming black shoes with gold buckles.

In spite of her deterrently flawless exterior, Jude got on very well with Tamsin's mother. Gillie was sensitive, compassionate, warm; she possessed all of the qualities that her appearance seemed to make unlikely. And, from the moment it first manifested itself, she had been deeply anxious about her daughter's illness.

But that Monday morning she seemed no more anxious than she had been when Tamsin disappeared from the family house four months previously. So unworried did Gillie Lutteridge seem that Jude wondered whether she had actually heard the rumours about the bones in South Welling Barn. Having no skills in prevarication, that was the first thing Jude asked her about.

'Yes, I heard,' Gillie replied. 'But that's just village gossip. I'm sure the bones have nothing to do with Tamsin. Tamsin's not dead.'

The words were spoken with firmness and a degree of calm. But was that just the desperate resolution of a mother unable to believe her child was no longer alive?

'Still, it must be hurtful for you even to hear people make the suggestion.'

Gillie Lutteridge shrugged her perfectly tailored shoulders. 'People are not very bright – certainly not here in Weldisham,' she said. 'They tend to go for the obvious. A dead body's found. A girl's missing. If you haven't got much imagination, then you assume the two must be related.'

'Have the police talked to you?'

'Yes. Nice young man, Lennie Baylis. I've often seen him round the village. I think he even used to live here. Anyway, he came. He was very reassuring.'

'What, you mean they've identified the bones and they definitely know they're not Tamsin's?'

'No. Apparently that'll take a bit longer. The . . .' For a moment her equilibrium was shaken by the thought of what she was saying. 'The . . . remains are at the police laboratories. But Lennie said there was nothing so far to connect them with Tamsin. There was no reason for us to panic.'

'It looks as if panicking is the last thing you're doing.'

'I'm very optimistic by nature, Jude. I'm positive Tamsin's still alive. Miles, though . . . Miles is taking it rather hard.' Gillie Lutteridge sank into an irreproachable armchair, giving for the first time some hint of the strain that she was under. 'Miles sees this as kind of . . . the end of a process.'

'What process?'

'The process that began with Tamsin's illness. That hit him very hard. Everything had always gone well for us. We'd been fortunate. Tamsin had always done well . . . school, university, walked straight into her job in magazine publishing. When she got ill, it was the first reverse in her life, in our lives too, I suppose. Miles couldn't really cope with the idea. He saw it as a reproach, almost as if it was his fault.'

'Of course, he never really believed in Tamsin's illness, did he?'

'No, he thought it was psychosomatic, that she was malingering. Everything's very black and white for Miles.'

'And very black at the moment?'

Gillie nodded. 'It's dreadful to see him like this. He's always been so positive. He's not gone into work today. The weekend was dreadful. Ever since Lennie Baylis told us about what had been found in South Welling Barn, Miles has just been twitching round the house, waiting for the phone to ring.'

'Is he here now?'

'In the garden. Pretending to be busy. He won't stay out there long.'

As if to prove her point, Miles Lutteridge appeared in the doorway. He looked at Jude with undisguised disappointment. 'Oh, it's you.'

The husband manifested the same brochure-like quality as his house and his wife. He was expensively dressed in a pale lilac jumper with a designer logo which hid the designer logo on the cream polo shirt he wore underneath. The creases in his beige trousers were as sharp as his wife's and his brown slip-on shoes carried the same shine.

The only things that would have kept him out of a leisurewear catalogue were his thinning hair on top and the expression of grey anxiety on his face.

'Good morning, Miles,' said Jude.

She knew he didn't like her – or perhaps just didn't trust her. She was too forcible a reminder of his daughter's illness, the very existence of which he sought to deny. He had met her once or twice when she'd come up for exploratory chats with Tamsin and hadn't disguised the fact that he thought her only one step away from charlatanism.

'I'm very sorry to hear about the rumours going round the village,' Jude continued. 'I'm sure it's nothing to do with Tamsin.'

'What do you know about it?' Miles Lutteridge demanded brusquely. In their previous encounters he'd always managed to stay the right side of politeness. Worry was taking its toll on his civility.

'I don't know anything for certain,' Jude replied evenly. 'I just think it very unlikely that Tamsin would have stayed around this area.'

'Do you mean you know where she did go?' The glint in his eye revealed both hope and suspicion. 'I bet she went off with one of your lot.'

'By "my lot", do you mean some alternative therapist who was trying to help her with her illness?'

'If "alternative therapist" is what you want to call it, yes. I mean some New Age quack doctor who took my daughter for everything she was worth by giving her false hopes he'd find her a cure.'

'Are you talking about someone specific?' asked Jude.

But Gillie decided the conversation had become too adversarial for polite society. 'Miles,' she intervened, 'it'll be all right, I promise.'

'How can you make promises like that? What meaning do they have? You aren't a god. You can't bring Tamsin back to life, Gillie.' He was getting very overwrought now. Tears glinted in his eyes.

'I don't need to bring her back to life. She is still alive.'

'Can you give me any proof of that?' he bellowed.

There was a long silence while husband and wife held each other's gaze. Gillie seemed about to say something, but decided against it. She looked down and shook her head.

'See!' He spat the word out. 'Why does it happen to my daughter? First she gets some phoney illness. Then she starts mixing with *alternative therapists.*' He loaded the words with contempt. 'And now she's probably dead!'

'Miles, she isn't!'

But he'd gone. Afraid to have his tears witnessed, Miles Lutteridge had stormed out of the room.

Jude talked to Gillie for a while, but little new was said. The mother retained her conviction her daughter was alive; the father was convinced she was dead. And all Jude was aware of was how much this new situation had driven a wedge into their marriage. While everything had been going well, Miles and Gillie Lutteridge seemed to have been fine. Tamsin's illness made the first crack in their unity, pointing up the differences between them – Gillie's belief in the illness and her search for a cure, Miles's disbelief and desire to pretend it wasn't happening. And the discovery of the bones at South Welling Barn had made that rift wider still.

Chapter Ten

Having cracked that first clue, Carole's mind moved up a gear and she had nearly completed the *Times* crossword by the time Jude joined her in the Hare and Hounds. They ordered cottage pie and yes, both did have a glass of white wine.

'Just the one,' said Carole automatically. 'Driving.' Then she asked about her friend's visit to the Lutteridges.

'Odd. Very odd.' Jude screwed up the skin around her large brown eyes. 'Miles was in a terrible state of panic, but Gillie seemed unnaturally calm.'

'Is she normally a calm person?'

'From the outside, yes. If you didn't know her, you'd have no idea what she's thinking. But over the time I spent with her and Tamsin, I did get to know her quite well, and she's not calm – at least not where her daughter's concerned. But this morning she kept saying she *knew* Tamsin was all right.'

'Positive thinking.'

'Maybe it's just that. I kept wondering whether maybe she was telling the truth. She knows that Tamsin's all right.'

'But if she did know that, surely she'd tell her husband? If he's in as bad a state as you say.'

'Yes. She would. Gillie's always been very supportive

72

to Miles. She wouldn't let him suffer unnecessarily.' Jude took a thoughtful sip of wine. 'That's what's so odd about it.'

Their cottage pies arrived, each neat in its oval earthenware dish on a wooden platter. Another earthenware dish contained carefully apportioned vegetables, exactly the same number for each of them. The food looked fine. But the gloss was taken off it by the fact that Carole knew identical portions were being served at the same moment in every one of the Home Hostelries chain.

'Tell me more about these bones,' said Jude, as they started to eat.

'I've told you most of it. There were just these recognizably human bones in two fertilizer bags.'

'But you didn't get any feeling how old they were?'

'I'm not a forensic pathologist, Jude.'

'No, but ... I was just thinking ... Tamsin's been missing for four months. Left her parents' house on the night of Hallowe'en. I remember, because at one stage Miles thought that might have some significance.'

'Why?'

'He's very confused about complementary medicine. He assumed it had something to do with witchcraft.'

'I see.'

'Anyway, say Tamsin was abducted and murdered that very evening ... which is the first possible time she could have been ... would there have been time since then for the bones to get as clean as you said they were?'

'Depends where they were left. Out in the open on the Downs ... there are plenty of predators who'd pick all the flesh off them.'

'But if the body had been left in the open, someone would have seen it, surely?'

'Possibly not. I'm sure there are lots of secret places round here . . . copses, streams, old chalk pits. I should think it'd be easy enough to hide a body if you set your mind to it. I don't know, though . . . We don't really have enough information.'

As if putting a full stop to the conversation, Carole took a large spoonful of cottage pie.

'No. But think about it,' Jude persisted. 'The world is full of missing persons – vagrants, tramps, travellers . . . The bones could belong to any one of them. And yet everyone's assuming they're Tamsin's.'

'Village mentality for you.'

'I suppose so. And until Tamsin is actually found alive – or until the police prove the bones belong to someone else – they'll go on thinking it's her.' Jude speared a head of Home Hostelries broccoli and looked at it pensively. 'I think I'd better find Tamsin.'

'Where would you start looking?'

'I know some of the people she might have contacted.'

'What kind of people?'

'Miles Lutteridge and a lot of other blinkered locals would probably call them "New Age quack doctors".'

'Ah.' Carole didn't like to admit that she was probably one of the 'other blinkered locals'. 'And what would you call them?'

'I'd call them "alternative therapists". And some of them are good, and some of them are not very good, but none of them is deliberately trying to do harm. They're trying to help people . . . and very often they succeed. Anyway, I'll make some enquiries.' And she popped the piece of broccoli into her mouth.

'I think you should market it as one of the murder villages of the South Downs.'

Both women turned at the sound of the loud voice from near the bar. Indeed, most of the customers in the pub stopped talking and turned towards the sound.

The man who had spoken did not seem averse to being the centre of attention. His face was thin, its skin apparently drawn towards the point of a sharp nose. Probably in his forties, with wild hair that hadn't seen a brush – or shampoo – since he got up that morning, he wore a black beret and a long cracked leather coat of the style favoured by Gestapo officers in British war movies. His thin legs in faded jeans ended in large laceless boots which splayed out from his ankles. The glass in his hand looked as though it contained gin and tonic. He was nominally in conversation with Will Maples, who had appeared behind the bar, but clearly his observations were meant for the whole assembled company.

'No, it's good marketing, Will. Lot of people with ghoulish tastes around these days. Look at the way horror movies sell. You want to get some literature out to market this place. I'll write it for you, give it that professional gloss – for the right money. You know horror's my speciality. Eat your heart out, Stephen King. You haven't begun to see nasty until you've read my stuff.

'So what should I write for you, Will? "Come to the Hare and Hounds in Weldisham, the village of murder. Sit in the quaint bar, where the local serial killer supped his foaming pint while he targeted his next victim." ' The man giggled.

'Don't be silly, Brian.' The manager's manner was embarrassed, as if he wanted to ignore the speaker, but for some reason couldn't. His body language was trying to draw him away, but the man called Brian held him.

'We're not talking about serial killers. We don't know there's even been one murder yet.'

'Are you telling me that people who die natural deaths are in the habit of neatly stacking up their own bones in fertilizer bags?'

Though the man called Brian was speaking as loudly as ever, conversations around the pub had started up again. There was an air of that embarrassment that people often manifest in the presence of the mentally ill. The man didn't seem completely sane. Despite the jocularity of his manner, there was an edginess to him, a sense that his mood could shift very suddenly.

'And as to what you were saying about serial killers, Will my old darling . . .' The manager didn't look pleased to be the recipient of such an endearment. 'They've all got to start somewhere. You need the first murder before you can move on to all the others. We've only had the first one so far here in Weldisham, but that's the one with which he defined his ritual. Mm, I think I might make a very close study of this case – could be the basis for my next bestseller. Very gory it'll be. Watch out, young girls. The Weldisham serial killer is going to spend the rest of his days repeating in exact detail the way he killed Tamsin Lutteridge.'

Jude thanked any god who might be listening that Gillie and Miles weren't in the pub at that moment.

After she had dropped Jude at her home, Woodside Cottage, Carole put the car in the garage and went inside to the martyred whimpering of Gulliver. She felt frustrated. Jude had something to do. She was going to try to get a lead on the whereabouts of Tamsin Lutteridge. But there was nothing Carole could do that was in any way connected with the case.

Case? Was there a case? And if there was, what could it possibly have to do with her?

The telephone rang.

'Hello. This is Graham Forbes. We met in the pub just now.'

'Yes, of course.'

'I mentioned the possibility of your coming to dinner with us at Warren Lodge. Well, as soon as I got home, my wife, Irene, said she'd had a call from one of our friends who was going to join us this coming Friday. Been called away by a family bereavement. And I apologize that it's awfully short notice . . . but I wondered, Carole, if you might by any chance be free that evening?'

She accepted. But, as she put the phone down, she thought, that was quick.

Chapter Eleven

Jude was glad Carole wasn't with her. Much as she liked her new friend, she recognized that there were subjects on which they were unlikely ever to see eye to eye. And though Carole hadn't said much when talk of alternative therapies arose, her expression and body language had immediately invoked scepticism.

Jude's attitude was more tolerant. She knew the dangers of being too susceptible and relished the quote she'd heard somewhere that 'if you have an open mind, people will throw all kinds of rubbish into it'. But she was prepared to approach an idea without prejudice and assess it on its merits. The fact that something didn't work for her never led her to reject it out of hand. She didn't rule out the possibility that it might work for someone else.

Jude had never been drawn to organized religion and the belief system she held was one built up over more than fifty years of life. It wasn't rigid; as new thoughts came and old ones slipped away, the contents changed, but its overall principle remained the same. Jude believed that there was some purpose in human life, that it had been designed and was monitored by some kind of greater power. She believed that the most important relationships in life were not with that greater power, but with her fellow human beings.

And some of those relationships were easy and some were difficult. The relationship with the man who she'd just been travelling with fell into the second category. That one, Jude knew, was going to need sorting out soon. The prospect was not one she relished. She was glad she had the search for Tamsin Lutteridge to occupy her mind.

As a result of her instinctive tolerance, wandering round Soul Nourishment in Brighton's North Lanes, Jude saw nothing that prompted her to ridicule. She enjoyed the smell of incense and was untroubled by the sound of wind-chimes. Most of the stock in the tiny shop was books – studies of astrology, crystallography, ley lines, synchronicity and the meaning of dreams. *The Road Less Travelled, The Prophet. The Alchemist.*

But Soul Nourishment also sold New Age life-aids. Some of them had worked for Jude and some hadn't. Though admiring their beauty, she had never received anything spiritual from crystals, but she knew people to whom they meant a lot. The same went for the tarot and angel cards. But she had benefited from aromatherapy and so checked Soul Nourishment's stock of oils with interest. Acupuncture she believed in strongly, though she questioned the wisdom of selling needles and charts to the unqualified.

As with all tools for medical or spiritual healing, they were only as good as the practitioners using them. In her contacts with New Age healers, Jude had met very few out-and-out charlatans, but she'd met a distressing number of incompetents.

And few of them had been helped by the kind of patients attracted to such alternative approaches. Many of these were 'therapy junkies', men and women who felt there was something wrong with their lives and were looking for the quick fix that would, at a stroke, sort everything out. Such people tended to butterfly from one alternative solution to another, moving speedily from yoga to shiatsu to reiki healing to reflexology to colonic irrigation. It was the patients, more than the healers, who gave New Age remedies such a bad public image.

Silver, the owner of Soul Nourishment, was busy behind the counter, showing a display of scarabs to a bearded Californian tourist, so Jude moved to the back of the shop, where there was a cork board dotted with cards from counsellors, healers and therapists. Most of them offered solutions to problems of stress management, anxiety, phobias, personal relationships, alcohol and smoking dependency. Personal growth and major life changes were also catered for. Other cards raised the hopes of a cure for more specifically medical problems – eating disorders, depression, irritable bowel syndrome. Jude took down the numbers of the two that specifically mentioned ME or chronic fatigue syndrome.

'Jude, how're you doing?'

Silver had finished with his Californian and she had his full attention. As she planted a kiss on his cheek and gave him a warm hug, Jude wished, not for the first time, that he didn't dress so much like a stereotype. Everything about Silver seemed to say 'owner of New Age shop', from the Turkish cap on his head, past the chunky silver rings threaded into his ears, over the Indian cotton shirt, worn under a thick Bolivian waistcoat, down across the shiny striped harem pants to the thonged Greek leather sandals. His pale eyes blinked through blue-tinted thin-rimmed spectacles. How could Silver hope for his ideas to be taken seriously if he insisted on dressing like a caricature?

On the other hand, thought Jude, ever slow to

condemn, perhaps it goes with the territory. Just as the checkout girls in Sainsbury's wear hygienic, almost medical-looking tabards, so Silver was dressed in livery appropriate to his surroundings. One thing she did know, it wasn't done for effect. Silver was wearing the clothes he liked wearing and – even more remarkably, given their cacophony of styles – clothes he must have thought he looked good in.

Maybe he still got the thrill of nonconformity every morning when he got up and dressed. Silver, then known as 'Mr Silver', had spent twenty-two years teaching geography in comprehensive schools before he saw the glint of alternative light at the end of the tunnel. He had earned the right to make whatever sartorial statement he chose.

'I heard you were in Spain,' said Silver.

'Just got back on Sunday.'

'Terry said he saw you.'

'He was teaching yoga first week I was out there.'

'Did you do the whole fortnight?'

'No, just the first week. Did some body- and voice-work. Second week I went off to the coast. Seafood therapy.'

'On your own?'

'With a friend.'

She was upset by the pang even the mention of him caused her, but Silver didn't probe. Jude's private life was her own affair.

'You been busy?'

He nodded. 'Not bad. Particularly running up to Christmas.'

'Funny, really, isn't it . . . the major Christian festival of the year and people come here to buy things that very positively have nothing to do with Christianity.'

Silver shrugged. 'I'm cool with that.'

'Me too.'

He indicated the cork board. 'You thinking of enrolling in something? I'm doing a course in transcendental meditation. He's really good, the guy who leads it.'

Jude shook her head. 'I know the basics. Don't need to take a course.'

'No.' He blinked at her, clearly interested, but too laid-back actually to ask why she'd come.

'In fact, I was trying to trace someone. Girl I came in here with once. Probably last September, October ... Name's Tamsin.'

He shook his head. 'Lot of people come through, Jude.'

'I know. Tall, blonde girl ... very pale ... very pretty ...'

'Oh, now that does ring a bell. She was ill, wasn't she?'

'Chronic fatigue syndrome.'

'Yes, I do remember. Because she came in with you that time, and then, only a few days later, she was here again, on her own.'

'Oh? What was she after?'

'She was looking for some books, you know, on the relationship between mind and body. I pointed out a few titles for her.'

'Did she buy any?'

'She got *Setting Free the Soul*.'

'Charles Hilton?'

'Right.'

Jude looked at the board. One card was larger than the others and better printed. Beneath a picture of a large country house, she read:

Weekend Breaks for the Body and the Mind

SANDALLS MANOR
WESTRIDGE

Get Close to Nature and Close to Your Own Nature
Find the Self That Sometimes Can Get Lost

Proprietors: Charles and Anne Hilton

There was a Brighton-area phone number. Jude looked at Silver.

'Did Tamsin know about this?'

'Yes. I pointed it out to her.'

Jude nodded grimly.

Chapter Twelve

Silver had given her a brochure for Sandalls Manor and Jude looked at it in the taxi on the way there. She knew Carole would happily have given her a lift, but she still felt that this part of the investigation should be private.

The Tuesday morning was clear, the green of the Downs and the blue of the sky brittle in their brightness. Outside the car, Jude knew the cold would sting her cheeks. They were driving north of Brighton, where West Sussex and East Sussex meet and the Downs change identity, flattening out in preparation for mixing into the Weald of Kent.

The Sandalls brochure, like the card in Soul Nourishment, was expensively produced. It wasn't aimed at dispossessed hippies; instead it offered a taste of New Age attitudes to rich city dwellers.

Is your life so busy you haven't time to know you're alive? Have success and materialism taken away your identity as a human being? Have you lost your relationship with the earth that bore you and that nurtures you still?

If that's the case, then the Sandalls Manor experience could be for you. On one of our Midweek or Weekend Breaks, get back in tune with the rhythm of the seasons. What's more, get back in tune with your own rhythms. Spend some time with the self that you want to spend time with.

Sandalls Manor is set in the splendour of the South Downs, an area rich in history and spiritualism. Leave the cares of the city behind and look at nature as if for the first time. With small groups of like-minded people, enjoy vigorous – but not too vigorous – walks in some of England's most beautiful countryside. Then, with your appetite sharpened by all that fresh air, sit down to a nourishing organic dinner, lovingly prepared from the freshest local ingredients by our award-winning chef.

And, while the concerns of your body are being catered for, we do not neglect your more spiritual dimension. You're under no obligation to participate, but during your stay there will be a regular programme of classes in meditation, relaxation, yoga, body-mapping, soul-journeying and other consciousness-raising exercises. All of these are conducted by Charles Hilton, a fully qualified Jungian psychotherapist and teacher, whose book *Setting Free the Soul* has become an international bestseller.

Sandalls Manor may help you to shed your other addictions, but you'll certainly find its own atmosphere addictive. Many of our guests come back time and again, knowing that they'll leave, as one participant put it, 'feeling that I'd just had a full MOT on my Body and on my Soul'. Sandalls Manor can provide that kind of cleansing experience for you too.

Arrive as the person who gives you problems.

Leave as the person you want to spend the rest of your life with.

There was then a list of dates and prices. The latter confirmed Jude's opinion that Sandalls Manor certainly was an experience for the well-heeled.

The house, approached by a long gravel drive, was impressive. It had been the centre-point of an extensive farm, owned by Anne Hilton's parents in the days when farming was both respectable and profitable. They'd sold most of the land, leaving their only daughter extremely well provided for when they died within three months of each other. At the time of their deaths they had assumed she would soon marry one of her own kind, ex-Army perhaps, and stay at Sandalls Manor, breeding children and golden retrievers.

Had they known that Anne would end up marrying Charles Hilton, her parents would have turned in their graves with enough vigour to power the National Grid.

She'd met him through a friend who, as Anne herself put it, 'had gone a bit doolally' and set out to 'find her soul'. Since most of the people Anne mixed with were unconcerned about whether they had souls or not so long as there was plenty of champers, at first her friend's quest seemed 'an absolute hoot'. But all that changed when she accompanied her 'doolally' friend to a north London literary institute, where a session on 'soul-searching' was being conducted by Charles Hilton.

It was love at first sight – certainly as far as Anne was concerned. If the subject ever arose – and they were the kind of couple who brought it up with regrettable frequency – Charles maintained that he'd felt exactly the same.

But Jude, not normally given to cynicism, questioned the truth of his claim. She had the blasphemous thought that, for Charles, it might have been love at second sight, once he had found out about Sandalls Manor and the generous provisions Anne's parents had made for her.

She also found it hard to take at face value the seamlessly perfect – though childless – marriage about which the Hiltons went on so much. There were suggestions that Charles was not above taking advantage of the emotional one-to-one situations in which he frequently found himself with young women. His recurrent travels abroad on conference and teaching assignments provided him with plentiful opportunities, and sometimes he came back from these surrounded by a whiff of rumour.

Under normal circumstances, Jude was extremely resistant to rumour, but in this case she gave it credence. Once, when they'd been alone doing a co-counselling exercise, Charles Hilton had made a pass at her – so unambiguous that it was in fact more of a pounce than a pass. She had dealt summarily with the advance, pointing out to Charles that he was married, that she didn't fancy him at all, and that, even if he had been attractive to her, the manner of his approach would very quickly have cancelled that out.

But that moment of embarrassment gave them a history and even, Jude felt, gave her a sense of power over him. There was always the potential threat that she might tell Anne. It was for that reason that Jude had arrived unannounced at Sandalls Manor that Tuesday morning. She felt confident Charles Hilton would make the time to see her.

She paid the cab driver, but agreed that he'd come to pick her up in an hour, unless she gave him a call on her mobile to make other arrangements. He looked up at the impressive frontage of Sandalls Manor and shook his head wryly. 'Number of loonies I've brought up to this place you wouldn't believe.'

Jude was gratified that what he'd said presumably meant he didn't include her in the category. 'What do they do up here then?' she asked, faux naïve.

'You name it. Frolicking around naked in the summer, painting themselves, banging drums, screaming and shouting a lot. Down in Lewes,' he confided, 'I've heard people say they're into black magic.'

'Really?'

'Oh yes.' He chuckled. 'So if I come back in an hour and you're not here . . . I'll know you've been used as a human sacrifice, won't I, darling?'

He was still chuckling as his car sped off in an unnecessary flurry of gravel.

Chapter Thirteen

Though in many ways run like a hotel, Sandalls Manor kept its front door closed and Jude had to ring the bell. Anne Hilton came to open it. Jude had met Charles's wife before, but she didn't expect to be remembered.

She was right. There was no recognition in the woman's blue eyes as she uttered a deterrently interrogative 'Good morning?'

Anne Hilton was a large woman, designed for the heavy labour that had supported her family in previous generations. Although dressed in a long purple crushed-velvet dress, she would have looked more comfortable in a tweed skirt, jumper and pearls.

'Good morning. My name's Jude.' She spoke breathlessly, as if in the grip of anxiety. 'There's something I need to talk to Charles about.'

The approach had been carefully pitched. Charles Hilton, as a psychotherapist, would have a lot of patients unknown to his wife. And, though Anne's natural instinct might have been to send such unexpected arrivals packing, her husband would have instructed her to be more careful. He dealt with damaged people, and knew how destructive rejection could be to some of them. The last thing he wanted professionally was a suicide on his hands.

'It's extremely inconvenient,' said Anne Hilton, asserting what she really felt, before grudgingly standing back to let Jude enter the hall. 'Charles is busy conducting a session at the moment. You'll have to wait. And he won't be able to give you long when they do break.'

'I won't need long. I just need a quick word with him.'

'Do sit down.' Anne Hilton indicated a hard wooden settle. Jude wasn't going to be allowed to feel welcome. No invitation to wait in a sitting room. She must be reminded of the inconvenience she was causing.

'You haven't done any of the courses here at Sandalls Manor, have you?'

Jude shook her head.

'You should try one. Charles would be much more able to help you in a structured session than he will in a few moments' chat. Have a look at some of our literature.' She thrust across a handful of brochures. 'Now, if you'll excuse me, I've things to do. They break at half past eleven. I've got to get their coffee ready.'

The way this was said made it clear that Jude wasn't going to be offered a cup. Ungraciously, Anne Hilton marched off to the kitchen, closing the door behind her with emphatic force.

Jude looked round the hall of Sandalls Manor. The door Anne had gone through was marked 'Kitchen'; another closed door was identified as the 'Karma Room'. A framed painting of some Indian guru was fixed to the wall and in the stairwell hung a circle of metal tubes with a suspended wooden clapper in the middle. But these were the only concessions to the house's New Age incarnation. Otherwise the furniture and décor were solid and respectable, the kind passed from generation to generation of gentleman farmers. A redoubtable mahogany

staircase dominated the space. Through an open door –
in contrast to the promise of the sign reading 'Chakra
Room' – large chintzy sofas and swagged brocade curtains
could be seen. The impression was as far from the shabby
mysticism of Soul Nourishment as could be imagined.

But for the bonus of a little light therapy thrown in,
Sandalls Manor was like any other country house hotel,
and this was borne out by the 'literature' that Jude had
been given. As in the brochure she had read in the taxi,
all the fliers and photocopies of magazine articles empha-
sized the level of comfort offered by 'the Sandalls Manor
experience'.

One of them identified the 'award-winning chef' as
Anne Hilton herself. Jude got the feeling that Anne was
the dynamo behind the operation. She enjoyed running
an upmarket hotel. Had she married the sort of man her
parents had wanted for her, Sandalls Manor would have
offered activities such as horse-riding and clay-pigeon-
shooting. It was only because she had fallen in love with
Charles Hilton that soul journeys were on the agenda.

A muffled scream interrupted Jude's thoughts, and
reminded her that a soul journey was taking place at that
very moment. But a scream at Sandalls Manor was not a
cause for anxiety. Indeed, Charles Hilton would regard
screaming and hysterics as a validation of what he was
trying to achieve. Inside the Karma Room the participants
were getting in touch with their inner children, and if
those confrontations undammed some repressed emotions, then the therapy was working.

Jude looked round the hall, quickly to be rewarded
by the sight she was expecting. A box of tissues stood on
a highly polished dresser. A new sheet was fanned out in
readiness for the next participant to be overcome by tears.

Jude felt sure that the Karma Room and the Chakra Room would be equipped with similar boxes. In therapeutic processes like those conducted by Charles Hilton, tissues were always a discreet presence.

There was a clatter at the door. Jude turned to see a little cataract of letters tumble from the letter-box slit. Mostly completed booking forms, she reckoned. More exhausted city dwellers applying to sit out the rat race for a few days at Sandalls Manor.

Curiosity gnawed at her. She looked across at the kitchen and the Karma Room. Both doors remained resolutely shut.

Jude was always obedient to strong instincts and something told her she was in a significant moment. She moved swiftly to the front door. With her foot, she spread the uneven pile of letters. Most of them were, as expected, bookings sent in reply-paid envelopes.

But one of them wasn't. She looked at it closely to double-check, then crossed back to sit on her hard settle.

A few minutes later, the door to the Karma Room opened. The first session of the morning had ended. Only Charles Hilton stood in the doorway, so Jude deduced that there must be another way out to the room where the participants had their coffee. Also to the toilets. She knew that intense soul-baring frequently had an effect on the participants' bladders.

Charles looked exactly as she remembered him, a little below average height with a low centre of gravity. Olive skin, the thinning hair on his head very black, and liquid eyes the colour of horse chestnuts. He wore jeans and a loosely hanging grey knitted cardigan.

He also wore an expression of anxiety, that very traditional and distinctive anxiety assumed by a married man who fears his wife is about to find out something she shouldn't.

'Jude. Why have you come here? You haven't said anything to Anne, have you?'

She thought it was rather funny to see the state he was in. Here was a man with an international reputation for helping people find serenity in their relationships, and he was scared witless that his wife was about to be told he'd once groped another woman. The guru reduced to a gibbering guilty husband from a bedroom farce.

'What are you worried I might say to Anne?' asked Jude, extending his discomfort. She wasn't by nature vindictive, but Charles Hilton's double standards got up her nose.

'Well, I don't know, do I?' he replied petulantly. 'Why have you come here?'

'I thought you might have some idea where Tamsin Lutteridge is.'

'Tamsin Lutteridge?'

'You remember her. Girl with ME. Silver in Soul Nourishment said she'd got in touch with you.'

'Yes, I remember her. We did have a consultation. She thought I might be able to help with her condition.'

'And did you think you could?'

Her tone had not been sceptical, but Charles Hilton's professional pride was still stung. 'I've had a lot of successes in the chronic fatigue area!'

'I'm sure you have. I'm asking whether you had any success with Tamsin Lutteridge.'

His face assumed a complacent mask. 'Jude, you know I can't possibly talk about an individual patient. Medical ethics. Confidentiality.'

'All right. I'm not asking whether you've managed to

cure her. I'm asking whether you know where she is at this moment.'

He shook his head, his expression still complacent. 'Sorry, Jude. I'm afraid I can't help you.'

'Look, if you do hear anything . . . let me know. Her parents are very worried about her.' Well, no, they're not, actually, thought Jude. Her *father's* very worried about her.

'Of course I'll let you know.'

'Do you have my new address? I'm living in Fethering now.'

'Really? Almost neighbours.' He smiled. Now he knew she wasn't about to blow the whistle to Anne about him, Charles Hilton's customary cockiness had returned. He moved straight into chatting-up mode. 'Maybe we could meet for a meal or something one of these days . . .' Jude gave his proposition no encouragement. 'Give me your number.'

She did so.

'I must get back,' he said. 'Just done a really good session. Don't want the participants to lose their concentration.'

'No. Can't risk that.' Jude grinned. 'How's this lot going?'

'Good group. Getting through to them. Really stirring the soup, we are. *Ciao*, Jude. Great to see you again.'

He took her hand and held it just that little bit too long, fixing her eyes in a penetrating gaze. Why is it, thought Jude, that certain men – in the teeth of the evidence – think they're irresistible to women? Maybe Charles Hilton believed that his almost shamanistic powers gave him an added magnetism. And maybe, on some women, he did have that effect. Not on her, however.

It was too cold to wait outside for her taxi, but the car arrived dead on time. Anne Hilton came out of the kitchen to answer the driver's ring at the doorbell. She shuffled up the post and bade farewell to Jude with the minimum civility her upbringing allowed.

In the cab, Jude tuned out the driver's views on alternative medicine and black magic, two concepts that his mind seemed unable to separate. All she could think about was what she'd seen on the doormat of Sandalls Manor.

Among the returned booking forms had been a letter addressed to Tamsin Lutteridge.

Jude would have challenged Charles Hilton with that fact, if she had not recognized the writing on the envelope. The letter had been sent by Tamsin's mother.

Chapter Fourteen

Detective Sergeant Baylis sat comfortably in front of Carole's log-effect gas fire. Gulliver, with that immediate trust of strangers that made him such an ineffectual guard dog, fawned around the policeman, trying repeatedly to put his bandaged paw up on Baylis's knee. The dressing was much smaller now. On the Friday Carole had an appointment when the vet would remove it completely.

'I was really just calling to see that you were all right,' the sergeant said.

'That's very kind of you. I'm fine.'

'The effects of shock can sometimes be delayed, Mrs Seddon. If you do need any help . . . counselling or . . .'

God, thought Carole, isn't there anything these days you aren't offered counselling for? 'Really, I'm fine. It was just a nasty moment, but it's gone. I mean, it'd be different if she'd been someone I knew.'

'She?'

'The . . . The body . . . The person whose remains I found.'

'How do you know it was a she?'

'Why? Isn't that common knowledge?'

'It is, but only just. That's one of the things I was coming to tell you, Mrs Seddon. They were the remains of a woman's body.'

Now it had been confirmed, Carole did feel a shiver of something not unlike shock. 'Poor girl,' she said.

'Poor girl?'

'Yes, Tamsin Lutteridge.'

Detective Sergeant Baylis shook his head wearily. 'Oh, they're not still saying that, are they? Bloody Weldisham gossips.'

'You mean it's not true?'

'The bones are in the labs now. There'll be more detailed information soon. But the preliminary path. report tells us they belonged to a woman, probably aged thirty to fifty, and she died at least five years ago.'

Carole found it strange how much relief the news brought her. She'd never known Tamsin Lutteridge, but had felt Jude's affection for the girl and compassion for her illness. Whoever the bones did belong to, she was glad it wasn't Tamsin.

'So, Sergeant, they've no idea who the dead woman was?'

He shook his head. 'Take some time. We do have procedures, you know. Start with talking to people locally.'

'Like the person who owns the South Welling Barn?'

'Phil Ayling. Yes, we've talked to him. Needless to say, he doesn't know anything about it. Why should he? Probably those bones belonged to someone who's never been to the village. Which means of course that we will have to go through missing persons files, all that stuff.' He sighed in disbelief. 'Tamsin Lutteridge, though . . . Doesn't change, Weldisham. However many ends a stick has, the people in that village can be guaranteed to get hold of the wrong one. Always had a reputation for gossip, even when I was growing up there.' In response to Carole's interrogative look, he went on, 'Yes, I'm a local boy. My parents used to live in one of the cottages by the pub.'

'Near Heron Cottage?'

'That's right. Mind you, we're talking when all that lot belonged to the Estate. My dad worked for the Estate. All his life. Started at age fourteen, dropped dead driving a tractor when he was fifty-seven. And the cottages weren't all tarted up when we lived there, I can tell you. Estate sold them off about fifteen years ago. That's when the central heating came in, and the fitted kitchens, and the double-glazing – and the fancy prices.'

He seemed to realize he was digressing. 'So . . . Tamsin Lutteridge. I didn't even know the girl was missing.'

'Has been three, four months, I gather.'

'Not been reported missing.'

'Ah.'

Baylis caught her eye and said shrewdly, 'Lot of parents don't report it when their kids go missing. Either they think it's an admission of failure on their part – which it very probably is – or they know full well where the child is, but don't want anyone else to know. Again they may keep schtum because their child's actions, or the company they're keeping, might be seen to reflect badly on their parents.'

'I wouldn't know if that's the case with the Lutteridges. We've never met. But a friend of mine who knows them says the girl hasn't been seen for four months.'

'Well, at least the Weldisham gossips will have to change their tune now. We've issued a press statement about everything we know so far. Be on the local news this evening, I should think. Anytime then the phones'll start ringing.'

'With people who think they can identify the dead woman?'

'Yes, Mrs Seddon. We'll get every poor sad bastard in the country who's lost someone. Mass media are great, all that *Crimewatch* stuff, encouraging the public to ring in, but it does infinitely increase the loony count.' He looked momentarily abashed. 'Sorry, perhaps I shouldn't have said that.'

'It's all right, Sergeant. I know exactly what you mean.'

Baylis grinned and ruffled the loose skin of the head of Gulliver, who had by now fallen heavily in love with him.

'Incidentally,' Carole went on, reckoning she'd never get a better opportunity to satisfy her curiosity about the life of Weldisham, 'the woman who owns Heron Cottage . . .'

'Pauline Helling. What about her?'

'Nothing. Well, nothing serious. It's just . . . I haven't even met her properly, just come across her a couple of times, but on both occasions she's made me feel extremely unwelcome in the village.'

Baylis chuckled. 'Don't take it personally. She makes everyone feel unwelcome in the village – even the people who live there.'

'My car got left outside Heron Cottage overnight when you and I went to the pub.'

'And I bet you got one of Pauline's little notes on your windscreen?'

Carole nodded.

'You wouldn't be the first to have had that treatment, nor the last. It's a nuisance, I know, but there's nothing we can do about it.'

'Oh, I wasn't meaning it was a police matter. I just wondered why she was so antisocial.'

'You should raise the question next time you're in the Hare and Hounds, and I'm sure you'll get as many answers as there are people present.'

'And what would your answer be, Sergeant?'

'As to why Pauline's such a bad-tempered old bat? My answer would be a rather old-fashioned one, in these supposedly classless times. I think Pauline's "living above her station". She grew up poor, in a council house on the Downside Estate—'

'In Fethering?'

'That's right. Then her husband left her with a son to bring up. I think that's when she developed both the chip on her shoulder and her ambitions to be upwardly mobile. As a result, the minute she got some money, she bought Heron Cottage. The good folks of Weldisham didn't like that. People of Pauline Helling's sort, they reckoned, should know their place. They'd be the same with me too. Because my old man worked on the Estate. And I didn't go to *private school.*' He couldn't keep the scorn out of his voice. 'Not that it worries me,' he went on, once again disclaiming a hurt that he clearly still felt. 'The new people come to the village, saying that they want to get close to the old rural England, but they don't want any reminders of the people who used to live in that old rural England. And the prices get pushed up so high, none of the former residents can afford to live in these villages anyway. So that's why Pauline Helling makes everyone feel unwelcome in Weldisham – because she's always been made to feel unwelcome there herself.'

'How did she get her money?' asked Carole.

'They didn't like that either. If you live in Weldisham,

it's all right to get money from stocks and shares, or inherit it from Mummeigh and Daddeigh . . .' Baylis's jokey manner could not disguise the deep bitterness with which he was speaking. 'But Pauline Helling got her money from winning the pools! The pools! Weldisham reckons it's bad form even to know what a pools coupon is, and actually to win on one . . . well, that's the height of vulgarity. So from day one they'd got Pauline marked down as "common".'

'Were people rude to her?'

'Not insulting to her face, no. Not like they would be somewhere a bit more honest. In Weldisham you freeze people out with politeness. You smile when you meet them, you give them a nod, but you never invite them into your house.'

Carole grinned wryly. She'd encountered some of that aloofness in Fethering.

'So I would imagine,' Detective Sergeant Baylis concluded, 'that for the past twenty years the only person Pauline Helling has talked to is her son.'

'He's still around?'

'Brian? Oh yes, he's still around.' The sergeant spoke as if this was not an entirely satisfactory state of affairs.

'He isn't a writer, is he?' asked Carole, with sudden insight.

'He calls himself a writer, though there doesn't seem to be much evidence that he's ever actually written anything.'

'I think I overheard him in the Hare and Hounds yesterday.'

'It's quite possible. Hard not to overhear Brian. He's always been of the view that everyone within earshot should have the benefit of his conversation. He was like that at school. I was in the same class as him. Nasty sneaky little bastard then, and I don't think the passage of the years has changed him that much.'

'What kind of nasty?'

'Vicious to other kids. And to animals. Most people who grow up round here know how to treat animals. They're not sentimental about them, but they don't hurt them deliberately.'

'And Brian Helling did?'

'When he was a kid, yes. Killed a couple of cats in a way I still can't forgive him for. He thought it was a game. The rest of us didn't play that kind of game.'

'Oh?' Carole put her next remark as sensitively as she could. 'In the Hare and Hounds he did seem to be . . . a little eccentric.'

'Eccentric's generous. He's a self-appointed eccentric, just as he's a self-appointed writer. Brian Helling has never been able to hold down a proper job. If his mother hadn't had the pools money to support him, God knows what he'd have lived on. He's always been getting into trouble of one sort or another.'

'Trouble that's involved the police?'

'Not often. Occasionally drunk. Reckless driving once, I think.'

'What about drugs?'

A shadow of caution crossed the sergeant's face. 'I'm fairly sure he dabbles in drugs, but he's never been convicted for it. No, he's not into anything that you'd call major-league criminal. Brian's always been a bloody nuisance, though – just like he was at school. Always trying to join everyone else's gang – and nobody wanted anything to do with him, because he was . . . I don't know . . . creepy.'

'In the Hare and Hounds yesterday,' said Carole, 'he was talking about the possibility of there being a serial killer in Weldisham.'

'Was he?' Detective Sergeant Baylis turned very pale. 'Was he really?'

Chapter Fifteen

'The bones weren't Tamsin Lutteridge's!' Carole and Jude spoke the words simultaneously.

Baylis had gone and Carole had hurried to answer the doorbell's summons, hoping it was Jude. She was dying to share her news. And amazed that Jude had the same news to impart.

'What do you mean? Come in. It's cold.'

'What do *you* mean? How do you know it's not Tamsin?'

'Just had Detective Sergeant Baylis round. Can I get you a coffee?'

'No, thanks.'

They went through into the sitting room and Carole quickly brought her friend up to date with what Baylis had said about the bones. 'I should have realized at the time. When I think about it, the bones looked old. Older than four months, anyway.'

'You weren't to know. You're not a pathologist. And there are all kinds of factors that can affect how quickly a body decomposes . . . whether it's left in water . . . if scavengers can get at it . . .'

'Maybe. I still think I should have known.' Carole had never enjoyed looking stupid – or, perhaps more accurately, thinking she looked stupid. 'Anyway, Jude, how did you find out they weren't Tamsin's bones.'

'Because I'm pretty certain Tamsin's still alive.' And she gave an edited version of her morning's visit to Sandalls Manor.

'Do you think she's being kept there against her will?'

'No, I'm sure her stay is entirely voluntary.'

'But you hear of these cases of young women getting caught up in cults . . . You know, falling under the spell of some guru and—'

'Carole!' Jude sounded uncharacteristically annoyed. 'This is nothing to do with a cult. It makes me really angry when people lump every alternative lifestyle in together. We're not talking about some crazed religious zealot here; we're talking about a psychotherapist with legitimate qualifications.'

'But from your tone of voice, it doesn't sound as though you like him very much.'

'I may not like him, and I may not like some of the things he does, but that doesn't stop me respecting him as a healer. Charles Hilton has had a great deal of success with bringing people back to health, both emotional and physical.'

Carole suspected that her friend was protesting a little too much in her respect for the therapist, but she didn't mention it. 'If Tamsin is up at Sandalls Manor, undergoing legitimate treatment, then why did he deny she was there?'

'Maybe he was respecting her wishes. If a patient asks for confidentiality, it's a therapist's duty to provide it.'

'But she's only a child. And her parents are so worried.'

'Tamsin's twenty-four years old. Quite old enough to make her own decisions. And I think it's only one of her parents who's worried.' Jude stood up with sudden resolve. 'Anyway, I'm about to find out.'

'Hm?'

'I'm going to pay another visit to Gillie Lutteridge.'

Jude accepted the offer of a lift up to Weldisham, but didn't respond to the unspoken request for them to do the interview together. Carole knew she shouldn't even have had the thought – Jude had Gillie Lutteridge's trust and they had discussed Tamsin's illness together – but, in spite of herself, Carole was getting excited about the case and didn't want to be excluded from any part of the investigation. However, she didn't raise the issue when she dropped Jude outside the Lutteridges' irreproachable house.

'Give me an hour,' said Jude. She looked up at the sky. It was only four, but already nearly dark. 'Don't know what you'll do.'

'It's all right,' said Carole, unwilling to appear resourceless. 'I've got time to make a quick raid on Sainsbury's.'

'OK. Then we can maybe go to the pub and see where we've got to – if anywhere.'

'The Hare and Hounds?'

'I was thinking the Crown and Anchor.'

For some reason, Carole didn't object to that idea.

Gillie Lutteridge looked once again as if the cellophane had just been removed from her package. This time she was wearing a burgundy chenille waistcoat over a cream silk shirt and black linen trousers, which, like every other pair she possessed, defied creasing. Flat black shoes with a little burgundy bow across the front.

Jude had phoned ahead, so she was expected. Before Gillie even had time to offer tea, she asked, 'Have you heard from the police about the bones?'

'Yes. I think they must have known earlier that they couldn't have been Tamsin's. It can't have been definite when Detective Sergeant Baylis came to see us, or he'd have said. But I suppose they didn't know about the rumours in the village, so they had no idea what we'd been thinking.'

'Miles must have been very relieved.'

'He's totally transformed. You cannot believe the difference between knowing your daughter's missing and thinking that she's dead. Now would you like some tea?'

Jude ignored the question and looked piercingly at Tamsin's mother. 'You, on the other hand, Gillie, don't look totally transformed.'

'Sorry?'

'You look exactly the same as you did yesterday.'

'Yes. Well, one has to keep up some kind of front, however much one's hurting inside.'

'What I'm saying, Gillie, is that I think you've known all along that Tamsin's alive.'

The shock in Gillie Lutteridge's face took a moment to establish itself. 'How could I?'

'Easily, if you were in touch with her.' Before the denial could come, Jude pressed on. 'I've been at Sandalls Manor this morning.'

'Ah.' The surrender was immediate. Gillie Lutteridge did not try to argue.

'By chance a letter in your handwriting arrived. Addressed to Tamsin.'

'Did you see her?' The question was full of maternal eagerness, desperate for any news of her daughter.

'Charles Hilton said she wasn't there.'

Gillie nodded, partly resigned, partly relieved. 'We'd agreed that. I was afraid that Miles might find out, and Tamsin . . . Well, she didn't want anyone to know she was there either.'

'Because she was ashamed of her illness?'

'No. She just . . . she said she wanted to vanish off the face of the earth for a while.'

'That's a rather strange thing to say.' Gillie shrugged. 'You don't think she meant she was suicidal?'

'No, Jude! Certainly not!' The girl's mother was appalled by the suggestion. 'Tamsin's got a bit depressed while she's been ill, but she's never thought like that. All she wants to do is get better, so that she can get back to her normal life. She'd never do anything to harm herself.'

'Good. So Charles is curing her, is he?'

'I hope to God he is, yes. She's having long sessions with him, and doing an exercise routine, and she's on a special diet. She has been getting better.'

'Has she?'

'Yes. Last week she was much stronger. She even came here.'

'What did Miles say?'

'He was away on business. Otherwise she wouldn't have come. Even then, she came in a taxi, after dark, so no one would see her. We just wanted to find out if she could cope.'

'And could she?'

The perfectly coiffed head drooped. 'No. Next morning she had gone right back. She seemed worse than ever. No energy, terribly jumpy and depressed. She didn't want to stay here a minute longer than necessary, went straight back to Sandalls Manor. That's what's so cruel about this wretched illness. Tamsin can go a day or two with hardly any symptoms at all, and then, just when she starts to make plans for the future, it comes back again.'

'But, in spite of that relapse, you still think Charles can cure her?'

'I'm praying that he can.' She read in Jude's face a scepticism that wasn't there. 'We've tried everything else! We've tried doctor after doctor. Tamsin's been in hospital for every test known to man. She's been prescribed vitamin supplements, tonics, antidepressant after antidepressant. Nothing has made her any better. Nothing has brought back her energy. Charles Hilton offers an alternative possibility. I'd say it was worth trying.'

'Yes. Yes, of course it is. Presumably the course will take quite a long time?'

'Chronic fatigue syndrome is a complex illness. There are no quick fixes.'

'I know. But I dare say one-to-one therapy with Charles Hilton doesn't come cheap.'

'I can afford it,' said Gillie defiantly. 'I got some money of my own when my mother died.'

'Ah.' Jude nodded her blonde head. 'I see.'

'See what?'

'You're using money of your own. You and Tamsin have agreed to this cloak of secrecy so that Miles doesn't find out.'

'Is that so odd? You've heard him on the subject of alternative therapists. Miles doesn't even believe Tamsin's illness exists. Just imagine what he'd make of someone like Charles Hilton.'

'Yes.' Jude understood completely. 'But, Gillie . . . what

I can't understand . . . when the rumours in the village started about the bones being Tamsin's . . . when you could see how much pain Miles was suffering . . . you could have set his mind at rest with just a few words . . . and you didn't. You could have told him you knew that Tamsin was still alive.'

'But then he'd have wanted to know how I knew. He'd have tracked her down, and destroyed her last chance of getting better!'

'Are you sure he would, Gillie? Couldn't you have talked to him about it?'

'No. I can't talk to Miles. I can't talk to Miles about anything.'

And, without the slightest tremor of her body, Gillie Lutteridge began to weep. Tears spilled and coursed down her cheeks, destroying the perfection of her make-up and spotting the immaculate collar of her silk blouse.

Chapter Sixteen

They watched the local news in Jude's cluttered sitting room. Although they'd already arranged to go to the Crown and Anchor, each had a glass of white wine in their hand. To Carole that seemed like the height of decadence. She also couldn't help stroking the new jumper she'd put on when she'd nipped back into High Tor to feed Gulliver. It was only Marks & Spencer's, but there was a bit of cashmere in the weave. And it was Cambridge Blue, a colour bolder than most in Carole's sartorial spectrum.

Jude's television was still a tiny portable perched on a pile of wine crates. And it still required a hearty thump before the snow on the screen resolved into pictures. Carole wondered why her neighbour hadn't replaced the set for something more modern. Could it be that Jude hadn't got the money to do so? One of the old gnawing questions reasserted itself. What did Jude live on? And how did she spend the majority of her time when she wasn't with Carole? Come to that, where had she been for the past few weeks? And with whom?

Carole realized she'd let the obvious cues for that last question slip past her. Well, never mind, that could still be remedied. She'd ask Jude straight: Where have you been the last fortnight? Such a direct question couldn't be evaded.

'Here we go,' said Jude, as the signature tune for the local news started.

And another cue had slipped past.

The news presenter had never quite got over being described as 'vivacious' in a school report. Probably at some point she'd also been said to have a 'bubbly personality'. As a result her lip and eyebrow movements were far too big for the television screen.

'Further to our report at the weekend of human remains being found near the West Sussex village of Weldisham, at a press conference today police . . .'

She hadn't much more to tell than they already knew. The skeleton was of a woman, aged between thirty and fifty, and she was reckoned to have died at least five years before. Police forensic investigations were continuing.

There was a clip from the news conference. As ever on the local bulletin, it was too short to have any meaning. Carole had a moment of surprise not to see Detective Sergeant Baylis on the screen, but quickly rationalized his absence. He was too junior in the investigation for such a role.

The detective inspector leading the inquiry, a face unfamiliar to her, said how committed the police were to finding out who the dead woman was and what had happened to her.

Then the presenter moved bumptiously on to introduce an item about a Jack Russell terrier in Gosport who had learned to use the cat-flap.

*

'It seems to me that there isn't a case,' said Ted Crisp, holding a pint glass he'd just cleaned up to the light.

'Oh, come on. There are the bones,' Jude insisted. 'They're real. They once belonged to someone.'

'Still do belong to someone, I suppose . . . depending of course on your religious persuasion. But the way I see it, there was this girl in Weldisham who everyone thought had disappeared, and so long as no one knew to the contrary, there might have been a link between her and what Carole found in the barn. But now you've lost that link, you're back to the much more likely scenario – that the bones have nothing to do with anyone in this area.'

'Surely—'

'No, listen, young Jude. In my long and varied career, I may have done a lot of things, but I've never actually committed a murder. Wanted to a few times, maybe, but I never succumbed to the temptation. And the fact that my former wife's still walking about is living proof of that. But even I – with my limited knowledge of murderers' know-how – can work out that if I *had* topped someone, I'd want to put as much distance as I could between me and the body. So it's much more likely that Carole's bones were paying their first visit to Weldisham – first visit to West Sussex, quite possibly.

'This is how I see it. You kill someone in Brixton, say . . . Don't know what – gangland turf war, drugs, whatever. Well, once you've done that, if you got any sense, first thing you do is get the evidence away from Brixton. South Downs, you think, that sounds nice, miles from anywhere. Dump the remains on the South Downs and scarper back home to Brixton quick as you can. That's what I'd do.'

Carole felt dispirited. For a start, what Ted Crisp was

saying was probably true. But also there was the way he was behaving towards her. Exactly as he always had in the past. She felt stupid for her misinterpretation of his manner to her last Friday, and even more stupid about the thoughts she had since allowed to flow from that encounter. If anything, Ted was paying more attention to Jude than he was to her.

But that was always going to be the case. Jude was more outgoing than she could ever be. People responded to Jude. They found her fun to be with. They found her sexy.

Carole had long since written off the possibility that anyone would ever find her sexy.

Anyway, Ted Crisp was very far from her type of man. He was scruffy, possibly not even very clean. His hair and beard looked beyond hairdressers' help. And he had no intellectual credentials. A publican who had formerly been a stand-up comedian. He was hardly the kind of man with whom Carole could see herself swapping clues from the *Times* crossword.

Jude, needless to say, wasn't cast down by Ted's arguments. 'No, there's more to it. Let's go with your murderer from Brixton, if you like . . . OK, all he knows about the South Downs is that they're a long way away from Brixton . . . So he drives down here, body in the boot, and he goes *by chance* up the lane to Weldisham, and once he's there he drives off into the wild, and *by chance* he finds this barn in the middle of nowhere. "Ooh," he thinks, "what a great hiding place for my body." Sorry, Ted, it doesn't work for me.'

In spite of herself, Carole had become caught up in the argument. 'What's more, where did he find fertilizer bags in Brixton? The fertilizer bags are the most interesting feature of the case.'

Ted opened his mouth.

'And before you say anything, I am absolutely certain there is a case. Those fertilizer bags give us two important pieces of information. One, they possibly connect the bones with this area. Two – and this is more significant – they prove that the bones had been *moved*. Which also raises the possibility that two people could have been involved – one who committed the murder years ago and another who, at a later date, moved the evidence so that it wouldn't be found.'

'Except,' Jude pointed out, 'the evidence was found. You found it, and you didn't have much difficulty doing so. Which raises an even more interesting possibility . . .'

Carole caught the sparkle in Jude's eye and nodded. 'That the bones were moved deliberately so that they *would* be found.'

The two women turned triumphantly towards the landlord. He shook his shaggy head. 'Too many guesses in that. Too many details we don't know. We certainly don't know there's been a murder. No proof of that at all. The person whose flesh was once wrapped around those bones could easily have died in an accident . . . Could even have died a natural death, been ceremoniously buried with all the pomp and circumstance of religion, and then been dug up in the churchyard by some dog.'

'A dog who then stacked up the bones in fertilizer bags?' demanded Carole sceptically. 'I must see if I can teach Gulliver that trick.'

'No, no. I'm not saying that's what happened. I accept that some human agency was involved in gift-wrapping the bones and popping them in the barn, but we have no means of knowing where the body came from or what happened to it.'

Jude chewed her lip. 'Frustrating, isn't it? I bet the police know more about it than we do.'

'It is their job,' Carole pointed out, reasonably enough.

'Not fair,' said Jude. 'They have all those advantages of forensic labs and fingerprints and DNA and they still get it wrong most of the time.'

Ted Crisp chuckled. 'Well, that's good for you, isn't it?'

'What?'

'Police getting it wrong. If they got it right every time, wouldn't be any openings for talented amateurs, would there?' And the wink he gave seemed to be specifically targeted at Carole.

'Oh, shut up,' she said.

Jude pursed her lips and slowly shook her head. 'If only we had one piece of information, we could move forward . . .'

'What piece of information's that?' Ted pointed at their glasses. 'Another large white wine in there, is it, Jude?'

'Yeah, go for it.'

'Carole?'

'Certainly.'

As he turned to open a new wine bottle, he called over his shoulder, 'Sorry, Jude. You said you needed one piece of information. What's that then?'

'Exactly how old the bones were. When the person died. The police must know that by now.'

'Oh, well, why don't you just ring up and ask them? Keep reading in the papers how user-friendly the police're trying to make themselves, how touchy-feely. I'm sure they'd be only too pleased to share their laboratory reports with you.'

'Ha, ha.' Jude stuck her tongue out at him. 'But if we did have that information, then we could concentrate our enquiries on that specific time . . . You know, find out who went missing from Weldisham round then.'

'"Concentrate our enquiries"?' Ted echoed. 'Who do you think you are – the West Sussex Constabulary.'

'No, we're just interested, that's all,' said Carole.

'Interested's one way of putting it. Another's bloody nosy.'

'Don't listen to him. We'll find out what happened up in that village, don't you worry.' As she spoke, Jude patted her arm. Carole found the gesture of solidarity strangely reassuring. 'Ooh, I'm starving,' Jude went on. 'I'm going to order something to eat. What about you?'

Carole's freezer contained a clingfilm-wrapped portion of fish designated for that evening, but it wasn't a plan that couldn't be shelved. 'Yes. Excellent idea.'

'What's good to eat tonight?' asked Jude as Ted put their wine glasses down on the counter.

'Apart from me?' Ted Crisp simpered coyly, but, getting no reaction, moved quickly on. 'You won't go wrong with the Kate and Sidney.'

'Sounds great to me. I'll have one of those.' Jude picked up her glass. 'We'll be sitting over there by the fire – OK?'

'Sure,' he called after her. 'I'll find you. Not exactly crowded out tonight, am I? And what are you going to eat, Carole?'

'I think I'll have the steak and kidney too.'

'You won't regret it. Two Kate and Sidneys, right.' He was silent for a moment, holding her eye. Then he said,

'Nice jumper you got on,' before abruptly turning away to the kitchen.

As she moved across to join her friend, Carole Seddon thought that Ted Crisp wasn't really such an unattractive man, after all.

Chapter Seventeen

It was clear from the moment Carole walked through the door on the Friday evening that the Forbeses were very used to giving dinner parties. There was a professionalism about the way Graham greeted her and took her coat which revealed him as a veteran of much entertaining. The beautifully tailored dark suit he wore had the look of a dinner jacket and his shoes were highly polished. In his various British Council postings, he must have played host to innumerable writers, musicians, dance groups, theatre-companies and conference delegates. An easy social manner was an essential qualification for the job.

In a way, that seemed to diminish Carole's invitation a little. Through the week, part of her had thought that Graham Forbes had asked her to dinner because, on very brief acquaintance, he'd found her intelligent and inter-esting. But the professionalism of his manner suggested simply that someone had dropped out and she'd been invited to make up the numbers.

To counterbalance that, though, Carole felt a degree of relief. She'd always found it daunting to walk into a room full of people she did not know, and since David's defection that anxiety had increased. But she knew a host as professional as Graham Forbes would ensure she was meticulously introduced to everyone and offered starting points for conversation.

Warren Lodge, situated next door to the Lutteridges' Conyers, was one of the Weldisham middle range. Probably at first a farm worker's cottage, it had grown organically, as different owners had added rooms and extensions. The result was a hotchpotch of architectural styles. Though the original cottage would have been flint-faced, the whole exterior had been pebble-dashed to give some kind of conformity.

If the outside was not a thing of beauty, inside the house breathed taste and character. It was full of mementoes of a long life spent mostly abroad. On the walls of the hall hung African masks and Japanese silk paintings. A plate rack supported dishes of Indian silver. Graham Forbes was a collector of beautiful things.

But the most treasured item in his collection was in the sitting room. Adoration glowed in his faded brown eyes as he introduced Carole to his wife, Irene.

She must have been a good twenty years younger than her husband. Dressed in a cheongsam of scarlet and gold, she was dwarfed by him. Her thick black hair was cut in a neat helmet and her eyes when she looked at Graham left no doubt that their adoration was mutual.

'Hello, Carole. A great pleasure to meet you,' she said as she stretched out her hand. Her English was excellent, but with that slight chopped-vowel quality that the Chinese have. 'Now what will you have to drink?'

And she gestured elegantly to a stout woman in waitress uniform who stood by the drinks table. As Carole asked for a white wine, she looked again at her hostess.

There was no doubt about it. Irene Forbes was the

woman Carole had encountered sobbing in St Michael and All Angels.

As anticipated, Graham Forbes's social efficiency provided instant introductions to other guests. His task was made easier, though, by the fact that only one other couple had arrived. The man, thick-necked and crammed into a double-breasted suit, and his wife, vague and beaky, like a seabird blown off-course, were introduced as Harry and Jenny Grant. He was ruddy in complexion, she very pale, as if the husband had appropriated all of the available family colour.

'I'm sure you'll have seen some of Harry's work around the area,' said Graham Forbes jovially. 'He's been responsible for some of the biggest residential developments along the South Coast.'

'Except in Weldisham.' The man's voice was big, as if his suit had difficulty holding that in too.

'Except in Weldisham,' Graham agreed, and chuckled, as at some private joke. The way Harry Grant smiled suggested it was a joke his host found funnier than he did.

This impression was confirmed, when Graham Forbes went off to answer the doorbell and Irene took Jenny aside to compliment her on what was in fact an over-fussy dress. 'No, they don't take to my ideas in Weldisham, Caroline,' said Harry Grant grimly.

'Carole.'

'Sorry. Misheard. As I say, I'm not welcome here, professionally. What's that thing about prophets being without honour in their own country?'

Carole was surprised. He didn't look like the sort of

man who'd know the reference. Once again she repri-
manded herself for her habit of too readily pigeonholing
people. 'Do you mean that you were actually brought up
here?'

'Yes, my father worked for the Estate. I lived here till
I was twenty-four.'

'So you must have known Detective Sergeant Baylis?'

'Lennie Baylis? Sure. His family lived two doors along.
We were at school together. Always out on the Downs,
playing these elaborate war games, me, him and the
others. Always building forts, we were, thinking up daft
names for them. Fort Welling. Fort Pittsburgh. Fort
Deathtrap.'

'It must've been a great place to grow up.'

'Mm.' He didn't look certain about that. 'Quite spooky
at times. There are some nasty places out on the
Downs . . . Marshy bits . . . Chalk pits . . . Caves . . . We used
to scare ourselves witless, some of the games we played.
Tying each other up, that kind of stuff. Not very nice
to each other, kids . . . Certainly we lot weren't.' With an
effort, he pulled himself out of these recollections. 'How
do you come to know Lennie, though?' For the first time
there was a twinkle in his eye as he said, 'You don't look
the sort to get on the wrong side of the law.'

Quickly Carole explained how she had met the
sergeant.

'Oh, it was you who found them, was it? Must've been
a nasty moment.'

'Bit of a shock, yes.'

'I bet. I'm not surprised Lennie Baylis is interested,
though.'

'What do you mean?'

'Well, I don't know if you heard, but his mother ran off when he was round fifteen.'

'I hadn't heard that, no.'

'The dad was a real brute, and no one blamed her for going. But, at the time..' He lowered his voice to a whisper. 'There were people in the village said she'd never have left Lennie on his own and in fact . . . the old man must have done away with her.'

'Good heavens. Was there a police investigation?'

'No, it was just village gossip. Probably rubbish, like most village gossip. I'm sure Ma Baylis'd had enough, went off with some fancy man and set up home at the other end of the country.'

'But you're suggesting it might have been her bones that I found?'

'I'm not suggesting anything. I'm just saying it's a thought.' He seemed to regret having gone so far, and steered the conversation in another direction. 'I doubt if you were in much of a state to appreciate it, but that South Welling Barn's a nice structure. Make a good conversion into a house. Except, of course, the Estate still owns that one, and they'd never agree to it. And if they ever did, then the Village Committee'd put a spanner in the works, like they keep doing with the other one.'

'Other one?'

'Don't know if you've seen it, but there's an old barn behind this house..'

'I have seen it.'

'Well, I bought that from the Estate six years back.' Anger and frustration grew in his voice, as he went on, 'And since I've been the owner, I've tried time and again to get planning permission to turn it into a house. I want to live there. But every time the planning inquiry comes up, the Village Committee gets it kicked out.'

'Bad luck. You must rather regret your investment.'

'No way. Even in that state, the barn's appreciating by the minute.' The thought of profit soothed his anger. 'And we've now got a government who's urging more housing in West Sussex. And new people get appointed to the County Council Planning Committee and . . . they may be persuaded to take a less blinkered view . . .

'Oh no, don't worry. I'll get what I want in the end . . . Maybe even next week – there's a planning meeting on Thursday. And when I do succeed and move into my own barn conversion in Weldisham . . . then people like Mr Graham Forbes may be laughing the other side of their faces, eh?'

He smiled triumphantly, just as the subject of his conversation approached, leading a thin-faced pinstriped man with the expression of someone who always counted his change.

'Carole, may I introduce Barry Stillwell. Barry – Carole Seddon.'

The newcomer was effusively polite in his greeting.

'And of course you two know each other.'

Harry Grant nodded.

'I dare say Barry's done some of your conveyancing for you, Harry.'

'No way. He's too bloody slow for me. When I want some legal work done, I go to a specialist.'

Graham Forbes might have used his diplomatic skills to ease this rather sticky opening to their conversation had not the doorbell once again rung. He scurried off, leaving the three of them together.

But not for long. Harry Grant moved away with a

mumbled, 'Oh well, better circulate.' Since his wife and Irene Forbes were the only other people available to circulate with, it could be deduced that Barry Stillwell was not his favourite person.

'I gather you're a solicitor,' said Carole, clutching at the conversational hint Graham Forbes had dropped for her.

'Yes, that's right. Partner in a practice in Worthing.'

'Ah.'

There was a silence. Carole had a nasty feeling she knew exactly the kind of man she was up against. Barry Stillwell, she reckoned, like many country solicitors, having limped through some exams in his early twenties, had thereafter made a comfortable living involving no intellectual effort of any kind. And, so long as people continued to buy houses, divorce and die, that comfortable living would remain secure.

'Are you connected with the law at all, Carole? I may call you Carole, I hope?'

'Please do. No, I'm not a lawyer myself. I used to come in contact with a lot of lawyers when I worked for the Home Office.'

'The Home Office? That's interesting.' She'd suspected Barry Stillwell would be a dreadful bore, and his use of the word 'interesting' confirmed it. The seriously boring claim to find everything interesting, maybe in the hope that some of it may rub off and they'll be found interesting too.

'But you're not still there?' he went on.

'No. Retired.'

He curled his lips into a thin smile. 'It must have been a very early retirement.'

Oh dear, thought Carole. Is there only one compliment available in Weldisham?

'It was a bit early,' she conceded. 'Have you thought about when you'll retire, Barry?'

'Oh, I don't know. I might not.' He assumed an expression of pious suffering. 'Since my wife died a couple of years back, my work has rather been my life.'

'Ah.'

'Though I live in hope of course that I will one day recover my *joie de vivre*.' He simpered.

Oh, my God, thought Carole. I know why I've been invited to this dinner party. He's a spare man.

Chapter Eighteen

She was relieved that the seating plan did not put her next to Barry Stillwell. In fact, she was well placed between her host and Harry Grant, but it was Graham Forbes who enlivened her evening. She was surprised. In the Hare and Hounds the evening she'd found the bones, he'd sounded very right-wing and intolerant. Maybe he'd taken on that role for the benefit of the regulars, because in his home environment he showed himself to be a man of genuine wit and sophistication. At first Carole thought he might have a tendency to name-drop, but after a while she realized that he did actually know all the people he was talking about. His work at the British Council meant that he had acted as host to some of the most eminent figures in the arts world.

He'd just concluded a hilarious anecdote about William Golding at an event in Cairo, when Carole said apologetically, 'I'm afraid I don't know many writers.'

'Your loss, my dear lady. They're most of them paranoid depressives, serial philanderers and improvident alcoholics, but *enormous fun*. I think I've had more pure unadulterated fun getting drunk with writers than from anything else in my life . . .' He grinned at Irene across the table. 'Possibly excluding sex.'

Graham Forbes certainly had a relish for drink and a

well-educated taste in wine. He was putting away a lot himself and ensuring that none of his guests ever had an empty glass for long. Carole had to keep putting her hand across the top of hers, or she was never going to drive safely back to Fethering. The West Sussex police, she knew, were notoriously vigilant about drink-driving.

'There was another rather amusing incident,' Graham went on, 'while I was based in Kuala Lumpur, where, um . . . I'd better call her a distinguished literary novelist out on a tour . . . developed a passion for one of the British Council drivers. Lovely chap called Shiva, my absolute favourite, I always got him to drive me everywhere. So, our, um . . . lady novelist . . . Sorry, the story'd be a lot better if I used her name, but I really can't. Anyway, she started in unambiguous pursuit of Shiva, and I could see she was making life very difficult for him. I think her culture and sexual mores were rather less inhibited than his. Then one day, quite suddenly, she appeared to have lost interest in him, and when I was next alone with Shiva in the car I asked how he'd managed to get her off his back. And Shiva said . . .' He dropped into the slightest of Indian accents, '"Very easily, Mr Forbes. I told her I had started one of her books and that I had found it unreadable."' He chuckled. 'Very sensitive plant, you know – writer's vanity.'

Carole thought she should try to contribute to the conversation. 'I met – well, I saw – a writer in the Hare and Hounds the other day. Local writer.'

'We haven't got any local writers,' said Graham. 'Not what I'd call writers, anyway. Who was this?'

'His name's Brian Helling.'

'Brian Helling? Oh, for heaven's sake, I said "writers"!' In spite of the vehemence, he managed to retain his charm and courtesy. 'I'm sorry, Carole, but I'm afraid you can't mention Brian Helling in the same breath as William Golding, Ted Hughes, Margaret Drabble and the other people I've been talking about. Brian Helling is a . . . is a . .'

For once Graham Forbes seemed lost for words. Harry Grant was happy to provide them. 'He's a useless bloody sponger.'

Their host nodded. 'I couldn't have put it better myself. Brian Helling is not the kind of person we want in a village like Weldisham.'

'I hope you won't ever say that to his face.'

It was Irene who had spoken. There was a look of concern on her smooth Oriental features.

'Why shouldn't I say it to his face? I'm not afraid of Brian Helling.'

'No, but there is no need to antagonize him.'

'What on earth are you talking about, Irene, my love?'

'I just don't think Brian Helling is someone you should rub up the wrong way, Graham. He's potentially violent.'

'He's never threatened you with violence, has he?'

'No.' For a moment, the eyes of husband and wife interlocked across the table. Graham's were puzzled, but in Irene's there was something close to fear.

Then she looked away to continue her duty as hostess and talk to the man on her right. He was Freddie Pointon, the newcomer to the village whom Carole had seen in the Hare and Hounds the previous Friday. Before they sat down, she had been introduced to him and his large, loud wife, Pam, whose dress vied with Jenny Grant's for the Christmas tree decoration stakes. The wine, Carole noticed, seemed to have made Pam Pointon even louder.

Their conversation about Brian Helling had been a

definite moment between Graham and Irene Forbes, though no outsider could judge its resonance within their marriage. After his wife had looked away, Graham slumped back and slightly petulantly continued his demolition of Weldisham's so-called 'local writer'.

'Brian Helling's all mannerisms and no substance. Always makes me think of that Chesterton line: "The artistic temperament is a disease that afflicts amateurs." Brian's that worst of combinations – a layabout and a poseur.'

'But what's he actually written?' asked Carole.

'Oh, plenty. And he still goes on writing it. He once asked me to read a *magnum opus* of his, and I was foolish enough to say yes. It was quite, quite horrible.'

'Horrible in what way? The writing?'

'No. The writing was functional, if not much more. But the subject matter . . . ugh. It all seemed to involve tying women up, imprisoning them and using them just as bodies on which to practise any number of disgusting tortures. Mutilations, amputations, eviscerations . . . It was all quite, quite ghastly . . .'

'There's apparently quite a market for that kind of horror stuff.'

'I can't imagine what Brian Helling had written having any market outside the inmates of Broadmoor. Anyway, in answer to your enquiry, *that*'s the kind of stuff he's actually written. But the more pertinent question is: What's he actually had published? And the answer to that one is, I'm pretty sure, nothing.'

'So he just lives on the proceeds of his mother's pools win, does he?'

'Something like that,' said Graham Forbes and, almost abruptly, turned to talk to Jenny Grant, who'd become isolated by Irene's conversation with Freddie Pointon, and looked more forlorn than ever.

Carole concentrated on her food. It was really excellent – roast pheasant with game chips and all the right trimmings. All the right wines too. The meal had been served by the woman dressed as a waitress, but Graham Forbes had made sure they all knew that Irene had done the cooking. A very English style of menu to be cooked by someone who looks like that, thought Carole, and once again kicked herself for the habit of stereotyping.

Her eye was caught by a pair of photographs on the dresser the other side of the table. Both were in beautiful frames of Indian silver and both were of weddings. One had clearly been taken in a hot climate and showed Graham, absurdly handsome in a linen suit, looming protectively over Irene. She wore a simple white dress and held a small posy of flowers.

But the second photograph was the more intriguing. A traditional English wedding with the full panoply of morning dress and bridesmaids is difficult to date precisely, but the quality of the print made this one a lot older than the other. The sharp-featured face of the bride felt distantly familiar to Carole, not familiar as a person she'd actually met might be, but familiar in the way of someone once glimpsed in a television documentary.

The remarkable fact was that the tall young groom was undoubtedly Graham Forbes.

At the moment Carole recognized this, it coincidentally became a matter of general discussion. Pam Pointon, her minimal inhibitions eroded by wine, called across the table, 'So, Graham, I gather you two are in the same boat as we are.'

He looked up, offended to have had his conversation

with Jenny Grant interrupted in this way, but far too well brought up to take issue. 'I'm sorry?'

'I gather from Irene that you're like Freddie and me.' He looked bewildered. 'Second-time-arounders.'

'Well—'

'Freddie and I have both been married before, haven't we, darling?'

'Yes,' her husband agreed, though at that moment he looked doubtful about the wisdom of his second venture into matrimony. He tried to signal minimal shut-up messages to his wife.

But Pam either didn't see them or was too far gone to care. 'My first husband was a complete bastard, Freddie's first wife was a complete cow. What was your first-time-arounder like, Graham?'

There was an uncomfortable silence. Carole cringed. She felt sure her host was about to say his first wife had died of a lingering illness in tragic circumstances.

But no. 'My first wife,' said Graham Forbes, with considerable dignity, 'left me for another man.'

The silence that followed that was more uncomfortable still. Even Pam Pointon looked momentarily abashed. But another slurp of wine restored her confidence and volubility. 'See?' she said. 'So yours fits into the "complete cow" category, just like Freddie's.'

Graham Forbes fixed her with expressionless brown eyes. 'You know nothing about my first wife, so I'd be grateful if you stopped talking about her.'

There was no ambiguity about this rebuff, and an even longer silence was only prevented by Freddie coming in with an attempt to save some Pointon dignity. He had the look of a man who was by now certain he should have stuck with his first-time-arounder.

'I must say, Pam and I are really getting to feel like we've lived in Weldisham for ever. It just feels so right. You know, when I got off that train from London this evening and felt the country air filling my lungs, I thought to myself, "Freddie, old man, you've arrived. This is where you were meant to be."'

Not an inspired piece of fence-mending, but it served its purpose. Individual conversations restarted. Graham Forbes continued the uphill task of finding a subject of mutual interest with Jenny Grant. Carole couldn't stop herself from turning to Harry and asking quietly, 'Did you know the first Mrs Forbes?'

'Oh yes. In fact, she was some relation of my wife's. Aunt, second cousin or something. Jenny comes from one of those local families who're all related to everyone else. Mind you, I never knew Sheila that well. Moved in different circles from us lot – particularly after she married Graham.'

'But you saw a lot of her round the village?'

'Not that much. They were abroad most of the time.'

'Of course. With Graham's British Council work.'

'Right. So they'd just be here for holidays and things. They let the house some of the time. He'd bought it quite early in his career, I think, to have a base in this country. Had private money. Or at least he did then. I don't think that he's got much of it left.'

'And did you know the man who Sheila Forbes ran off with?'

'No. He was—'

But further revelations about their host's private life were prevented by the man himself clapping his hands. 'Now, as Barry and the Grants will know, Irene and I have a little custom at our Friday night dinners . . .'

Oh God, Carole groaned. Please don't say it's going to be party games.

The threat was quickly removed. 'After the main course we do a little revision of the seating plan, so that you all get a chance to speak to everyone.' That old thing, thought Carole, bet they used to do it at all their British Council dinners. 'Now, with only eight of us, it does mean a few husbands and wives will end up sitting together, but I'm sure you can cope with that.

'Ladies, you'll be glad to hear you don't have to move at all. But, gentlemen, I would ask you to pick up your glasses and take the seat four to your right. So, effectively, Harry and Freddie change places, and I change places with . . .'

Oh no. I get Barry, thought Carole.

She did. He sat ingratiatingly beside her, his mouth once again curled into a smile, and set about the serious business of making conversation.

'So . . . what are your leisure pursuits, Carole?'

'Oh, not a lot. Reading, crosswords, taking my dog for walks.'

'That's interesting,' said Barry Stillwell.

Chapter Nineteen

'But I don't like him,' Carole objected.

'You don't know him. You might find he has likeable qualities when you know him better.'

'I doubt it, Jude.'

'Anyway, that's not the point. Barry Stillwell's invited you out. You've no reason to say no. You're not attached to anyone. You're not holding a candle for some unrequited love.'

Carole blushed.

'Are you?'

'No, of course I'm not.'

'Then why not go out with him? It's only a dinner, after all.'

'Yes, but it's a . . .' Carole hesitated before she brought out the word 'date'.

'You've been on dates before.'

'Not for a long time.'

Carole tried to think how long. She supposed the last date she had been on was with David, at the stage when they were . . . What were they doing? 'Courting' didn't sound the right word. 'Circling each other warily and both contemplating the possibility of getting married'? Yes, that was about it.

'Well, you've been in restaurants before, Carole. It's

not as if you won't be able to understand the menu or will start setting fire to the tablecloth.'

'No, I think I can probably avoid those pitfalls.'

'Then where's your problem?'

Before Carole could begin the catalogue of problems she had about the very thought of going on a date with the solicitor, Jude went on, 'You've got to do it, because Barry Stillwell probably has a lot of information about the case. And you can pump it out of him.'

'How? Using my "feminine wiles"?'

'Yes.'

'I'm afraid, when it came to the handing out "feminine wiles" stage of creation, God was a bit mean to me. Anyway, you talk of a "case". I'm moving round to Ted's view that there isn't a "case".'

'Of course there is. There's still an unidentified pile of female bones.'

'Yes, but that's a case for the police and their forensic pathologists. I meant there isn't a case that has anything to do with you and me.'

'You mean you're not interested?'

'Of course I'm interested. But I don't see that it's our business.'

'Oh, come on, Carole, if people only concerned themselves with things that were their business, what a very dull world it would be. I want to find out who those bones belonged to. And I want to find out what happened to her.' She fixed Carole with her big brown eyes, less dreamy than usual and more powerful. 'As do you.'

'Yes, all right. I do.'

'So ring Barry Stillwell back and say yes, you'd love to go out to dinner with him on Thursday.'

'Very well.' Carole jutted out a rueful lower lip. 'Against my better judgement.'

Early on the Wednesday morning, Carole took Gulliver for his first walk on Fethering Beach since his injury. The dressing had been removed, and he scampered over the shingle and sand like a thing possessed. He snuffled frantically at every piece of flotsam and jetsam, as though determined to find another rusty can on which to cut his paw.

The tryst was at an Italian restaurant in Worthing, where clearly Barry was known. 'Signor Stillwell,' fawned the owner, a helpful visual aid to language students who didn't understand the meaning of the word 'oleaginous'.

'I used to come here a lot,' said Barry, once they were seated, 'in happier times . . .'

Oh no, thought Carole. Am I going to be treated to the fully grieving widower routine all evening until he finally makes a pounce at the end?

His next remark did not bode well. 'But I haven't been here much in the last couple of years.' Then, seeming with an effort to pull himself out of introspection, he went on, 'You're looking extremely elegant this evening, Carole.'

Extremely schoolmistressy, she thought. She'd considered the new Marks & Spencer jumper, but thought the Cambridge Blue might present a misleadingly racy image, so she'd dressed in an almost black navy-blue suit over a white blouse. No, probably she didn't look like a schoolmistress these days. They all tended to dress down. A personal banking manager, perhaps?

Barry was wearing another pinstriped suit. For a second Carole entertained the fantasy that every garment he possessed was pinstriped. Maybe he even had pinstriped underwear. She hoped it was not something he was expecting her to check out.

'You said you used to work in the Home Office . . .' But, before he could get further into his 'so tell me about yourself' routine, a waiter presented them with menus the size of billboards and Barry Stillwell assumed the mantle of a suave and sophisticated habitué of Worthing's restaurants.

'Now, I'm sure we'll have a drink, Mario. What's it to be, Carole?'

'Oh, a dry white wine, thanks.'

She'd planned to make two glasses last the whole evening, because she had the car with her. Resisting Barry's offer to pick her up at home, she'd said instinctively that they'd meet at the restaurant. Only after she'd put the phone down did she realize what a snub this had been. So out of practice was she with going on dates that she'd forgotten that picking up the quarry and – more importantly – driving her back home and then maybe 'coming in for a coffee' were part of the accepted ritual.

Still, she didn't really care about any offence she might have caused. For someone so rusty in courtship procedures, hurrying things would be a bad idea. And the chances of her ever wanting to see Barry Stillwell again after that evening were extremely slender.

Carole reminded herself of the rationalization for the dinner. She was there simply to get information out of him for the 'case' that she and Jude were pursuing. And, in that cause, she might be required to use some 'feminine wiles'. The idea gave her a charge of guilty excitement. It was like being an undercover agent – certainly not a situation she had been in before.

Barry made a big deal of the ordering, weighing the virtues of the *vitello alla marsala* against the *saltimbocca alla romana*, and constantly telling Carole how good Giorgio the cook was and how eating at this restaurant 'transports me back to being in Italy, where I spent so many happy times'. Since she'd decided after one glance at the menu to order *zuppa di frutti di mare* and *lasagne con funghi e prosciutto*, all this recommendation was a bit superfluous.

When she gave her order, he tried to persuade her that she really wanted meat or fish as a main course, as though her selecting one of the cheaper items on the menu was in some way an aspersion on his masculinity. Carole, who from an early age had known her own mind, did not change it.

She concurred with his choice of a Chianti Classico, though warned him that he would have to drink most of it. Barry seemed unworried about going over the limit for driving. When Carole raised the matter, he said, 'One of the advantages of being attached to the legal profession is that one does have a lot of dealings with the local police.'

'Are you saying they'd turn a blind eye if you failed a breathalyser test?'

She had asked the question in a way that invited staunch denial, but that was not how Barry Stillwell took it. With a smug smile and a tap to his nose, he said, 'Ooh, I don't think it'd get as far as the breathalyser . . . once they knew who I was.'

'Really?'

This time he interpreted her reaction of contempt as

one of being impressed. 'Oh yes, I've got some very useful local contacts, Carole. When you've been in Rotary as long as I have, you tend to know everyone.'

If he's capable of misinterpreting my signals so totally, thought Carole, thank God I'm travelling home in my own car.

'I'm a past president,' he confided modestly.

'Of what?'

'Rotary. In Worthing.'

He left a pause for her awestruck response to this revelation.

'Goodness,' said Carole. 'Really?'

Then, before he could interrogate her about work at the Home Office and tell her how interesting that sounded, she pitched in. 'Charming couple, the Forbeses.'

'Oh yes. Charming.'

'Have you known them long?'

'Quite a while. I've acted professionally for Graham since he first moved to the area. I did the conveyancing when he bought the house in Weldisham.'

Wow, that must have been exciting, thought Carole, because it was the reaction Barry Stillwell's tone of voice demanded.

'It's very gratifying,' he went on, 'when clients become friends.'

'Yes, it must be. So have you continued to do all Graham's legal work since then?'

'Oh yes. When you've got a good relationship with a client . . .' Barry Stillwell let out a thin chuckle. 'If it ain't broken, don't fix it.'

'Broke,' Carole couldn't help saying.

'Sorry?'

'I think the idiom is, "If it ain't *broke*, don't fix it."'

'But that's not correct English. The past participle of "break" is "broken".'

'Yes,' Carole agreed, wishing she hadn't set off up this particular cul-de-sac.

'I'm very interested in grammar,' said Barry.

You bloody would be.

'It's very interesting.'

'Yes.' She pressed on. 'So did you do Graham's divorce?'

'Sorry?'

'As a lawyer, did you act for Graham when he got divorced from his first wife?'

'Ah, see what you mean.'

Was she being hyper-sensitive to detect a slight hesitation in his manner? Maybe the abruptness of her questioning had thrown him.

'I've managed all the legal side of Graham's life,' Barry concluded smugly.

Mario arrived with their starters. The restaurant owner himself oozed over with the Chianti Classico. There was much elaborate ceremonial with the corkscrew and with a peppermill like the bell-tower of a minor Italian cathedral. Barry Stillwell sniffed and sipped the wine as if it were the elixir of eternal life.

After a long, lip-licking pause, he pronounced himself satisfied.

Carole had to put up with an extensive questionnaire about the Home Office and how she liked living in Fethering, before she could get back to the subject that interested her: Weldisham, its inhabitants and their history. Common politeness meant her interrogation was unavoidable, but she got a bit sick of the way Barry kept punctuating the conversation with references to his late wife.

Carole didn't lack respect for bereavement, but Barry Stillwell's deployment of it seemed calculated. As if he was trying to prove what a caring man he was, as if the late wife (her name, it soon became apparent, had been Vivienne) had become part of an elaborate chat-up routine. Carole had a nasty feeling that, if he ever met someone he was really interested in, Barry would very quickly be into the patter of, 'After Vivienne died, I never thought I could feel anything for another woman, but you're bringing to life feelings I feared were long dead and buried.'

She hoped to God she was never cast in the role of the woman who had to hear that manifesto.

When Barry reached the end – or maybe it wasn't the end – of a recollection about how lonely he'd been when he went on a Rotary Club exchange visit to Cologne just after Vivienne died, Carole seized the opportunity and leapt back in.

'Does Graham Forbes have any children?'

'What?' Barry was thrown by the sudden change of direction.

'From either marriage? I just wondered.'

'No, no, he doesn't.' He still looked bewildered. 'What about you, Carole? I know you said you were divorced, but do you have any children?'

'A son. Stephen.'

'Ah.'

'I don't see him that often.'

'But surely you must? Surely he's still living at home?'

It was Carole's turn to look bewildered. Barry had a strange expectant expression on his face and she tried to work out what on earth it was meant to communicate. Not easy. She didn't think she'd ever met anyone with whom she'd had less mental connection. In conversation with Barry Stillwell, everything needed to be interpreted and explained.

Suddenly she realized. What he'd said had been a compliment. Cumbersome, contrived and lateral, but nonetheless a compliment. Barry was suggesting that no one of her age could possibly have a child old enough to have left home. It was in the same vein as the 'early retirement' compliment.

'Stephen's nearly thirty,' she said brusquely.

Barry looked thoughtfully pained. 'Sadly, Vivienne and I were not blessed.'

'Sorry?'

'With the gift of offspring.' A melancholy sigh. 'I'd like to have had children,' he simpered. 'Still live in hope.'

Well, don't look at me, Carole wanted to say. I'm well past my impregnate-by date.

Chapter Twenty

'Still thinking about Graham Forbes,' she went on.

'You seem to keep thinking about him,' Barry Stillwell observed, with a winsome chuckle. 'Should I be worried? Should I start thinking you're more interested in him than you are in me?'

If only you knew . . . Carole couldn't think of anything appropriate to say, so she came up with a chuckle of her own. Barry continued his. Oh no, she thought, he imagines we're sharing a joke. He thinks we're getting on well together.

She pressed on. 'Did you know his first wife?'

'Yes, I did. Not well, because they didn't spend a lot of time in Sussex while they were working abroad, but I did meet Sheila.' His face took on a pious expression. 'Tragic, isn't it, the way some bad marriages break up and the partners both survive . . . and then a marriage that does work can be suddenly ended by the cruel hand of fate . . .'

He was about to get on to Vivienne again. Carole was now convinced that these references were part of Barry's seduction technique, though she wondered how well advised they were. A woman, though possibly impressed by the tenderness implied in these constant mentions of his late wife, would surely be warned off the possibility of a relationship with someone over whom the memory of Vivienne loomed so powerfully. The *Rebecca* syndrome.

Not, of course, that any of this concerned Carole. The evening had only confirmed her first adverse impressions. She'd rather have a relationship with Bill Sykes than with Barry Stillwell.

Before the sainted Vivienne had the chance to re-enter the conversation, Carole demanded, 'So when did his first marriage end?'

Barry gave a prim smile. 'Well, as it happens, I can give you an exact answer to that. Not that I was present when they did split up. Might have been difficult to engineer, because that happened when they were in Kuala Lumpur.' He snickered at his rather amusing remark. 'But I did see them the weekend before they went off on that fateful trip.'

'Oh?'

'Graham wanted me to draw up a new lease for the house, because they were letting it again. So . . . always ready to mix business with pleasure . .' He grinned an arch, man-of-the-world grin. ' . . . I suggested we meet in the Hare and Hounds to thrash things out. The Hare and Hounds in those days, by the way, was rather primitive. Rough wooden floors, only a couple of beers to choose from and a menu of ploughman's lunch or sandwiches. Not sophisticated like it is since Will Maples has been in charge. It's so much better now.'

The evening was becoming a challenge to Carole. Was Barry Stillwell going to express one single opinion with which she didn't disagree?

'Anyway, I saw Sheila when I arrived to pick up Graham. She wasn't coming to the pub with us – too busy packing. Big undertaking when you're going to have tenants in for the best part of a year. Sheila was ordering the cleaning woman around like nobody's business. But I chatted to her while I waited for Graham... Very important in my line of business to get on with everyone, you know.'

'And at that stage you weren't aware of any cracks in the marriage?'

'Good heavens, no. They behaved together exactly as they always had done. They were always very polite, you know, very correct, very good at entertaining people..'

'Part of the job they had to do abroad.'

'I imagine so. Graham was brought up to that, of course – the right schools, universities and so on, moneyed background, you know.'

'At their dinner party, Harry Grant implied Graham had lost a lot of money.'

'Well, I believe he caught a bit of a cold at Lloyd's, but, you know, he's not the sort to talk about that kind of thing. Anyway, as I say, Graham was from a very privileged family, and Sheila must have caught up very quickly after they got married.'

'You mean she didn't come from his kind of family?'

'No, local girl, in spite of her posh schools. Lots of relatives in Weldisham and all round here. There are some families that never seem to move from this area, however much—'

But Carole wasn't interested in Barry Stillwell's views on the demographics of West Sussex. 'And was that the last time you saw them together, Graham and Sheila?'

'Yes,' Barry replied a little sourly. He didn't like being hurried in his story-telling. 'Anyway, the reason I have cause to remember – and this is interesting – is that I had lunch with Graham in the Hare and Hounds on the

Thursday.' He paused portentously. 'Thursday 15 October 1987. And that weekend was the weekend of the Great Storm. You remember the Great Storm, do you, Carole?'

She assured him she did. It was the weekend when the south of England had been devastated by a most un-English hurricane. Thousands of trees had been uprooted, roofs lifted, greenhouses smashed. A BBC weatherman by the name of Michael Fish had become famous overnight for pooh-poohing the warning from a viewer that such an event was likely to happen. And cosmic conspiracy theorists were rewarded on the following Monday when the Great Storm's climatic augury produced the biggest London Stock Market crash of recent years.

Although she hadn't lived in the area at the time, Carole Seddon certainly knew all about it. There wasn't a man or woman in West Sussex who hadn't got their own story to tell about the Great Storm.

And she had a horrible feeling she was about to hear Barry Stillwell's.

'Have you any idea what the storm did to my conservatory?' he began.

'No,' said Carole. 'Tell me about Graham and Sheila Forbes first. Then tell me about your conservatory.'

Barry was so surprised by her bossiness that he did exactly what he had been told. 'Well, there's not much to say, really. They were due off to Kuala Lumpur on the Monday, the 19th, and though the village was briefly cut off by trees across the lane, they'd been cleared by then, so presumably they got to the airport all right. It was six months before they were next due back in Weldisham, and when they did arrive . . . Graham was on his own.'

'Sheila had left him?'

'Yes. It came out slowly, but obviously, as soon as he'd told one person, everyone in the village knew.'

'Do you know who she went off with?'

'Apparently some academic from a university in Kuala Lumpur.'

'Had they been having an affair before?'

'I've no idea.' The solicitor shrugged his shoulders testily. He was getting increasingly irritated by her interest in Graham and Sheila Forbes. He was her host, after all; she ought to be showing interest in him. Carole knew she hadn't got much longer to continue her grilling.

'Do you know where they are now?'

'Of course I don't.' There was petulance in his voice. 'I gather after a time the man got a job at a university in Singapore. Whether they're still there or not, I've no idea.'

'Sheila was the same sort of age as Graham?' Barry Stillwell nodded. 'So she could be dead by now.'

'I don't think so. There would be legal implications if she were. Graham would have told me.'

'If he knew.'

'Yes. Look, I didn't come here this evening to talk about Graham Forbes. I'm much more interested in *you*, Carole.' He leered across the table.

'Yes, and I'm much more interested in *you*, Barry,' she lied. 'But, just before we leave the subject . . . can you tell me when you first met Irene?'

'Oh, very well.' Her saying she was interested in him had bought Carole a little more goodwill. 'It was when Graham retired. After 1987, he came back to Weldisham for a few weeks each year, always on his own, always very lonely and miserable. Then in 1989 he told me he was retiring from the British Council the next year and all lettings of the house would cease, because he was going to live in it all the time. Well, he must have got lucky during that last tour in Kuala Lumpur, because when he did come back, he had a new bride in tow. The lovely Irene.'

Carole really didn't think she could push it any further. She tried to justify her unusual conversational approach. 'Thank you so much, Barry. I'm a nosy old thing, but I do love knowing all the details about people.'

'There are lots of interesting details you don't know about me yet,' he said coyly.

'I know.' She gave him a smile which she hoped would qualify as a 'feminine wile'. Jude should be proud of her. 'So many interesting details I don't know about you . . . Where to begin?'

He sat back with a complacent smile on his thin lips. 'Up to you, Carole.'

'Tell me, Barry . . . what *did* happen to your conservatory during the Great Storm?'

She couldn't have picked a better subject. He leaned forward with relish and began, 'Well, this is extremely interesting . . .'

Carole's mind was racing and she didn't take in anything he said. She didn't really notice the end of the meal. She was still distracted when Barry asked her if she'd like to meet up again, and dangerously vague in her answer.

And she hardly noticed as he leaned down to kiss her when she was safely ensconced in the Renault. All she was aware of was a sensation as if her cheek had been wiped by a soapy facecloth.

Chapter Twenty-one

The downstairs light in Woodside Cottage was still on when Carole drove past on the way back from the restaurant. As she parked the Renault, what for her was a daring thought crept into her mind. Suppose she went round straight away to see if Jude was still up . . .

It was a very un-Fethering idea. In Fethering no one except the police or a family member who had lost their key would knock on a door after nine o'clock at night. And ten o'clock was very definitely the curfew for phone calls. These rules did not trouble Carole – she had instinctively abided by them all her life. But, emboldened by two glasses of wine and bubbling with the ideas her conversation with Barry Stillwell had engendered, she went straight round and tapped on the wooden front door of Woodside Cottage. Even though it was nearly half past eleven.

Jude was, of course, totally unfazed when she let her neighbour in. 'Oh, thank goodness you've come. You've made a decision for me.'

'What decision?'

'I'd just finished a bottle of wine. I was divided between opening another one and going to bed. Now opening another one is no longer mere self-indulgence; it's become a social necessity. Do sit.'

As she went through to the kitchen, Jude waved vaguely to the array of sofas and armchairs, all covered with brightly coloured drapes and bedspreads. Carole sank tentatively into one. It was surprisingly comfortable. She couldn't feel the outlines of the structure that lay beneath the patchwork quilt, but the contours settled easily around her thin body.

Jude returned carrying a moisture-beaded bottle of white wine and a corkscrew. 'You open this. I'll get some life back into the fire.'

A few seconds' ministration with coal, logs and poker set up a promising blaze. Jude squatted back on her heels and looked teasingly across at her friend. 'So what have you come to tell me? That you completely misjudged Barry Stillwell? That he is the Mr Right you have been searching for all these years? And that you are going to spend the rest of your lives together?'

'God, no. I've got something much more interesting than that. I think I know who . . .' But she stopped herself. Carole reckoned she had a good story to tell and she didn't want to give away the best bit first. 'You remember the Great Storm, don't you, Jude?'

'Well, I heard about it. I was living in Australia when it happened.'

'What were you doing in Austr—?'

'But what's the Great Storm got to do with the case?'

Never mind Australia. Carole could find out about that another time. What she had to say was much more interesting.

'I think the weekend of the Great Storm has a huge significance in the case. I think that was the date of the murder, the evidence of which I found in South Welling Barn.'

'And you got this from Barry Stillwell? Well, that is a turn-up. You turned the heat on him and he confessed to you, did he?'

'God, no. Barry's far too boring to do anything as interesting as murder.'

'So who is your murderer?'

'Let's start with the victim. You know I told you that Graham Forbes had been married twice . . .'

'Yes.'

'I think the victim was his first wife, Sheila.'

'What do you base that on?'

'Instinct.'

A sceptical lower lip was jutted out.

'What's the matter with you? Why aren't you excited?'

Jude slowly shook her head, in some bewilderment. 'There's something wrong here, Carole. I'm the one who's supposed to respond to instinct. I thought, of the two of us, you were the rationalist.'

'I am.'

'Well, then give me your rationale for saying that the bones belonged to Sheila Forbes.'

'All right. They're a woman's bones for a start. Aged between thirty and fifty. That fits.'

'OK.' Jude looked at the fire through the wine she was swirling in her glass. 'What else?'

'Graham Forbes is deeply in love with his second wife, Irene.'

'Are you saying that means he must've murdered his first wife?'

'I'm saying it would give him a motive to do so.'

'Only if he had met Irene before his first wife died.'

'He must've done.'

'We don't know that.'

'Well, let's assume he did.' Carole ignored Jude's sardonic expression as she hurried on, 'So, the weekend of the Great Storm, Graham Forbes, tortured by his love for Irene and infuriated by the loveless marriage he shares with Sheila, decides to solve all his problems at a stroke. He murders his wife, hides her body somewhere in the village and on the Monday travels back to Kuala Lumpur alone. Everyone in Weldisham imagines that Sheila went with him. Then on his next leave, he comes back without her and tells everyone she's dumped him and run off with this academic. Everyone believes him. Why shouldn't they? He's a pillar of the local community. When he's out in Malaysia he happily spends all his time with Irene. Back in England, he does his impression of the miserable abandoned husband. Then when he retires, he brings Irene back to Weldisham as his new bride, maintaining he's only recently met her.'

There was a long silence. At first Carole was disappointed not to see Jude carried along by her enthusiasm. Then she started wondering quite how watertight the scenario she'd presented was.

Finally, Jude spoke. Shaking her head wryly, she said, 'How much did you have to drink this evening, Carole?'

'Only a couple of glasses. What're you on about? Can't you see the logic of what I've just spelled out?'

'I can see *a* logic,' said Jude, 'but I don't think it'll stand up to very close scrutiny. I know Malaysia's a long way away, but I'm sure somebody would have noticed if Graham Forbes's wife suddenly vanished off the face of the earth. I mean, they must've had staff out there, friends, who'd notice her absence.

'Also, if her body's been hidden since 1987, why do her bones suddenly turn up now? And, if they are Sheila

Forbes's bones, why haven't the police been to question her husband?'

'We don't know they haven't,' said Carole truculently. She had been so excited by the edifice of conjecture she'd constructed that she wasn't enjoying seeing it demolished brick by brick.

'I'm sorry. I'd need more evidence before I could go along the route you're suggesting. I'd need proof that Sheila Forbes wasn't seen out in Kuala Lumpur after the weekend of the Great Storm. I'd need proof that Graham Forbes did know Irene before he supposedly murdered his wife. I'd need . . . I'm sorry, Carole. I'd just need so much more information.'

'What kind of information?'

'Information that presumably the police have access to. Surely these days they can identify human remains by DNA, apart from anything else.'

'Only if they have some sample of DNA to match it with,' said Carole, with a feeble attempt at triumph in her voice. 'And if Sheila Forbes had totally disappeared they wouldn't have that.'

Jude's mouth was still crinkled with scepticism. 'No, but they could probably link the DNA to her through relatives, other family members. We need something a bit more positive. As I say, if we had evidence from someone in Kuala Lumpur that Graham did arrive out there in 1987 on his own . . .'

'Well, I'll get that,' said Carole defiantly. 'I've got a friend who works in the British Council.' It didn't seem worth mentioning that she hadn't been in touch with Trevor Malcolm for nearly thirty years.

'OK.' Jude grinned one of her huge, all-embracing grins. 'I'm ready to be convinced. Convince me.'

*

Carole woke the next morning with a hangover. It was partly physical – she and Jude had finished the bottle – but more it was mental. She felt embarrassed by the way she had let her ideas run away with her the night before. Jude was right. The scenario she'd expounded, casting Graham Forbes in the role of murderer, was a fabrication of unsupported conjecture. Its logic was full of holes, and in the cold light of day looked even more threadbare.

Where, Carole thought, did I get the idea that I have any aptitude for criminal investigation? The evidence at the moment does not support the claim. Solving murders should be left to the professionals. The police have all the information; no one who hasn't got all the information stands a chance.

But greater than all the mental discomforts she felt was the fact that she'd behaved out of character. Carole Seddon had always prided herself on having a rational mind, but the previous evening she had ignored its dictates and followed a path of whimsy. What hurt was that, by her behaviour, she'd lost any intellectual ascendancy she might have had over her next-door neighbour.

Carole had made a fool of herself, and Jude had been the one who was all sober and sensible.

Chapter Twenty-two

Still, she could at least do the one bit of follow-up she'd promised. She found the number of the British Council office in Spring Gardens and rang through. It was a long chance that Trevor Malcolm had remained in the organization he'd started with in his early twenties and, even if he had, a long chance that he was still there. As Carole knew to her cost, there were a lot of early retirements around. And, in the unlikely event that Trevor was still employed by the British Council, he would almost certainly be working abroad.

But her gloomy prognostications proved unfounded. When she asked for the name, she was put through without hesitation and the girl at the other end certainly knew who she was talking about. But Trevor was out at a meeting. He'd be back after lunch . . . 'Probably best to leave it till three-thirty or so.'

Oh well, thought Carole as she put the phone down, might give him a call then. But she didn't think it with great determination. Whatever she'd felt about the case the night before had dwindled away into a vague residue of dissatisfaction. It was a police matter. Unidentified bones were their job.

*

Only shortly after that, her doorbell rang. Jude was standing there, swathed in a long burgundy velvet coat. A peach-coloured scarf was wrapped around her face so high that only her bird's-nest of blonde hair and her brown eyes showed over the top.

'Came round to say sorry.'

'Sorry?'

'For being a wet blanket last night.'

'Oh, I don't know that you were. You were just sensible.'

'There are already enough sensible people in the world without me joining their ranks. No, I was just feeling down.'

'You? Down?' It was a novel concept. Jude always seemed to be on top of everything.

'Yes. Some bloody man.'

'Which bloody man?'

'Doesn't matter which when they behave like that. They're all the bloody same, aren't they?'

'Well . . . Surely you can tell me what—?'

But this new window for an insight into Jude's private life was quickly closed. 'Never mind. Perdition to the lot of them, eh? I want to make amends by taking you out for lunch . . .'

'What?'

'And I have to confess, Carole, my motivation is not entirely altruistic. I just had a call from Gillie Lutteridge, and I promised to go and see her. So I'm offering you lunch in the Hare and Hounds at Weldisham . . .'

'In return for a lift up there?'

'Exactly.'

After some havering, Carole decided not to take Gulliver, in spite of the agonized importunity in his endearingly stupid face. He still couldn't be trusted up on the Downs, and he would hate being shut in the Renault behind the Hare and Hounds while they had lunch.

There was a man leaving the pub as they reached the door. He wore a grubby denim jacket over a tartan working shirt. He crossed to a tractor with an enclosed cab that was parked opposite the pub.

'Who's that?' Jude whispered. 'You looked like you recognized him.'

'Name's Nick. He was in the Hare and Hounds first evening I came here. One of the Estate workers, I think. Extremely taciturn . . . or he certainly was that night.'

Inside the pub, although it was only twelve-thirty, tables were already full of pension-happy lunchers munching their way through the Home Hostelries blackboard specials. There was also a figure standing by the log-effect fire in the main bar whom Carole recognized from the Forbeses' dinner party.

'Hello, Harry,' she said, as Jude went to get the drinks and order the food.

He gave her a bemused look, unfocused, as if he had already been drinking. 'Oh yes . .' he said vaguely. But even using it vaguely, his voice was loud.

'We met at Graham and Irene's last Friday.'

He nodded, recollection slowly returning. 'Of course. Caroline, wasn't it?'

'Carole.' Big impression she'd made.

Harry Grant grinned. 'I'm actually in here waiting to see Graham. Always comes in for his pre-lunch snifter. Isn't that right, Will?'

The manager, who had just given Jude her change, looked across. 'Sorry?'

'I said Graham always comes in for a pre-lunch snifter, isn't that right?'

'Every day, regular as clockwork.' And Will Maples turned back to chivvy one of his barmaids.

Jude was standing beside her with their two glasses of white wine. 'This is my friend, Jude.' Ridiculous, thought Carole, I still don't know her surname. I really must ask. 'Harry Grant.'

'Nice to see you.'

A grin spread across Harry's broad face. He fancied Jude, Carole could tell. Jude was the type men fell for. Whereas she . . . Her exploratory use of 'feminine wiles' on Barry Stillwell felt a bit shabby in retrospect.

'All well with you and Jenny?' asked Carole, not sure whether she was deliberately mentioning his wife's name to stop him ogling Jude.

'Yes, yes, fine.' He turned his thick neck and slowly refocused on her. There was no doubt. He had been drinking. 'More than fine, in fact.' He raised a half-empty pint in salute. 'I am celebrating my return to "the land of my fathers".'

'You mean you're Welsh?' asked Jude.

He found this funnier than it was. 'No, no, no,' he said finally, wiping the spittle from his lips. 'I was born here in Weldisham . . . and I'm coming back to live right here in Weldisham.'

Carole understood immediately. 'You've got the planning permission on your barn?'

'Exactly. The application has finally been accepted. Yesterday's meeting. Composition of the Planning Committee had changed a bit, one or two people I knew had joined . . . Suddenly they're looking on my plans with a much more friendly eye. As everywhere else in the world, round these parts it's not what you know, it's who you know. And when I was growing up here, the only people I knew were Lennie and Nick. They might have been good at building forts and things, but otherwise . . . useless people. Now, though, I know the right people. At last I know the right people. So now all the toffee-nosed prigs of Weldisham are going to have Harry Grant as their neighbour . . . like it or not!'

He didn't realize how much his excitement had raised his voice and looked embarrassed by the silence he'd created in the pub. He leaned close to Carole and Jude and confided, in an elaborate whisper, 'So that's why I'm waiting in here for Graham Forbes . . . just for the pleasure of seeing him laugh on the other side of his face.'

Triumphantly, Harry Grant swilled down the rest of his beer and turned back to the bar. 'Think I could manage another of those, thank you, young Will.'

Carole and Jude made good the opportunity to take one of the few remaining empty tables. The developer didn't seem to notice their absence. He stayed leaning against the bar, making desultory conversation with Will Maples when the manager wasn't busy serving his customers.

Harry Grant wasn't on his own for long, however. Detective Sergeant Baylis came into the bar and joined him. The meeting did not appear to have been pre-arranged, but Carole remembered that the two of them had grown up together in the village. They'd have plenty to talk about. Two Weldisham boys, both resentful that they couldn't live there any more. Except, of course, for Harry Grant that exclusion was now at an end.

Lennie Baylis ordered a pint and got another one for Harry. To the scrutiny of Carole's beady eye, once again no money seemed to change hands. What was the hold that the sergeant had over Will Maples? Was she witnessing some minor level of police corruption? And once again, Baylis didn't seem to suffer from the 'not while I'm on duty' attitude to drink.

Carole chided herself. After the previous night's exhibition, she should be a little more wary of leaping to conclusions. She kept an eye on the bar, but although the two men were deep in conversation, she had no inkling of what they might be discussing. Once or twice, Harry Grant turned round to look at the door and then consult his watch. Graham Forbes was evidently late for what she remembered he'd called his 'pre-lunch tincture', and so the developer's moment of glory was postponed.

Downing the remains of his pint, Detective Sergeant Baylis turned away from the bar, and that was the first time he noticed Carole. With a word to Harry, he came across to join them.

'Sergeant, this is my friend Jude.'

Baylis seemed as impressed with Jude's looks as Harry Grant had been.

'Jude, this is Detective Sergeant Baylis . . . Remember, the one I told you was so kind after my . . . after my unpleasant experience.'

'Yes. Nice to meet you, Sergeant.'

'I think you should both be calling me Lennie.'

He hadn't suggested that when there was just me, came Carole's knee-jerk reaction.

'This becoming your regular, is it, Mrs Seddon?'

'Carole, please,' she said in a way which, to her hyper-sensitive ear, sounded clumsy. 'No, just happened to be up here. Jude's visiting a friend in Weldisham.'

'I see,' said Baylis, easily enough. But he gave Carole a rather sharp look.

'Is there anything more you can tell us about the bones Carole found?' asked Jude, direct as ever.

Like everyone else, he responded to her manner. 'Try me.'

'Well, for instance . . . are you any nearer to finding out who the woman was?'

'We're getting there.' Lennie Baylis suddenly cocked a challenging eye at them. 'Why? Have you got any ideas of who it might be?'

Carole felt Jude's eyes boring into her as she looked down at her wine. 'No,' she mumbled. 'No idea at all.'

'I can guarantee that, as soon as we know anything definite, it'll be all over the television and radio,' he said, as if drawing the conversation to an end.

'Presumably . . .' Jude held his attention. 'Presumably these days it's fairly simple to identify bodies by DNA?'

He grimaced. 'Dead easy if you've got a record of their DNA, certainly. Or if you know who their relatives are. If you're starting from scratch, you're no further advanced than a copper any time over the last couple of centuries . . . relying on educated guesswork.' He glanced at his watch, straightened up and looked around the pub. 'No sign of him. Told me on the phone he'd be in here.' He shrugged. 'Oh well, if the mountain won't come to Mohammed, then Mohammed must go to the mountain.'

'Are you casting yourself as Mohammed in this scenario?' asked Jude.

'Guess so.'

'Then who's the mountain?'

'Graham Forbes. Goodbye, ladies.'

As Detective Sergeant Baylis left the pub, the two women exchanged looks. In Jude's there was an element of apology, and in Carole's something that approached triumph.

Chapter Twenty-three

When they emerged from the Hare and Hounds, the weather was brighter than it had any right to be in the middle of March. A cloudless sky and sunlight gave a false promise of summer. Moving into the shadows, however, they still felt as if they had stepped into a vault.

Carole and Jude didn't say any more about the case as they walked down to Conyers. There was a kind of tacit agreement between them that they'd discuss it later. Even though Tamsin's retreat to Sandalls Manor now seemed to be an irrelevance, Gillie had sounded urgent on the phone. What she had to impart to Jude might be important.

Carole had briefly contemplated another dutiful trip to Sainsbury's, but her kitchen shelves were adequately stocked. There was nothing she couldn't get at Allinstore in Fethering. And, as she said to Jude, it was wicked not to take advantage of such an afternoon for a walk on the Downs. So they parted at the Lutteridges' gate, agreeing to meet back at the car in an hour.

Carole felt a guilty excitement as she watched her friend cross the immaculate gravel up to the front door. Her talk of a walk, though not entirely inaccurate, had been incomplete. A little plan had been hatching in Carole's mind, an investigation opportunity right there in Weldisham. If her conjecture proved correct, when they next came to discuss the case she'd certainly have something that'd make Jude sit up.

From in front of the Lutteridges' house she could once again just see the sagging rooftop of the old barn behind. From lack of alternative candidates, it must be the one that Harry Grant had bought and for which he had finally received planning permission. From that position, in a few months' time he would be able to celebrate his return to Weldisham, one of the few local boys who'd made good enough to afford to live in his own village.

The decaying barn was set behind the row of houses that lined Weldisham's only street and there was no way through to it. That was one of the reasons that the Village Committee produced with such regularity to block the development of the old shell. The barn had no access. A new road would have to be built, with all the attendant disruption.

So Carole knew she'd have to walk down to the end of the village and double back, hoping there was a route to the site through the fields. Belting her Burberry tighter around her, she set out to do just that.

As she walked past the house next door to the Lutter-idges', Warren Lodge, she wondered what was happening inside. Detective Sergeant Baylis had said he was going to talk to Graham Forbes, but on what subject? Were the official enquiries moving in the same direction as her conjectures? How much did the police know?

Whatever the detailed answer to the last question, Carole knew one thing for certain. The police knew more than she and Jude did. Once again she felt the eternal frustration of the amateur, aware that she was on the back foot, pitting her wits against a highly organized and scientifically supported institution whose sole purpose was the investigation of crime.

The houses petered out and ahead of her Carole saw the track that led up over the Downs to South Welling Barn. The thought of that place and what she had found inside the fertilizer bags could still send a chill tremor through her body.

She turned right and walked along the road out of the village, along the garden wall of the first house in Weldisham. When the garden gave way to fields, the next stage of her route proved easier than she had anticipated. There was a stile, and a post with a wooden sign reading 'Public Footpath', which pointed in the direction of Harry Grant's barn. Lifting up the skirts of her Burberry, Carole stepped over the stile.

The path did not lead directly to the barn, but veered off to the left, taking a line between the fences and hedgerow which contained the fields on either side. But Carole had no difficulty leaving the path and continuing towards her destination. The depth to which the wire sagged at that point and the flattened earth on the other side suggested she was following a much-used short-cut. Though there hadn't been much rain since the downpours of her last walk on the Downs, the ground underfoot was still slippery and clogging. Her sensible walking shoes were soon heavy with mud.

She glanced up to her right. She could see the tops of the roofs in Weldisham High Street over the swell of the Downs, but no windows. The path was not overlooked.

As she got closer to the barn, Carole became more aware of how advanced was its dilapidation. The roof was not just sagging but broken-backed. Much of the greening thatch had slipped away completely, and what remained was rotten and slimy. A few disconnected rafters pointed up to the sky. The large double doors had crumbled away to nothing, leaving only lumps of blackened wood hanging like dead flesh from twisted skeletal hinges.

But the basic brick rectangle, though subsiding towards one end, looked solid enough. With sufficient injections of cash and building expertise, a developer like Harry Grant would have no problems in turning the barn into a dream home from which to crow at the other residents of Weldisham.

What would in time become Harry Grant's garden was a tangle of briars and other tendrils of undergrowth. In summer these would be interwoven with head-high nettles, but even now it was hard to make a way through to the gaping barn doors. Carole had to hold her hands up to shield her face from the lash of brambles and she felt the constant snag of thorns catching on the fabric of her Burberry.

She battered a path through to the doorway. Inside, alternate patches of gloom and bright March sunlight meant that her eyes took a moment to adjust.

Where the sun and rain could get through the holes in the roof to the ground were patches of growth, low and scrubby this time of year, but no doubt green and luxuriant in the summer. Elsewhere, there was a floor of trodden earth.

But the interior was very cluttered. In the shadows Carole could see the rusty limbs of long-dead farm machinery. There were bales of corroded barbed wire, stacks of blackened fencing posts and bellied, sagging plastic sacks.

The space had also been used as a rubbish tip by the people of Weldisham. Carole was amused by this manifestation of local hypocrisy. Residents who no doubt waxed righteously furious at Village Committee meetings about the vandalism of tourists, the detritus of bottles and crisp packets left in front of the Hare and Hounds, the drinks cartons scattered on the Green, had their own secret dumping ground. The old barn was home to a sad selection of broken furniture, wheel-less bicycles and the odd superannuated fridge.

Her eyes now used to the light, Carole picked her way cautiously through the clutter. She knew what she was looking for and, with a mixture of excitement and dread, she found it.

In one of the darkest recesses of the barn, where the sun never penetrated, there was a small patch of recently turned earth.

Chapter Twenty-four

Gillie Lutteridge's immaculate ensemble that Friday afternoon was a silk dress the colour of morello cherries. The open neck revealed a cluster of gold necklaces; a single gold chain hung from her wrist. Her make-up and the shape of her blonde hair were, as ever, irreproachable.

Jude, who'd just had a cup at the Hare and Hounds, refused the offer of coffee. Gillie gestured her to a freshly plumped armchair. 'I hope it wasn't inconvenient for you to come up here. I'm just not very good at talking on the telephone.'

'It's fine. I got a lift from a friend. She was coming up here anyway.' A minor lie, but necessary to put her hostess at ease. Jude was getting used to reading the tiny gradations in Gillie Lutteridge's manner, and had identified a considerable degree of agitation. 'It's about Tamsin, I take it,' she went on, still easing the passage for Gillie's revelation.

'Yes. I went to see her yesterday.'

'At Sandalls Manor?'

Gillie nodded. 'Miles was away on business, so I risked it.'

'And how're things going with Charles? Is he making her better?'

There was a shrug, almost of hopelessness. Gillie

169

Lutteridge seemed much less positive than Jude had ever seen her. Maybe, having once broken her façade by crying, Tamsin's mother felt she no longer had to maintain a front. What was the point, since Jude had already seen through it?

'I don't know. She seems to get better, she relapses. I keep wondering whether it's our fault.'

'What?'

'The illness. The chronic fatigue syndrome. I wonder if it's Tamsin's reaction to growing up in this house.'

'What's wrong with this house?'

Gillie's next shrug was nearly despairing. 'There's so much tension between me and Miles. I think there always has been. Ever since Tamsin was born, really. That . . . changed things between us. And, as she grew up, she can't have been unaware of the atmosphere.'

'So are you suggesting that the atmosphere in the house got to her, that that's what made her ill? As if she'd been infected by it?'

Gillie looked at Jude defiantly. 'It's possible. It seems as likely as any of the other explanations that have come up.'

'But Tamsin wasn't even living here when she got ill. She was in London.'

'Yes, but maybe she couldn't cope in London, couldn't cope with the job. Maybe living with us had kind of weakened her, so that she couldn't deal with real life.'

'Gillie, Gillie, Gillie . . .' Jude crossed from her chair and took the other woman's thin hand in hers. 'Chronic fatigue syndrome is a genuine illness. You know that. That's what you have arguments with Miles about. He's the one who thinks it's all psychosomatic. You know it's real.'

But Gillie Lutteridge was in too reduced a state to be persuaded by her own arguments. 'I don't know. It doesn't happen to other people's daughters. I keep thinking it must be my fault.'

'But then you've thought everything was your fault for a long, long time,' observed Jude quietly.

Gillie sniffed. Once again tears were not far away. Then she nodded. 'Well, it is. Most things are my fault.'

'No, Gillie. You're not well.'

'Me too?' she asked with a bitter smile.

'You're depressed if you blame yourself for everything that's wrong.'

'If that's the case, then I've been depressed for a very long time.'

'Perhaps you have.'

'No, of course I haven't!' Jude had never heard her speak so sharply. Gillie was quick to recover her usual level tone. 'Anyway, we don't want to talk about me. Tamsin's the one who's ill.'

'Are you sure she's the only one?'

'Yes.' Gillie Lutteridge moved on brusquely. 'Tamsin said something yesterday that worried me.'

'What?'

'She implied that she wanted to stay at Sandalls Manor for ever.'

'Ah. Well, I can understand why that would worry you. Given the kind of rates Charles Hilton charges for his—'

'No, it wasn't that!' Having snapped at Jude once, Gillie Lutteridge had no inhibitions about doing so again. 'It wasn't to do with Charles, not to do with her illness. It was something else and it had her absolutely terrified.'

'What?'

'Tamsin said, "Nobody knows I'm here. So I feel safe. As long as I'm here, I feel safe. But if people knew where to find me, then my life would be in danger."'

Chapter Twenty-five

When Carole got back from the footpath to Weldisham Lane, she was surprised to see that her venture to the barn had taken less than twenty minutes. Still forty to go before she'd agreed to meet her friend.

It was infuriating. She was dying to tell Jude what she'd seen and discuss the implications. Her thoughts were running too fast; she needed someone to bounce them off, someone to challenge their logic, someone to help her regain a sense of proportion. Once again she was bemused by this potential role reversal, the idea that she should look to Jude for stability. Carole was meant to be the sensible one.

Given the time she had to kill, Carole decided to walk back along the track she'd trodden two weeks before. If, as logic was telling her, the woman's body had once been buried in the wreck of the building that now belonged to Harry Grant, then someone had been along the same route to take the bones to South Welling Barn.

Ideas as to who that person might have been kept bubbling into her mind and she had to keep rigid control to stop those ideas from crystallizing in conclusions.

The track was still tacky underfoot, but not nearly as bad as it had been on her previous journey. And the mood of the Downs was very different. The menace she had felt under the louring rain-clouds was long gone, and Carole even wondered whether it was a feeling she had grafted on in retrospect, after her grisly discovery. The sun transformed the Downs from a hostile to a nurturing environment.

Her sensible shoes made a regular slapping sound on the mud as she strode forward. She felt fit and optimistic. Carole Seddon was only in her early fifties, after all. There was life in the old girl yet.

Sound travels strangely on the Downs, bounced from hillocks and funnelled by valleys. Frequently it's hard to tell exactly where a noise is coming from.

So Carole wasn't distracted by the screech of eroded gears until the vehicle was almost upon her. She turned to see an old Land Rover roaring up the track behind her. It was being driven as though the driver were blind to her existence.

Carole leapt to the verge at the side, mentally cursing the loutishness of whoever was driving, and expected to see the Land Rover career off along the track.

But it didn't. The vehicle braked fiercely in a flurry of mud. Then, in a grinding of gears, it reversed and came to a halt beside her. The flailing tyres spotted her freshly cleaned Burberry with mud.

Carole opened her mouth to remonstrate with whatever road-hog she was up against, but the words dried on her lips when she saw who got out of the driver's door.

She was not an accidental victim of someone's thoughtless high spirits. The man had been looking for her.

Carole Seddon didn't like the expression she saw in his eyes as he said, more statement than question, 'You're the one who found the bones, aren't you?'

Chapter Twenty-six

'All I could get out of Tamsin,' Gillie Lutteridge went on, 'was that something happened last time she came here.'

'That was only a few weeks ago, you said. Another time Miles was away on business.'

'Yes. Anyway, while she was in Weldisham, she saw something that frightened her to death.'

'But she wouldn't tell you what?'

Gillie shook her head.

'Well, who did she see while she was here?'

'That's the point. She didn't see anyone except me. She didn't want anyone to know she was here.'

'Did she use the phone?'

'Not so far as I know.'

'There weren't any letters waiting for her?'

'No. As soon as anything addressed to her arrives, I forward it to Sandalls Manor.'

Jude grimaced. 'Well, something must've happened to get her into such a state.' She rubbed her chin thoughtfully. 'She didn't go out?'

'I was with her all evening. We both went to bed at the same time.'

'So, without leaving the house or having contact with another human being, Tamsin managed to get the impression that someone wanted to kill her? It doesn't make sense.'

'No. There's only one thing I can think, Jude . . .'

'What's that?'

'Well, I just wonder if . . . With her illness, Tamsin's sleep patterns are all over the place. Sometimes she sleeps all the time, almost as if she were narcoleptic. And then she goes through phases when she's awake for hours in the night and . . .'

'You think she might have gone out?'

'She might.'

'What for?'

'To smoke a cigarette. She keeps telling me she's given up, but I'm not sure I believe her. She used to smoke like a chimney at university, and while she was working in London. When Miles and I made it pretty clear that we didn't like the smell of cigarettes in the house, Tamsin used to go outside.'

'Into the garden?'

'Yes. Or if it was cold or wet, she'd go a bit further.'

'Where?'

'There's an old barn just beyond the end of our garden. Tamsin sometimes used to go in there to smoke.'

Chapter Twenty-seven

Brian Helling was once again dressed in the leather coat and beret, uniform of the disaffected artist. Carole couldn't help recalling Graham Forbes's Chesterton quote about the artistic temperament being 'a disease that afflicts amateurs'. In other circumstances, she might have found the self-defined writer a figure of fun. But not with the expression that was currently on his thin face. Nor as she recollected the rest of her conversation with Graham Forbes, about the subject matter of Brian Helling's writing.

She answered his question, confirming that she was indeed the one who had found the bones.

'Carole somebody . . .'

'Carole Seddon.'

'Lennie Baylis told me it was you.'

'Ah.' Strange – or perhaps not strange, perhaps characteristic of the area – how all these Weldisham boys seemed to keep in touch. Brian Helling still living there with his mother; Harry Grant soon to move back in; Detective Sergeant Baylis living elsewhere, but still resentful of his exclusion from the village on economic grounds.

'And what do you know about them?' Brian Helling went on.

'Know about the bones?' Carole shrugged. She wasn't about to share the conjectures that had formed in her mind since visiting the dilapidated barn. 'I know what's been on the media. They're the bones of a woman aged between thirty and fifty. That's all anyone knows . . . except maybe the police pathologists . . . and they're not yet sharing their conclusions.'

'So you didn't go to South Welling Barn looking for them?'

'Looking for the bones?' Carole was incredulous. 'No. I was just sheltering from the rain. I'd never seen the barn before. I didn't even know it existed.'

'Right.' Brian Helling rubbed the back of his hand against his long nose. It could have been a gesture of relief. He certainly seemed less manic as he continued. 'I'm sorry. In a small place like Weldisham a lot of rumours get spread around. And some of them aren't very helpful rumours. They could be hurtful to local individuals.'

'Individuals like your mother?' Carole hazarded.

Her words snapped his mood back to paranoia. 'What do you know about my mother? How do you know who my mother is?'

'Detective Sergeant Baylis told me who you were,' replied Carole evenly. 'He said your mother was Pauline Helling, who lives in Heron Cottage.'

The answer was insufficient to allay all of his suspicion. 'Why did Lennie tell you about me?'

'Because I asked him.'

'Why?'

'Because, if you must know, I'd overheard you sounding off in the Hare and Hounds. I wondered who it could be who was talking so loudly and tastelessly about the bones I'd discovered.'

'Oh.' He seemed to accept that, and not to be offended

by it. Brian Helling knew he drew attention to himself in public. He even prided himself on the fact.

'Did Lennie say anything else about me?'

'Like what?'

'Oh. Nothing.'

Carole pressed on. She might as well get any information she could. 'So, have people been circulating nasty rumours about your mother?'

'What?' He looked distracted for a moment. 'No, no, of course they haven't.' A new unease came into his eyes. 'What makes you ask that? What makes you think my mother has anything to do with the bones?'

Carole noted the anxiety in his tone, but her answer was entirely palliative. 'Nothing, no reason.' She decided to play the 'silly woman' card. 'Sorry, but you make a discovery like I did at South Welling Barn and, needless to say, it sets your mind racing. You get all kinds of daft ideas.'

'So long as you recognize they are daft,' said Brian Helling, with an edge of threat in his voice.

'Yes,' Carole responded humbly. She was still trying to work out what Brian Helling's agenda might be. Why had he come chasing after her so dramatically? Was he trying to get information out of her or simply find out how much she knew? And why did how much she knew matter to him?

'Do you know many people in Weldisham?' he asked suddenly.

'I've met a few in the past couple of weeks. The Forbeses invited me to dinner.'

'Oh, did they?' For Brian Helling this seemed to categorize her. She was the sort of woman who got invited to dinner by Graham and Irene Forbes. 'And you haven't known them for long?'

'No. I'd hardly say I know them now. I mean, I never met Graham's first wife.'

'But you know what happened to her?' He was very alert now, fixing Carole with his eyes, as though her answer mattered a lot.

'The story goes she ran off with another man. In Malaysia.'

The words seemed to relax him. 'Yes,' he said. 'That's how the story goes.'

'Are you implying the story's not true?'

'Certainly not. Are you?'

Given the cue, Carole was insanely tempted to share the thoughts that had been building up inside about the first Mrs Forbes. But she restrained herself. To Jude maybe, but not to Brian Helling. He was the last person on earth she should make aware of her suspicions.

'Of course not,' she said.

He broke the eye contact between them. 'Who else do you know in the village?'

'I've told you. I didn't know anyone till two weeks ago.'

'Sure?'

'Of course I'm sure.'

'You don't know the Lutteridges?'

'No. I've heard the name, but I haven't met them.' Carole was about to say that she had a friend who knew them, but some instinct held her back.

'Mm. I see.' Some of the tension went from his thin face, as if he'd found out what he'd come to find out. He looked along the exposed chalk of the track. 'Were you going back to South Welling Barn?'

'No. I was just going for a walk. Killing time.'

'Why do you need to kill time?' he asked sharply.

Again she kept Jude's name out of it. Instead, she played for a bit of spurious sympathy. 'You have a lot of time to kill when you're retired.'

'Do you?' Some of the cockiness Brian Helling had shown in the pub returned to his manner. 'I won't have to worry about that.'

'Oh?'

'I'm a writer. Writers don't retire.'

'Ah.' Even those writers who never make any money from their writing?

He moved towards the Land Rover. 'Right. I must get back.'

'Mr Helling . . .'

He stopped and looked at her. There was still malevolence in his eyes.

'I just wanted to ask . . . given the fact that something like the discovery of these bones is, as you said, going to start a lot of rumours in a small place like Weldisham . . .'

He didn't help her. He just waited.

'Which of the rumours would you go along with?'

'How do you mean?'

'Who do you think the bones might have belonged to?'

He was about to give a brusque answer, but stopped himself. As he smiled, Carole noticed that he had almost no upper lip, just a line above his teeth where the flesh stopped. 'I think, to answer that,' he began slowly, 'you'd have to ask yourself who'd gone missing from Weldisham in the past twenty years . . .'

'Yes,' Carole prompted. That was the conclusion she'd reached herself.

Brian Helling let out a little grunt of a laugh. 'Wouldn't you say Lennie Baylis was taking rather a personal interest in this case?'

'In what way?'

'He seems to be around the village more than he needs to be.'

'But he used to live here, didn't he? Maybe that's the reason.'

'Yes, but Lennie's always been a snooper. I was at school with him, I know. Don't you think it's odd, though, the way he keeps checking up on everyone here in Weldisham, seeing if they're all right, finding out what they're thinking?'

It was true. Carole had put his solicitude for her down to compassionate professionalism, but what Brian Helling was hinting at also fitted the facts.

'Well, you probably don't know,' he went on, 'but more than twenty years ago, his mother walked out.'

'He did tell me that, yes.'

'Or was *supposed* to have walked out,' said Brian Helling slyly. 'It was a very unhappy marriage. Lennie's father beat her up ... That wasn't the kind of thing you could keep quiet in a place like Weldisham. Everyone knows everyone's business.'

'And you're suggesting Lennie Baylis's father may have killed his wife?'

He shrugged. 'There was talk at the time. I remember my mother talking about it. She's always known everything that went on in Weldisham.'

'But she wasn't living here when Mrs Baylis disappeared.'

'Not living here, but working here. Anyway, some of the rumours about Lennie's dad doing away with his old woman have resurfaced in the last couple of weeks . . . Might be worth investigating.'

'Yes.'

Abruptly Brian Helling stepped up into the cab of his Land Rover. He slammed the door and, as he peered fixedly at Carole, underwent another of his sudden mood changes. 'But not investigating by *you*,' he hissed. 'Weldisham is a tightly knit community. It doesn't like outsiders snooping into its affairs.'

He started the engine, slammed the Land Rover into reverse and set off at breakneck speed, skidding over the track back to Weldisham.

Leaving Carole in no doubt that she had been both warned off and threatened.

Chapter Twenty-eight

'But I'm sure I'm right,' Carole crowed.

'Hey, watch how you're driving!'

'Sorry, Jude.'

Carole slowed the Renault down. The Weldisham Lane was too narrow for the speed she'd been doing. She must slow herself down too. Relief after her unpleasant encounter with Brian Helling was compounding the excitement with which her mind was racing to make her heady and irresponsible. Stop it, she told herself. You are Carole Seddon. Boring, reliable old Carole Seddon. Carole Seddon doesn't behave like this.

With the Renault progressing as if to a funeral, she laid out her thinking with all the sobriety of a Home Office departmental strategy presentation. 'Jude, the clincher is that Lennie – Detective Sergeant Baylis – was going to see Graham Forbes. That must mean he's suspicious about what happened to Graham's first wife.'

'It could mean a lot of other things. Detective Sergeant Baylis has been to see you a couple of times, and that doesn't mean he's suspecting you of murder, does it?'

'No, all right,' said Carole testily.

Jude giggled.

'What's the joke?'

'I'm sorry. This is just such an unfamiliar role for me – playing devil's advocate.'

'It's becoming more familiar by the minute. You were doing exactly the same thing last night.'

'Maybe it's the part I'll play for the rest of my life. Is that my future – the eternal wet blanket?'

'I can't see it.' Carole was not going to be deflected. 'Look, just let me spell out my scenario, and don't stop me till I've finished. Then pick holes in it, by all means . . . Though,' she said with an uncharacteristic moment of cockiness, 'I don't think you'll find any.'

'Well, well, there's confidence for you. OK, spell away.'

'All right. I'll take the starting point I did last night. In 1987, on the night of the Great Storm, Graham Forbes, driven mad by the aridity of his marriage and the fact that he's fallen in love with Irene out in Kuala Lumpur, kills his wife, Sheila.'

Jude opened her mouth to make some comment, but managed to stop herself.

'He buries her body in the old barn. He puts it there, because the barn's right behind his house and nobody can see him from the rest of the village. Then, on the Monday morning he catches his flight to Kuala Lumpur and is reunited with his beloved Irene. When he next returns to England, he's alone and he has this hard-luck story about Sheila having gone off with another man. Three years is reckoned to be a decent interval, so when he retires in 1990, he brings back his new bride and they settle down to live permanently in Weldisham.'

Jude could restrain herself no longer. 'That's virtually exactly what you told me last night.'

'No. We have a very important new element – the fact that the body was buried in the barn.'

'Then why was it moved from the barn?'

Carole grinned triumphantly. 'I was just coming to that. Graham Forbes's secret is safe so long as the barn remains a dilapidated wreck. Various people, the latest of whom is Harry Grant, have plans to convert it into a dwelling. But each time the issue arises, the Village Committee makes such a fuss with local objections that planning permission is refused. And who's Chairman of the Village Committee? Graham Forbes. So he sees to it that every time his secret is threatened, he coordinates the opposition. And he always succeeds. Until this time.

'This time, a few different members on the Planning Committee and a new government policy about building more homes in Sussex mean that finally Harry Grant gets the go-ahead he's been waiting for all this time.

'But, of course, that has very serious implications for Graham Forbes. A house won't have an earth floor. A house will have proper foundations dug. And once those are dug, his thirteen-year-old skeleton in the cupboard – or rather under the barn – is going to be discovered.

'So, as soon as Graham Forbes gets the tip-off that the Planning Committee decision has gone against him, he has to move his wife's remains.' Carole was trying to sound all sober and objective, but she couldn't keep the excitement out of her voice as she went on, 'However, the night he chooses to perform the grisly task of exhumation happens to be the night that Tamsin Lutteridge, knowing her father's away on business, has come to visit her mother.'

Jude let out a little gasp as the excitement got to her too. She hadn't previously made the connection that Carole continued, with mounting triumph, to spell out.

'So now we fit in what you found out from Gillie

Lutteridge. That night Tamsin can't sleep. She's dying for a cigarette. She goes out into the garden. But it's cold. So, as she has often done in the past, she goes into the old barn.

'Inside she sees Graham Forbes and she sees what he's doing. There is a confrontation. He threatens to kill her if she ever breathes a word of what she's seen. Tamsin is so terrified that she hides herself back in Sandalls Manor, genuinely afraid that she'll be killed if she ever comes out.'

Carole Seddon stopped and looked across at the passenger seat. Jude was nodding her head slowly, as she tested the junctions of the logical progression her friend had just described. Finally, she said, 'No, Carole, that's good. It's very good.'

'Thank you.' Carole turned the Renault sedately out on to the main road towards Fethering. 'And you'd say that even with your devil's advocate hat on, would you?'

Wryly, Jude shook her head. 'Ooh no. The devil's advocate in me would want various points proved.'

'Oh. What points?'

'Let's just start with three obvious ones. The devil's advocate in me would want proof a) that Graham Forbes had met and fallen in love with Irene before he returned to England for the leave that ended on the weekend of the Great Storm, b) that he was definitely on his own when he travelled back to Kuala Lumpur the following Monday, and c), coming up to date, that he knew the likely outcome of the Planning Committee's meeting two weeks before it happened.'

There was a silence. Then, bitterly, Carole said, 'God, you're picky.'

*

'Darling, how too, too wonderful to hear from you!'

It was clear from Trevor Malcolm's opening words that he'd overcome any reticence he might once have suffered from about his sexual orientation. It was also clear that the lunch he'd returned from had been a good one.

'I'm sorry it's been such a long time.'

'Carole, my dear, what is thirty years between friends? Presumably you want something?'

'Well . . .'

'Oh, come on, dearie. I know I made a huge impression on you at Durham and you've been holding a candle for me all these years . . . no doubt in the snug security of your spinster bed . . .'

'I did actually get married, Trevor.'

'Did you? Little devil. Are you still?'

'No.'

'Thought not. That's the thing about me. I spoil people for other men. No one really matches up, you know.'

'Mm. You didn't get married, did you?'

He giggled a tinkling giggle. 'No, I don't think that would have been . . . um . . . appropriate. Why make one woman unhappy when you can make lots and lots of men happy?'

'Right.'

'So come on, what is it you want from me . . . now we seem to have ruled out the possibility that it's my body?'

'OK. I need some information about the movements of someone who used to work for the British Council.'

'Ooh, how very sinister. What is this, Carole – are you turning detective?'

She laughed. The suggestion was too silly.

'Or is it something to do with your work? Yes, you're at the Home Office, aren't you?'

'Was. I'm retired.'

'Oh, my God! I don't believe it. Anno Domini's so cruel, isn't she? The policemen're looking so young these days, I feel like I'm positively cradle-snatching. And you only have to scan the obituaries to see that people are dying at absurdly young ages. No, it's dreadful, Carole, I'm the only person of my age I know who's kept his looks.'

'Ah.'

'Mind you, the picture in the attic is positively *wizened*. OK, so tell me what you want to find out and I'll see if I can help you.'

Carole told him.

When she'd finished, he said, 'Ooh, how intriguing. I'm far too polite to ask you why you want to know. I'll just let my little mind buzz with conjecture.'

'Do you think you'll be able to help me?'

'Might.'

'Or is all that kind of information high security?'

'Of course it is, Carole dear.'

'Oh. I'm sorry.'

'But don't you worry about that. I'll find it. I always think discretion's such an overrated virtue . . . don't you?'

Chapter Twenty-nine

Trevor Malcolm rang back within the hour. It was nearly six o'clock. 'You're lucky to get me still in the office this late on a Friday.'

'I do appreciate it, Trevor.'

'Oh, don't worry about that. Nothing I like more than a little *intrigue*. And I'm afraid this evening I haven't got a whole raft of young Adonises fighting over my body.' For a moment, his façade slipped and he sounded a little wistful. 'In fact, young Adonises are a bit thin on the ground these days. I keep myself in shape, but do they notice?'

Carole cut through the potential introspection. 'Did you have any luck?'

'Not with the young Adonises, no.'

'I meant—'

'I know exactly what you meant, dear. And I wouldn't have rung you back if I hadn't got anything to tell you. The assignment wasn't easy, let me tell you—'

'I do appreciate your making the effort, Trevor. It's very generous of you.'

'Yes, I am generous. Not recognized as much as it should be, perhaps, but it gives me a warm inward glow. And you don't get many of those to the pound these days. Still, you want to know what I found out, don't you?'

'Would be nice.'

'Mm. Well, I had to be a bit lateral. Most of the relevant information would be in personnel files and the Council tends to be a bit anal with those, very unwilling to let all and sundry peer through them ... which I suppose you can understand. There are a few little details of my time in Morocco that I wouldn't necessarily want everyone to know about. By no means. That business with the two waiters and the camel ... hmm ... So, as I say, I had to think laterally ... I went to the Literature Department instead.'

'How would that help?'

'A lot of the work someone like Graham Forbes would have been doing out in Malaysia would be hosting tours by British writers, you see. So I thought, if there was anyone out there over the time you've asked about ... Well, Bob would be your male aunt, wouldn't she?'

'Yes,' said Carole, a little bewildered. 'Very clever.'

'Hm ... Yes, I always have been clever ... in every area except my private life ... Still, I don't want to *whinge*. That would just be too painful. No, it was wonderful. I hit pay-dirt straight away. There was a writer out on a tour in Malaysia at exactly the right time.'

'Brilliant. Do you have any means of contacting him?'

'All on his file. Address, telephone, fax ... It's even been updated with an e-mail address.'

'Trevor, you're a genius.'

'Yes, I am, aren't I? Not that you'd know it from the way the riff-raff round here treat me ... Some of us were born, you know, just not to be appreciated ...'

Carole had heard a blip on her Call Waiting towards the end of her conversation with Trevor Malcolm, but she hadn't bothered to respond to it. At the end of her call, she checked 1471.

At first she didn't know the number. Then she recognized it as Barry Stillwell's. It didn't seem like less than twenty-four hours since she'd had her date with him; could have been years before.

What on earth did Barry want? She didn't bother to ring him back.

Sebastian Trent was very happy to talk to them. Carole had rung on the Friday evening and he'd said in his laid-back, slightly aristocratic voice that he always did 'interviews and stuff' in the afternoon. 'I write in the mornings. Can only do three hours a day. If I do more, my writing just gets glib.'

He suggested three o'clock on the Monday. Carole tried to spell out to him what she wanted to ask about, but he waved the detail away with, 'I'm sure we can sort all that out when you come. House is dead easy to find. You are familiar with Hampstead, I assume?'

She didn't really know why she wanted Jude to come along with her for this part of the investigation. Maybe it was just that she felt uncertain of her own people skills and knew that everyone responded to Jude's easy manner. She was also keen to bring their enquiries together, so that they didn't get into another 'devil's advocate' situation. If they both got information at the same time, they might find making sense of it easier.

Jude agreed readily – indeed enthusiastically. 'Yes,' she said, 'I haven't had to go to London for a while. The timing's right.'

That was intriguing. Why did Jude *have* to go up to

London? But, as ever, Carole didn't have time to put the supplementary questions.

'But can we meet there – at Sebastian Trent's house?'

'Yes, if you like.'

Carole was slightly put out. She'd had in mind a girls' jolly, travelling up on the train from Fethering together and then perhaps a nice lunch somewhere. She didn't, however, let her disappointment show.

Jude went on, 'I think this was meant to happen.'

'What was meant to happen?'

'You suggesting I should go up to London. I'm clearly meant to go up there this weekend. It's a synchronicity thing. There's someone I ought to see.'

But, once again, before the compulsion to see this person – or indeed his or her identity – could be explored, the conversation had moved on.

On the Sunday morning, Carole took Gulliver for a long walk on Fethering Beach. He was completely recovered now from his injury and extravagantly grateful to her for the extended excursion.

Automatically, when she got back to High Tor, Carole went to the phone and checked 1471. Barry Stillwell had rung again. Again she didn't call him back.

Chapter Thirty

'I just feel story-telling is simplistic. There's so much one can do with language beyond merely passing on narratives. Rather than opening up the potentialities locked in language, plotting can limit them.'

Sebastian Trent stood with an arm resting nonchalantly along the mantelpiece of his artfully lived-in sitting room. His unruly grey curls were reflected in the large arched mirror over the fireplace. He was dressed, with calculated casualness, in chunky brown brogues, loose-cut chinos, a slightly frayed button-down Oxford shirt and a shapeless grey cardigan into whose pockets his fists were pushed down.

On a shelf behind him, adjacent to the mirror – conveniently, had a photographer been present – were copies of his thin literary oeuvre. Carole had thought it politic to consult a reference book before meeting the author, and found that Sebastian Trent had published five novels. They had all been critically lauded for 'playing with the concepts of magic realism and postmodernism and subverting both to produce a synthesis that is uniquely Trent'.

Carole was surprised that writing books of that kind made enough money for the three-storey Hampstead pile in which the author lived. But then she didn't know much about the world of publishing.

It was clearly his novels Sebastian Trent wished to pontificate on. Carole now understood why he had shooed away the details of what she wanted to ask him about. He would have said the same, whatever the questions. She and Jude were being treated to the authorial overview of his own work, and it was clearly a routine that he'd wheeled out many times before. No doubt his audiences in Malaysia in 1987 had been treated to something very similar.

His manner was that of a skilled lecturer or interviewee. The timing was practised, the jokes honed and the whole presented with that particular brand of self-depreciation which masks huge arrogance.

Carole recognized that they had a problem. Getting Sebastian Trent off his literary tramlines was not going to be easy.

'I am interested,' he continued, 'not in the mere meanings of words but in their resonance. In some ways, I suppose, I could be called a semioticist, except that I'm not solely interested in the adumbration of covert references which get attached to words. I am also concerned by their sounds, the anomalies of homonyms, the latent misunderstandings inherent in assonantal rhymes, the misleading potential of the word half-heard. This is what gives such a rich texture to my writing. And this is why I feel readers only get the full experience on a second reading of my novels. Take, for instance, the Tuscan idyll sequence in my—'

'I'm sorry,' said Jude, 'but this isn't what we came here to talk about.'

Sebastian Trent was so taken aback to be stopped in mid-flow that he could only mouth helplessly. This was the first time in his authorial experience that he'd been interrupted. Listeners usually hung with rapt attention on his every insight and *aperçu*, frequently taking notes.

Carole grinned inwardly. Now she knew why her instinct had told her to bring Jude along.

'The reason we came,' her friend went on with an engagingly innocent smile, 'was to talk about a trip you made for the British Council to Malaysia in 1987.'

'Oh.' The supremely articulate Sebastian Trent was still so much in shock that he was reduced to a mono-syllable.

'Now, as we understand it, Sebastian, you were in Malaysia in October of that year . . .'

He gave a bewildered nod.

'You spent most of your time in Kuala Lumpur, but also travelled to Ipoh and Penang.'

He couldn't deny that either.

'And while you were out there your British Council host was Graham Forbes.'

Another nod.

Carole wondered how long this could go on. It was wonderful while it lasted, but surely at some point Sebastian Trent was going to ask why he was being grilled in this way. She didn't have to wait long.

'I'm sorry,' he said, 'but what is this all about?'

'Oh, didn't Carole say on the phone?' asked Jude coolly.

No, thought Carole, she's not going to throw this over to me, is she? She needn't have worried.

Glibly, Jude continued, 'We're trying to contact Graham Forbes's wife, Sheila.'

He didn't ask why. Having apparently come to terms with the fact that they weren't after his pearls of literary wisdom, Sebastian Trent now seemed keen only to send them on their way. 'Presumably you contact her through Graham. He's retired now, but I think I've got an address for him. Somewhere in Sussex, I seem to remember.'

Carole came in to do her bit. 'You didn't know that he'd remarried?'

'No.' Sebastian Trent didn't sound particularly interested in the information. Graham Forbes may have been his host in Kuala Lumpur, but no closeness seemed to have developed between them.

'He remarried someone called Irene. Chinese woman. I wondered if you'd met her while you were out in Malaysia.'

He shrugged. 'I met a lot of people. And obviously, because I was giving lectures and things, they'd remember me a lot better than I'd remember them. I'd have made much more of an impression. Anyway, we are talking thirteen years ago. I can't be expected to remember all the names now, can I?'

'No,' Carole persisted, 'but you might have noticed if Graham Forbes was making a particular fuss of Irene, if he was treating her like a girlfriend . . .?'

'Well, he'd be unlikely to do that in public, wouldn't he? Whatever their private relationship might have been.'

'What do you mean?'

'Men don't usually flaunt their girlfriends when their wives are present.'

It was Carole's turn to be struck dumb. So it was left to Jude to clarify the situation. 'Sheila Forbes was in Kuala Lumpur with her husband while you were out there?'

'Yes. We even travelled from Heathrow on the same plane.'

'Really? On the morning of Monday 19 October 1987?' asked Carole.

'I can't remember the exact date, but if you say that's when it was, I'm sure you're right. I remember it was the Monday after that terrible storm, because my wife had to go off down to Hampshire to assess the damage to our country place.'

A country place too, thought Carole. There must be really serious money in writing experimental literary fiction.

'Did you know you'd be travelling out with Graham Forbes?'

'No. But he recognized me of course at Heathrow and introduced himself and his wife.'

'Ah.' Carole felt her whole edifice of conjecture tumbling around her ears.

'And at the other end, did you travel from the airport into Kuala Lumpur together?' asked Jude.

'I can't remember after all this time.' He tapped his chin testily, trying to dredge up the recollection. 'Oh, I think what actually happened was that Mrs Forbes went off in a taxi and Graham Forbes came with me in the British Council car to show me my hotel. The Ming Palace, as I recall. Yes, I remember now. There was a new driver, only just started that day. He didn't know the way to the hotel.'

'And did you see a lot of Sheila Forbes while you were in Kuala Lumpur?'

'Not a lot, no.'

'But you did see her?'

'I must have done. I can't honestly remember.'

'Did you get much impression of her personality?'

He shrugged. 'She seemed quiet, not very interesting.' Sebastian Trent gave the impression he didn't find many other people very interesting.

'But you couldn't judge whether she and her husband were getting on well?'

'No, I couldn't judge that.' He was beginning to find the interrogation irksome. 'For heaven's sake. Look, Graham Forbes was simply the British Council representative in Kuala Lumpur who made the arrangements for my tour. I didn't get to know him and I certainly didn't get to know his wife.'

And that was it, really. Sebastian Trent had nothing else to tell them. And though he could no doubt have been prompted by the proper cue to continue his dissertation on the genius of Sebastian Trent, Carole and Jude felt too shattered by his revelations to want to do anything other than leave as soon as possible.

In the large hallway, they met the author's wife coming in. She was instantly recognizable as the star of one of the country's most popular and dumbed-down television soaps.

So that was how a writer of recherché literary novels could afford a mansion in Hampstead and a country place in Hampshire.

Chapter Thirty-one

They travelled back together from Victoria to Fethering on a train that was crowded and filthy and rattled through endless stations, getting a little further behind schedule with each one. The market for public transport to that part of West Sussex has always been a finite one, so no effort has ever been made to improve the service. Carole Seddon had become inured to the third-world squalor of her local railway system and so travelled up to London as little as possible.

They didn't say much on the train. This was partly because the compartments were so full, loud with the hubbub of shrieking adolescents and businessmen on mobile phones.

But their silence was also, in a way, because there was nothing *to* say. The links of logic, so durable on the Friday, had been shattered by a single blow. The connection between the freshly turned earth in one old barn and the bones in another had been destroyed the instant Sebastian Trent said he'd travelled out to Kuala Lumpur with Graham Forbes and his wife.

Carole and Jude's investigation had run into a brick wall.

*

They could both have gone back to their separate houses in Fethering High Street, but the Crown and Anchor seemed a more cheerful prospect. Not that it felt particularly cheerful when they arrived. Apart from anything else, the landlord was in subdued mood.

'You two been having a good time then, have you?' he asked gloomily.

'Not bad,' said Jude.

'Carole?'

She was so caught up in her thoughts, trying to make new connections in the case, that it took her a moment to realize he was addressing her.

'What? Oh yes. You know, all right.'

Her tone must have sounded more deterrent than she'd intended, because Ted Crisp went off to serve another customer before returning to take their order. And then he was distinctly offhand, particularly with Carole. She couldn't think what she'd done to offend him, but Ted's behaviour seemed just another symptom of her uncanny ability to read signals wrong.

She sat down with Jude at a table some way away from the bar. Her friend yawned and raked her fingers through her blonde hair. Carole wondered what she'd been doing in London all weekend. Needless to say, Jude hadn't volunteered anything about the person whom she 'ought to see'.

But something seemed to have got her down. Carole had never seen Jude so subdued. Her customary energy had been replaced by a kind of lethargy.

'Is anything the matter?' Carole asked.

'What? Oh, nothing that won't get better.'

'Is it what happened with Sebastian Trent?'

Jude let out a little wry laugh. 'No, no. Obviously that

was disappointing, but . . . No, that's not what's got me down.'

'What then?'

'Oh, a bloody man. It usually is a bloody man, isn't it?'

This was closer to a confessional mood than any other moment Carole had shared with Jude. 'If you want to talk about it . . .' she said.

For a moment, Jude looked undecided. Then she shook her head. 'No. No need to burden you with my troubles.'

'I don't mind. And you're always saying that troubles should be shared.'

'Yes, thanks, Carole, but . . . not in this case, I think.' Another brisk shake of the head. 'No, there's a certain kind of man who gets pleasure from knowing he's upset you. It's some kind of validation of his masculinity, the fact that he can make women suffer . . .'

'Yes,' agreed Carole, hoping for more.

'And so talking about how much that kind of man has upset you is really just playing into his hands, joining his conspiracy, building up his self-image as a heart-breaker . . .'

'Well . . .'

'Which means the best thing is to think very deliber-ately about something else.' She swept her hands back from her nose, as if wiping away unpleasant memories. 'OK. Let's get back to your bones.'

'All right,' said Carole, disappointed.

'Well, it seems like your wonderful Graham Forbes wife-murderer theory is shot out of the water . . .'

'I'm afraid so.'

'But don't worry. Some of the thinking you've done

may still be relevant. I mean, that newly dug earth in the barn . . . It can't have anything to do with Graham Forbes, but it still might be where the bones were buried. And, if that is the case, then we've got to work out who else it was who dug them up.'

'Right.'

'Ooh, and there's one thing I can certainly follow up on.' Jude's vitality may not have been spontaneous, but she was willing it back with renewed energy as she took out her mobile phone and punched in a number. 'I can ask Tamsin Lutteridge what she saw in the barn that night when she was back in Weldisham. I should have done that earlier, but I was so caught up in thoughts of — Ah, hello,' she said, as she got through on the phone. 'Could I speak to Charles Hilton, please? How long will he be there? Right. Is that Anne? This is Jude. Jude. We met the other week when I came over to Sandalls Manor. Yes. In fact, it's not really Charles I'm trying to contact. I'd like to speak to Tamsin Lutteridge. No, as a matter of fact, Anne, I know she's there. I—'

But the phone had been put down on her. Jude grimaced as she switched off.

'Hung up on me. Charles's wife's maintaining the fiction that Tamsin's not there. I'll have to speak to Charles himself.'

'You can get round him?'

'Oh yes.'

Jude rubbed her hands over her brown eyes. Carole noticed how tired she looked. Her weekend had been tough. Whoever the man was, he had caused her a lot of stress.

Carole was about to make solicitous enquiries, but Jude steepled her hands up to her mouth and puffed through them in an irritated way. 'Right. What else can we do about the case? What other leads have we got to follow?'

'Nothing very definite. I'm afraid I've been so caught up in the Graham Forbes scenario, I haven't really considered any other options.'

'No . . . But, whatever really happened, the whole thing does go back quite a long time in the history of Weldisham . . .'

'Probably.'

'So we need to talk to people who've been around the village a long time.'

'Not that there are many of those. The majority of residents only moved there to retire.'

'Yes, but we still have the ones who grew up there . . .'

'Lennie Baylis and Harry Grant.'

'And wasn't there someone else? I'm sure when I met Harry in the Hare and Hounds, he said . . .' But Jude's thought was overtaken by a more urgent one. 'What about Brian Helling?'

Carole shuddered. She didn't want to be reminded of their encounter on the previous Friday. The wildness in Brian Helling's eyes still disturbed her. 'I'm not sure whether he actually did grow up in Weldisham. I think he was probably an adult by the time his mother had her pools win and bought Heron Cottage.'

'Hm. So she . . . what's her name?'

'Pauline Helling.'

'She didn't live in the village before that?'

'Don't think so. Mind you, Brian did say that she used to work there.'

'Really?' There was now almost a sparkle in Jude's eyes. 'Well, if the way she snooped at you is anything to go by, I should think Pauline Helling knows everything that's ever gone on in Weldisham.'

'Possibly.'

'So it's obvious what you have to do next, isn't it, Carole?'

'Is it? What?'

'You have to go and see Pauline Helling.'

Carole had spent the rest of the evening trying to find a reason that might justify a visit to the owner of Heron Cottage. She and Jude hadn't stayed at the Crown and Anchor for a meal. One more drink and they'd gone. Ted Crisp hadn't even looked up from the bar when they called out their goodbyes.

Carole woke on the Tuesday morning with her problem still unresolved. There was no plausible reason why she needed to call on Pauline Helling, other than the true one – that she wanted to pick the old woman's brains to help her unauthorized enquiries into the bones found in South Welling Barn.

She continued to chew through the possibilities as she took Gulliver for his early morning walk on Fethering Beach, and while she drove the few miles from Fethering to Weldisham.

But nothing came. And, given the antisocial malevolence which was all she had seen of Pauline Helling's behaviour, as she stood on the doorstep after ringing the bell of Heron Cottage, Carole fully expected to have the door slammed in her face.

Certainly the old woman's eyes, close-set on either side of her beaky nose, radiated suspicion. There was also recognition. If Pauline Helling was as much of a social outcast in Weldisham as Detective Sergeant Baylis had suggested, God only knew through what network she got her information, but she was definitely aware that the woman on her doorstep was the one who'd found the bones.

'Good morning?' The words may have been polite, but their delivery was distinctly deterrent.

Carole still had no plan of what to say. In desperation, she tried the truth. 'Mrs Helling, good morning. My name's Carole Seddon. I wanted to talk to you about something your son Brian said to me.'

There was a moment's impasse, then, with bad grace, Pauline Helling moved back into the gloom of her hall. 'You'd better come in.'

Chapter Thirty-two

Carole could hear barking as she entered Heron Cottage. Presumably Pauline Helling's black and white spaniel was locked away in the kitchen.

The sitting room into which she was ushered looked at odds with the exterior of the house. She had been in enough modernized country cottages to have certain expectations – white walls, exposed beams, open fireplaces, details which accentuated the building's rustic origins. Pauline Helling's home had none of these. If there were any beams – and the cottage's age suggested there must have been – they'd been covered over with plasterboard, and the fireplace had been filled in. The walls were a dyspeptic green colour, not a gentle eau-de-Nil, but a sharp acidic tone. On a carpet whose multi-hued swirly design was too large for the space sat a three-piece suite in purple velour. The same material was used for the orange curtains.

The room's only concession to its history was the lozenge criss-crossing on the leaded windows, but these were modern double-glazed units and had probably been demanded by the planning authorities when the cottage was converted.

Such extreme clashes of style might be used with postmodernist irony in a television decorating make-over programme. In Heron Cottage they seemed to reflect only the owner's lack of taste. The knee-jerk snobbish reaction which Carole could not quite curb was that someone who'd been brought up in a council house shouldn't aspire to the middle-class gentility of Weldisham. Like the other residents of the village, she was very quickly condemning Pauline Helling for having ideas above her station.

There were no pictures on the walls and very few ornaments. On the window sill perched the statuette which Carole had seen from outside. The shepherdess bent winsomely over her crook, lifting the hem of her long skirt, against which a fluffy lamb nuzzled. The piece wasn't even china, just a badly painted plaster figurine of the kind that might be won at a fair. Next to the shepherdess sat the pin-cushion in the shape of a fat Chinaman. His tiny head perched incongruously on the ball of his body. There were no pins or needles stuck into the fabric; the object was there purely as an ornament. On the side which faced the window the purple silk was almost bleached of colour. The two-tone effect reminded Carole of a childhood illustration she'd seen of the poisoned apple the Wicked Queen had presented to Snow White.

On the mantelpiece, bereft of its fireplace beneath, stood a couple of family photographs. One was clearly of some Helling family reunion, an amateur snap in faded black and white, dating back at least twenty years. Sitting uncomfortably in the centre were an elderly couple, while around them generations of descendants posed in various stages of unease. The Hellings, their body language seemed to say, were not good at social events and, what's more, they didn't like each other much. None of the family seemed to have escaped the Helling pointed nose.

The second picture was a school photograph of Brian. Though he had probably been only about nine when the picture was taken, the same nose and a slyness in his eyes made him instantly recognizable.

There was not a book in sight; the *Radio Times* beneath the small television was the only evidence of any kind of reading matter. How Brian Helling could have developed the desire to be a writer from this kind of background Carole's rather narrow mind could not imagine.

'All right,' demanded Pauline Helling, after she'd perfunctorily gestured her visitor into a purple armchair. 'What's he done this time?'

'What do you mean?'

'I know Brian gets in trouble from time to time. Has he stolen something from you or what?' Her local accent was strong, and she spoke like someone who was unused to talking. She didn't sit herself, but hovered uneasily by the stranded mantelpiece.

'He hasn't stolen anything from me.'

Pauline Helling looked a little puzzled. Then she said, 'He might call it "borrowing". He might say he just wanted to borrow something from you.'

'No, it's not that.'

'He doesn't owe you anything?'

'No.'

'Then what is it?'

'Brian stopped me on the track last Friday.'

'Track? What track's that?'

'The one on the way out of the village. Where Weldisham Lane turns right back down to the main road.' Pauline Helling still looked uncomprehending. 'The track that leads to South Welling Barn.'

That did it. The old woman's eyes narrowed with suspicion. Carole noticed that, like her son, she had no visible upper lip. 'Why were you going to South Welling Barn?'

'I wasn't. I was just going for a walk.'

'But why in that direction?'

Carole shrugged.

Pauline Helling enunciated her next words with great care. 'I know it was you who found the bones up there.'

This came as no surprise to Carole, but she still asked, 'How do you know?'

'That's my business.'

'It seems to me, Mrs Helling, that there's very little goes on in Weldisham you don't know about.'

The old woman didn't react to this. Instead, she asked in a voice that was almost fearful, 'Did Brian say anything to you about the bones?'

'Yes, he did.' From the expression on Pauline Helling's face, that was the news she was afraid to hear. For a moment, she seemed unable to speak. Carole went on, 'He effectively said I should mind my own business about them.'

Brian's mother found her voice again. 'Sounds like very good advice to me.'

'He also hinted to me who he thought the bones might have belonged to.'

'Did he?' The fear in the voice was now almost panic. 'Who?'

'He talked about Detective Sergeant Baylis . . .'

The panic grew. 'Lennie hadn't been questioning Brian, had he?'

'I don't know. He didn't mention that. But he said that Sergeant Baylis's mother had disappeared more than twenty years ago, and that some people at the time thought his father had done away with her.'

'Ah.' The thin shoulders sagged, as the tension went out of them. Carole felt sure she was witnessing a reaction of huge relief. Pauline Helling had been afraid she knew who the bones belonged to. What she'd just said ruled out that possibility. Whoever the victim had been, it wasn't Lennie Baylis's mother.

But Pauline Helling knew who it was.

Carole didn't reckon much for her chances of finding out, but it was worth trying. 'You've lived round the village for a long time, haven't you, Mrs Helling?'

'Only been in this cottage twelve years,' she replied defensively.

'But Brian said you used to work up here before that.'

'So? What's that to you?'

Carole tried to guess what kind of work someone like Pauline Helling could have done in a place like Weldisham. She could never have had the outgoing personality to serve in the Hare and Hounds, so that really left only one alternative. 'What did you do – cleaning?' There was no reply, but Carole knew she had got it right. 'Who did you clean for?'

'That's no business of yours.'

True, it wasn't, but Carole was far too caught up in her thoughts to stop there. 'Did you work for the Lutteridges?' No reply, and no flicker of reaction either. 'If you don't tell me, I can find out.'

'You do that then,' said Pauline Helling, defiantly malevolent. 'Come on, it's time you went. We haven't got anything else to say to each other.'

There was no pretence of politeness between them now, so, though Carole wasn't optimistic about getting answers, she felt she could ask any questions she wanted to. As if the old woman hadn't spoken, she said, 'I gather you had a big pools win . . .' No reaction. 'And that's how you bought this house . . .' The vestigial upper lip remained an unmoving line. 'When was that exactly?'

'Out.' Pauline Helling crossed to open the sitting-room door. 'You're not welcome here.'

She stood in the doorway and opened the front door. Carole stayed in her purple armchair and kept trying. 'But you're not welcome here either, are you, Mrs Helling? I gather the good folk of Weldisham don't think you fit in.'

'If you don't leave, I'll call Brian. He can be quite nasty when he needs to be.'

After her experience on the track, Carole didn't doubt it. Reluctantly, she rose from her armchair and moved towards the hall. She took one last look around the hideous sitting room.

Her eye was caught again by the Helling family reunion photograph.

And in it she saw something she should have noticed before, something that started a whole new set of exciting connections racing through her mind.

Chapter Thirty-three

Carole wasn't yet positively suspicious of Detective Sergeant Baylis, but she was surprised by the alacrity with which he responded to her phone call. The fact that he was sitting in front of her fire at three-thirty that afternoon could have borne out Brian Helling's hint that the detective was more concerned with monitoring other people's thinking on the case than with finding a solution to it himself. Which could, as Brian had implied, mean that Lennie Baylis's interest was a very personal one.

'So do I gather that you've got some new information, Mrs Seddon?'

He seemed at ease in her armchair, but watchful. Now she had recognized him as one of the boys in the Helling family photograph, the likeness was obvious. It was only his bulk that made his nose look small; in a thinner face it would have stood out as beakily as Pauline's or Brian's.

'I wouldn't say it was new information, really. New thinking, perhaps.' He'd been so prompt in answering her summons that Carole hadn't had time to refine her approach. She had to think on her feet. 'It seems to me,' she continued tentatively, 'that there's some Helling family connection in this whole thing.'

He was unshocked by the suggestion. 'Wouldn't be a great surprise if there was. The Hellings are a very extensive family round here. At all kinds of different levels. Farm owners, farm workers . . . These days doctors and solicitors. There are Hellings everywhere. Most local people have some distant connection with them.'

'Including you,' she dared to say.

He may have been surprised by her knowing this, but not fazed. 'Yes, my mother was a Helling.'

'So you're related to Pauline and Brian?'

'Not directly, so far as I know. We probably are if you go back a few generations.'

'But you didn't see a lot of Brian when you were growing up?'

'I told you we went to school together. But didn't mix much in our spare time. Never really got on. Had to meet at the occasional big Helling family reunion, but that was it.' He spoke almost as if he knew she'd made the connection from the photograph on Pauline's mantelpiece.

'The reason I mention it . . .' For a moment Carole almost lost her nerve, but she regained impetus. 'The reason I mention it is something that Brian Helling said to me.'

'When did you see Brian?'

'He came chasing after me on the Downs on Friday. In his Land Rover.'

Baylis looked alarmed. 'He didn't hurt you, did he?'

'No. He frightened me a bit, that's all.'

The sergeant relaxed back in his chair. 'Good. Keep clear of Brian Helling if you can. He's a nasty bit of work.'

'But not criminally nasty. Or at least that's what you implied before.'

'No, probably not criminally nasty. But you never know how someone like him might behave, given the right provocation.'

'I will do my level best to avoid meeting him again. And if I do meet him, I'll do my level best to avoid provoking him. Not that I actually sought out his company last Friday.'

'No. Of course not. But be careful. He's volatile and . . .' The sergeant stopped, as though he'd been about to go too far.

'Volatile *and* . . .?' Carole insisted.

'I've mentioned I think he's into drugs. I haven't got any proof yet, but . . .' He shook his head in exasperation. 'Why am I telling you this? I rely on your discretion to keep quiet about it.'

'Of course.' Well, to everyone except Jude.

'So what was it Brian said to you last Friday?'

Presented with the direct question, there was no way Carole could avoid the direct answer. 'He suggested that the bones I found might have belonged to your mother.'

Baylis nodded slowly. Again he appeared unshocked, almost as if he had been expecting that response. 'I see. Well, it's an old rumour. No surprise it should have resurfaced again.'

'And is it a rumour to which you give any credence?'

This time his face closed over. 'No,' he replied curtly. 'I'm not pretending my parents got on. If you think I'm about to say, "Never mind, we were poor but we were happy," forget it. We were bloody miserable. When I was a kid, I spent as much time out of the house as I could. Out on the Downs all the time.'

'Must've been a great place to play, though.'

'Oh yes, we had plenty of games.' The grin this time was wry. 'It's easy for kids to play out their fantasies up on the Downs. Except, as I say, I was only out there so's I didn't have to go back home. My dad was a violent

215

man, I don't deny that. And yes, my mother walked out when I was fifteen. Just upped and left.'

'I'm sorry.'

'Oh, don't bother. You get over things. I joined the police force, made my own mates, got my own life now. Never think about those times.' He was clearly lying when he said the words. 'As I say, my mother walked out on my father. He didn't kill her. Nor did I, in case that was going to be your next question.' Then, before Carole could respond, he went on, 'Interesting, though, that Brian should raise that suggestion to you.'

'Why?'

'Well, for one thing, why you? Apart from the fact that you discovered the bones, you have nothing to do with the case. Why should he bother to go chasing over the Downs after you?'

'I think he'd somehow got the impression that I was making my own private investigation.'

'And are you?'

Carole couldn't meet his sardonic eyes. 'No, of course I'm not.'

He didn't sound convinced. 'You've been around Weld-isham rather a lot the last couple of weeks. You and your chubby blonde friend.'

She'd never heard anyone describe Jude as 'chubby'. Least of all a man. Men seemed too immediately caught up in Jude's aura to be critical of her appearance. And when they'd been introduced, Baylis had apparently responded like the rest. Maybe in his vocabulary 'chubby' was a compliment.

Carole blushed. 'Well, obviously we're interested.'

'Yes, I suppose it's not every day you find a dead body.'

She wondered what access he'd had to her records, whether he knew that this was in fact the second dead body she'd found within the year. 'Not every day I find a neatly packed set of bones, no,' she responded cautiously, and then moved quickly on. 'You said "for one thing" . . .'

'Sorry?'

'You said "for one thing" it was odd Brian should target me. Was there "another thing"?'

'Well, I suppose . . .' He seemed undecided whether to tell her more, but then shrugged and grinned. 'Basic rule of police investigation. When someone volunteers a significant piece of information for no very good reason, they might well be doing it to divert suspicion from something else.'

For a moment, Carole considered an application of Baylis's words to what he himself had said about Brian Helling's possible drug habit. It was surely unprofessional for a policeman to drop that kind of hint. He'd have to have a very good reason for doing it . . . like, say, deliberately building up suspicions of Brian Helling . . . in order to divert suspicions away from someone else . . . even from himself.

But Carole didn't pursue the thought out loud. 'So, Lennie, you're suggesting that Brian Helling raised the old rumour about your mother to me to stop me focusing my enquiries in any other direction?'

'Something like that.' He smiled at her ironically. 'Except, of course, you're not conducting an investigation, so you wouldn't be wanting to focus it in any direction . . . would you?'

'No.' Again she couldn't hold his gaze.

He rubbed his chin. 'Still, it's interesting that Brian should have bothered to try and divert your suspicions.

Maybe I should have a word with him . . . and with his mother . . .'

'The eyes and ears of Weldisham.'

'Yes. I've a feeling that the two of them know more about those bones than they're letting on.'

This exactly reflected Carole's views, but she didn't embark on further discussion. Her moment of doubt about Detective Sergeant Baylis's motivations had engendered caution. So she just asked, 'Can you tell me something about Pauline Helling?'

'If it's something to which I know the answer, yes. And if, of course, it's not classified information.'

'I don't think the answer to this is going to breach any security regulations. She used to work in Weldisham as a cleaner, didn't she?'

'Mm.'

'Who did she work for?'

'Graham Forbes. Graham and his first wife, Sheila.'

'It's very frustrating.' Jude was slumped in one of her shapeless draped armchairs, a glass of white wine in her hand.

Yes, she does look chubby, thought Carole. Something nobody's ever accused me of being.

'Charles Hilton's been away conducting this course in Ireland. He's not back till late tonight. So I can't ring him till tomorrow to fix a time to see Tamsin.'

'Are you sure you'll be able to, though? I thought last time you saw him he denied she was even at Sandalls Manor.'

'Yes, but now I know from Gillie that she definitely is there. Charles'll let me see her.'

'You sound very certain of that. Have you got some hold over him?'

'Yes.'

'What?'

Jude grinned. 'Don't ask.'

And, with a degree of unwillingness, Carole didn't.

'You say Lennie Baylis was going up to see Pauline Helling?'

'Yes. This evening. He rang her from my place. Said he needed to talk to her. To talk to Brian too, if he was going to be there.'

'And was he?'

'I don't know. Detective Sergeant – Lennie didn't say.'

'From what you've told me, Carole, Pauline Helling certainly knows something about those bones you found.'

'I'm sure she does. And Brian's involved too, somehow.' A gloom settled over Carole. She sighed. 'But I doubt if we'll ever find out in what way. Lennie Baylis will. The police will. They've got the information, they've got the technology. They'll sort it.'

'Don't be defeatist.' But the mood was infectious. Jude's response sounded automatic rather than heartfelt.

There was a silence.

'Do you want some more wine?'

'Shouldn't.'

'Go on.'

'Oh, all right.' After her glass had been recharged and she'd had taken a long sip, Carole said, 'Do you know, I had another call from Barry Stillwell earlier this evening . . .'

'Don't know why you sound so surprised about it.'

'He wants to take me out for dinner – again. I can't understand why he keeps pestering me.'

'Well, that's not very difficult. Obviously because he fancies you.'

'Don't be ridiculous.'

Jude looked flabbergasted. 'What's ridiculous about it?'

'Look, I'm in my early fifties. God knows whether I ever was attractive to men, but I'm certainly not now.'

'Are you saying that women in their early fifties can no longer be attractive to men? God, if I thought that, I'd top myself.'

'There are exceptions, obviously, but I'm sure, even you, when you get to my age—'

'Carole, Carole, stop. What's all this "when you get to my age"? I'm older than you are.'

'What?'

'I'm fifty-four. You're fifty-three, aren't you?'

'How did you know that?'

'Because you told me.'

'You never told me you were fifty-four.'

'You never asked.'

'There are lots of things I don't know about you, Jude.'

'Probably again because you never asked. There are no big secrets about me.'

'No, but—'

'I still can't get over this thing about you not thinking you're attractive. In the teeth of the evidence. There's Barry Stillwell panting to get his hands on you.'

'Yes, but who'd want Barry Stillwell's hands on them?'

'That's not the point. He may be the most boring creature on God's earth, but he's still a man. And as a man, he fancies you.'

'Maybe, but—'

'And then there's Ted . . .'

'Ted Crisp?' Carole blushed. 'He doesn't fancy me.'

'Of course he does.'

'But you saw how he behaved to me in the Crown and Anchor last night.'

'He was in a mood last night. Something had got up his nose. God knows what, but it certainly doesn't mean he's stopped fancying you.'

'Jude, don't be silly.'

'Silly? Oh, this really upsets me. Have you never thought of yourself as attractive?'

'Well, there were times, I suppose . . . Not since David walked out.'

'Really hit you hard, didn't it, Carole? You're still hurting from that.'

'Rubbish.' Carole tossed her head. 'It's happened to any number of women. And what you have to do when it does happen is just get on with things.'

'I would think when it does happen what you have to do is talk to someone about it.'

'Is that what you'd do? You said you'd had man trouble over this weekend. Have you talked to someone about that?'

'Yes, of course I have.'

Carole was taken aback, even a little hurt. 'Who?'

'Friends. I've hardly been off the phone for the last forty-eight hours.'

'Oh.' Carole's mood of gloom hardened into despair. She remembered, when she had offered a sympathetic ear, Jude had refused. 'Have you talked to the man himself?'

'No, of course I haven't. I need support, not more humiliation. Talking to supportive people helps. It really does. You should try it.'

Jude could not have known how much her words hurt. Unthinkingly, she had excluded her neighbour from the category of 'supportive people'. Carole felt very alienated, forced once again to realize how little she knew Jude. As a result, her response was scornful. 'That's not my style. I can't go all touchy-feely about things. I can't spill out my guts to some complete stranger.'

'Who said anything about complete strangers? Friends. For the last couple of days I've been talking to friends.'

The line of Carole's mouth hardened. 'I think I have to get on with my own life in my own way.'

'Who would you be letting down if you didn't?'

'Myself. I was brought up to believe that you should stand on your own two feet. You should be able to manage on your own.'

'Without ever asking for help from anyone else?'

'Ideally yes. I mean, obviously, if you're physically ill, you need help from a doctor.'

'And if you're mentally ill?'

Carole coloured with affront. 'I am not mentally ill!'

'I didn't say you were. I was talking in general terms.'

'Oh.'

'Presumably this – what shall I call it? – this independence of yours means you've never shared what you're really feeling with anyone?'

'Maybe not. As I said, I'm not the kind to wear my heart on my sleeve.'

'And presumably that's why your marriage broke up?'

Carole stopped in her tracks. The assessment was so accurate it almost winded her. And, to her amazement, she started to cry.

Chapter Thirty-four

Jude was ringing at her doorbell as soon as Carole got in the following morning. She'd just taken Gulliver for his walk on Fethering Beach. Her neighbour must've seen her go past the window and rushed round straight away. Carole was prepared to be embarrassed about the previous night's uncharacteristic lapse into weakness, until she saw the expression on Jude's face.

'What on earth is it?' Carole had never seen her friend's serenity so shot to pieces. The cheeks were red, the brown eyes wide with excitement and anxiety.

'Come back to my place. I'll show you.'

'What?'

'I videoed it. Quick!'

'What are you talking about?'

'The local news. They had a headline about it, so I switched the video on straight away. I got most of the report.'

'Look, I've got to take my coat off and give Gulliver a drink and—'

'Come *on*!'

Carole perched on the swathed arm of a chair while Jude fiddled with the video control to wind back the tape. The playback wheezed into life.

'. . . a terrible tragedy,' said a reporter's voice. 'The

fire, which is believed to have started on the ground floor, spread very quickly.'

The screen filled with a blackened shell, from which wisps of smoke still rose. It took Carole a moment to recognize Heron Cottage.

'Because Weldisham is so far from the main road and because the fire had taken such a firm hold before the alarm was raised at four o'clock this morning, the emergency services were able to do little. By the time they reached the cottage, it was already virtually demolished.

'One body, that of an elderly woman, was found on the premises in an upstairs room. She has yet to be formally identified.'

Chapter Thirty-five

'I'm only here because you went to Heron Cottage yesterday morning. I saw her in the evening. Apart from me, you're probably one of the last people to see Pauline Helling alive. I'm sorry, it's just a formality. I have to ask you a few questions.'

Since Brian Helling had planted the thought in her mind, Carole couldn't get rid of it. Detective Sergeant Baylis might well have an agenda of his own, outside his official duties. It did seem odd that he was constantly talking to her, and maybe his aim was not to get information but to assess her suspicions.

And why was it always him? Carole Seddon's knowledge of police procedure was rudimentary, but knew there'd be other officers involved in the investigation of the bones she'd found. And possibly even a whole new team investigating the incident – no one was yet calling it a crime – at Heron Cottage. So why was it once again Detective Sergeant Baylis who was sitting in her front room?

'Of course, you can ask me anything you like,' she replied smoothly, 'but I don't think there's much I can add to what I said when we last met.'

'No, but you didn't really tell me what kind of state Pauline Helling was in when you visited her.'

'I don't know what kind of state she was in normally. I've only seen her three times in my life, only spoken to her once, and on each occasion she was as antisocial to me as she could be. From all accounts, antisocial was her customary manner. So I suppose I'd have to say, when I visited her, she was quite normal.'

'She didn't seem ill or anything, did she?'

'I don't think so. Why do you ask?'

'Because if she had been particularly doddery, she might have been more likely to have knocked over something, not noticed an electrical spark flying out of the fire . . .'

'She didn't seem particularly doddery. Come on, you saw her yesterday evening. Surely you could judge for yourself.'

'I'm asking *you*, Mrs Seddon.'

'All right. Well, I've answered your question. Have they any idea how the fire started?'

He shook his head. 'Far too early to say.' It was easy for him. In terms of information, he held all the cards. Any time he wanted to avoid a question, Baylis could back away behind professional police-speak. Far too early to say . . . our enquiries are still progressing . . . we haven't had the results yet . . .

'You're waiting for the report from the forensic examination of the scene?'

'Exactly, Mrs Seddon.'

'And have you had the results of the other forensic examination yet?' she asked, challenging him with her pale blue eyes.

He looked uncomfortable. 'Which other forensic examination?' But he knew what she was talking about.

'The examination of the bones I found.'

He hid again behind his professional front. 'I'm afraid, even if I had such information, I wouldn't be able to divulge it until permission had been given.'

'No, but something must be known by now.' Carole recognized that she was getting increasingly reckless, but wasn't quite sure why. 'They'll have got a DNA profile from the bones.'

'But for that to have any meaning, they'd have to have tissue to match it to.'

'Might they not try to get a match through relatives of the deceased . . .?'

He chuckled at her absurdity. 'If you don't know who a victim is, it's sometimes very difficult to trace their relatives.'

'You haven't been asked to give a sample of DNA, have you, Sergeant?'

The expression on his face could not have changed more if Carole had slapped him.

'I was just meaning that there were rumours about your mother when—'

'I know exactly what you were meaning, Mrs Seddon.' He stood up. 'I came here to talk about the fire at Heron Cottage and I think there's nothing else I need to ask you.' He moved towards the door. 'Oh, there was one other question . . . When you went to see Pauline Helling yesterday morning, did you see Brian?'

Carole shook her head, and then her hand leapt to her mouth. 'He wasn't killed too, was he? They didn't find Brian's body in the ruins of the cottage?'

'No. No, they didn't.'

'So where is he?'

'A very good question, Mrs Seddon. And one which we hope, in the not too distant future, to answer.'

Carole had risen from her chair too, as if to show the sergeant out, but still he lingered, swaying slightly, by the door.

'We've established that Pauline Helling was profoundly antisocial . . .'

'Yes.'

'I knew she was before, and your experience with her has only borne that out . . .' Still he swayed, uncertain. 'And yet she let you, a complete stranger, into Heron Cottage. Why?'

Was he suspicious of her, Carole wondered. Did he think she'd been lying, that in fact she had some association with Pauline Helling going back a long way into the past?

'She let me in,' came the unflustered reply, 'because I mentioned something that Brian had said to me.'

'Ah, Brian,' said Baylis, almost to himself. 'Everything comes back to Brian.'

'What do you mean?'

'I'm getting the feeling that Brian Helling had a lot of enemies . . . that his mother knew he had a lot of enemies . . . and she was trying to protect him. That's why she had to listen to what you said about him.'

'Why?'

'Because she thought you might be one of his enemies . . . or that you might have been sent by one of his enemies. That's why she objected so much to you snooping around the village.'

'I thought she behaved like that to everyone. I didn't think I'd been particularly singled out.'

'I think you may have been.'

'But why me? Did I look like one of Brian's enemies? What kind of enemies did he have, come to that?'

'Drug dealers in Brighton.'

'Well, *thank you* very much!' Carole Seddon was affronted to her middle-class core. 'Do I look like a . . . I don't know . . . like a drug dealer's moll?'

'You'd be surprised, Mrs Seddon. Maybe you imagine drug dealers are shifty half-castes in loud suits. Very few of them are. Most you wouldn't be able to tell apart from any other kind of businessman.'

'Oh.'

'We've just discovered this morning,' the sergeant went on, 'that Brian Helling owes a lot of money to one of the big boys in Brighton. A really enormous amount of money.'

'So are you suggesting that they were behind the torching of Heron Cottage? That it was Brian, and not his mother, who was the intended victim?'

A moment before, Detective Sergeant Baylis couldn't stop volunteering information. Suddenly, once again, he was all professional caution. 'We haven't established yet,' he said primly, 'that the fire was not accidental.'

'No,' Carole agreed, deflated.

He rubbed his hands together. 'I must be going. Thank you for bearing with me once again, Mrs Seddon. Sorry, a lot of police work is like this, routine enquiries, double-checking the facts . . . achieving little, I'm afraid.'

But after the sergeant had gone, Carole wondered whether he really had achieved little that morning. Again, she felt certain that his visit was part of a personal agenda. And that that agenda could well include diverting suspicion away from the circumstances of his mother's death.

*

She watched the lunchtime local news. She wished Jude had been there to see it with her, but Jude was on her way to Sandalls Manor.

The bulletin had more on the tragedy in Weldisham. Still, as Baylis had pointed out, it was far too early to say what had caused the blaze, although they did have an ID of the victim, Mrs Pauline Helling.

'One of her nearest neighbours,' said the presenter, 'manager of the Hare and Hounds pub in Weldisham, is Will Maples.'

The landlord was filmed behind the bar, in a report which started on the smouldering wreckage of Heron Cottage, then moved round to the jokey sign of the Hare and Hounds, before cutting to the interior. The directors of Home Hostelries must have been delighted; it looked just like a commercial.

'This is a terrible tragedy,' said Will Maples. 'Mrs Helling was not a regular here in the Hare and Hounds, but she was a familiar sight around the village, always out walking her dog. She'll be sorely missed.'

His words were formal and meaningless, like a retirement-party encomium from a managing director who'd never met the guest of honour. For a moment Carole thought how ridiculous it had been to get Will Maples to speak. He had no roots in the village, he was just passing through on the way to his next promotion. He didn't know Pauline Helling.

But then she reflected that it didn't matter. No one in Weldisham had known Pauline Helling, or at least no one had chosen to know her. Better perhaps platitudes from Will Maples than condescension from a more established resident.

Will's mention of the dog made Carole think. Pauline

Helling and the spaniel had been inseparable. Had the dog too perished in the blaze? If so, surprising that the local news, always keener on animal-interest than human-interest stories, hadn't mentioned the fact.

'Mrs Pauline Helling, who died in a fire at her cottage in Weldisham last night.'

The screen filled with a photograph. It must have been twenty years old, dating from before Pauline Helling's move to the village that subsequently ostracized her. The features were thinner, the sharpness of the nose more pronounced.

Carole gasped. It was a face she recognized.

At that moment the telephone rang.

'Carole Seddon?'

'Yes.'

'This is Brian Helling.'

The voice sent a chill through her. 'Oh. I was terribly sorry to hear about your mother.' Her condolence sounded clumsy.

'Sad,' said Brian, in a voice that gave no clue to his real feelings. 'Bit of a bummer, wasn't it?'

'Where are you, Brian?'

'I'm not going to tell anyone that – least of all you.'

'Why least of all me?'

'Because, Carole, I think you suffer from more than your share of curiosity . . . and less than your share of reticence.'

'Are you hiding somewhere?'

'You could say that. There are lots of good hiding places on the Downs, you know. I'm just keeping out of the way until it's safe for me to get back.'

'And when will that be?'

'When the people who threaten my safety have been brought to justice.'

The languor of his delivery was starting to annoy Carole. 'Why're you ringing me?'

'Just a bit of friendly advice.' His voice was still calm, nearly lazy, but with an underlying tension. Not the voice traditionally adopted by someone who'd just lost his mother.

'Like the friendly advice you gave me last Friday?'

'Not unlike that. In fact part of the advice is identical. Mind your own bloody business!'

'Or?'

'Or you might find yourself the third victim, Carole.'

'Are you threatening me?'

'Am *I* threatening you? No, not me. I didn't kill the other two.'

'Then who did?'

He chuckled indulgently. 'Ooh, now I can't make it too easy for you, can I? Amateur snoopers don't like to be told all the details. You have to leave something for them to work out on their own . . . otherwise it spoils their fun.'

'Maybe, but—'

'Were you watching the lunchtime news, Carole?' he interrupted brusquely.

'Yes, I was.'

'And did that photograph of my mother remind you of anyone?'

'Yes, it did.'

'Then I think you probably have all the information you require.'

And at that point Brian Helling rang off.

Chapter Thirty-six

This time Jude had rung ahead to Sandalls Manor and fixed a time to see Charles Hilton. Four o'clock in the afternoon.

Wednesday was the changeover day. One group of soul-searching participants had left on the Tuesday (slightly disappointed that due to the guru's absence in Ireland, they'd been taken on their soul journey by a sub); the next consignment would arrive on the Thursday. Wednesday was the day for Anne Hilton to shout at her staff as she supervised their bed-changing and laundry work. And a day when Charles Hilton retired to his study to get on with his writing.

It was to the study that Jude was shown, with no pretence at welcome, by the guru's wife. Charles sat behind a large desk of dark wood, at which Anne's father had no doubt checked the farm's accounts. The old man would have been shocked, though, to see the range of objects which neatly littered the desk's surface. There were pebbles and crystals, fossils and face masks, evil eyes and tiny totems – a mini-museum of the world's alternative belief systems.

On the wall behind Charles were pristine editions of *Setting Free the Soul* and others of his publications. There were framed texts in squiggly Oriental writing, and some in English, calligraphed and illustrated no doubt by besotted acolytes. Jude couldn't help noticing one that read: 'WE ARE ALL IRRELEVANT, AND THAT'S WHAT MAKES US ALL MATTER SO MUCH.'

She was reminded of her recent encounter with Sebastian Trent. He had stood in his Hampstead sitting room as if posing for a photograph. Jude had a feeling the neatly framed scene she was looking at might well appear on the jacket of Charles Hilton's books.

He himself was all solicitous charm as he rose to greet the supplicant. 'Jude, great to see you again. Would you care for some coffee?'

She could sense Anne Hilton's disapproval of the offer, but that wasn't why she declined it. If all went well, Jude didn't intend to be in Charles Hilton's study long enough to drink coffee. She hoped to be taken straight to see the object of her quest.

Relieved that at least she wasn't going to have to get bloody coffee – though of course far too well brought up to verbalize any such opinion – Anne Hilton stomped out of the room, closing the door heavily behind her. Jude wondered whether this was to make a point or if she always did it like that. Anne Hilton's upbringing had made her the kind of woman who talked loudly in public places. Maybe slamming doors came with the genetic territory.

Charles Hilton seemed visibly to relax once his wife was out of the room. Maybe he had still been afraid Jude might make some reference to his ill-considered grope of long ago. He was dressed again in neat jeans, though today's cardigan was of an ethnic design that looked vaguely Peruvian.

'So . . . what can I do for you?' His smile was as bland

and patronizing as he could make it, but with an under-tone of anxiety.

'I want to see Tamsin Lutteridge,' said Jude.

'I've told you, I can't discuss my patients' cases.'

'I'm not asking you to do that. If you'd listened, Charles, you would have heard me say I wanted to *see* her, not *discuss* her.'

'I don't know what makes you think I've any idea where she is. I'm not—'

She cut through his bluster. 'I know Tamsin's here, because her mother told me she's here. I did in fact ring Gillie this morning and tell her I was coming to see her daughter. She was quite happy about it.' Jude gestured to the telephone. 'Ring her if you don't believe me.'

'No, no, of course I believe you.' He seemed to recognize the pointlessness of further resistance. 'But I think you owe me the courtesy of telling me why you want to see Tamsin.'

'There's something I need to ask her.'

Charles Hilton looked even more anxious. 'Is it something to do with her treatment?'

'No, it has nothing to do with her treatment or her illness.'

'Then . . .?'

'Then it is on a subject that has nothing to do with you, Charles.'

'Fine.' But his expression suggested everything wasn't entirely fine. 'Jude . . . I've got to make a few ground rules for when you do see her.'

'Oh yes?'

'You're not to ask her anything about the treatment she's receiving here.'

'All right. I told you, that's not what interests me.'

'No . . !' He still wasn't fully reassured. 'The work I'm doing with Tamsin is experimental . . . exploratory perhaps is a better word . . . I don't want any details of it to be publicly known until the process is complete, until we've achieved some kind of closure.'

'Charles, will you stop worrying? I'm not a muck-raking journalist. I'm not interested in how you're treating Tamsin . . . Well, that is to say I'm only interested in how you're treating Tamsin if the treatment is successful.'

She hadn't managed to remove all residue of scepticism from her voice and Charles Hilton flared up. 'Look, what I'm doing is perfectly legitimate and may go on to help many other sufferers from an illness that is one of the most complex and disturbing to have emerged in recent decades. I'm a serious therapist, Jude, and I really care about helping people, making them better. It'd be so easy to pigeonhole me as a charlatan, a devious guru, a false prophet, but you can't do that, because it's not true!'

Jude was amazed and not a little amused by this outburst. She would have thought Charles Hilton's training as a psychotherapist might have given him a little more self-knowledge. She hadn't made any of the accusations against which he had so vigorously defended himself. If anyone was dubious about the validity of his treatments, then that person had to be Charles himself. His insecurity was so overt, it was almost endearing.

But she didn't say anything. There was nothing that needed saying. Charles had already said it all.

'Right. Could I see Tamsin then, please?'

'Yes. Yes, of course.'

He rose from his little area of film set and picked up a bunch of keys from the desk.

'You're not telling me you keep her locked up, are you, like someone out of a Victorian asylum?'

He was oblivious of the jokiness in her tone and almost screamed, 'No of course I don't keep her locked up!'

Charles Hilton looked at Jude. He saw the smile on her lips and his eyes slipped away from hers. He opened the door of his study.

As she passed through, he put a hand that was a little more than avuncular on the soft curve of her shoulder. Jude gave him a look far more articulate than many novels. Charles Hilton removed his hand.

Chapter Thirty-seven

Carole Seddon tried to be calm, but the thoughts bubbling up in her mind threatened her self-image as a sensible woman. The idea had already taken root in her mind before Brian Helling's phone call had encouraged its growth and now it was running wild, spreading out more and more shoots of suspicion and implication.

She still needed more facts, though, facts that might corroborate her conjectures and fill in details of the evolving scenario. And she needed to get those facts from someone who knew Weldisham well, who had known it before Pauline Helling had taken up residence in Heron Cottage.

She came back to the three boys who'd been at school together. Lennie Baylis, Harry Grant and Brian Helling. The first two had actually lived in the village, and Brian's mother had worked there as a cleaner. Each one of them, she felt certain, knew something that would be relevant to her enquiries.

But Carole had no means of recontacting Brian Helling. She guessed he'd been calling from a mobile, but when she tried 1471 she was told, 'The caller withheld their number.'

Lennie Baylis was the obvious person with whom to discuss the case. He kept encouraging her to do just that, but that very eagerness disqualified him as the perfect confidant. Carole still reckoned the sergeant had a personal as well as a professional agenda and, though she wouldn't go as far as considering him a suspect, she wanted to define his connection with the bones she'd found before volunteering more of her suspicions to him.

So that left Harry Grant. Or indeed Harry Grant's wife . . . Suddenly Carole had a vivid image of the nervous, overdressed woman she'd met at the Forbeses' dinner party. Though Jenny Grant represented a paler carbon than Pauline Helling, she was still unmistakably stamped with the same facial characteristics. The beaky nose dominated her thin pale face.

Carole remembered Harry saying that his wife had been related to Graham Forbes's first wife. Perhaps Jenny too had been in the family photograph on the wall of Heron Cottage. She could be a close relative, a first cousin even, of Pauline Helling. Jenny Grant might be able to reveal everything Carole wanted to know about the old woman and her son.

There was only one 'H. Grant' in the local phone book. The address was nearer Fethering than Weldisham. Jenny Grant answered the phone. She sounded unsurprised by Carole's call, and not particularly interested. Yes, it was a tragedy about Pauline. And yes, if Carole wanted to come round and talk to her about the old woman, that was fine. Jenny's voice was flat, containing no curiosity as to why. In one way, that was good for Carole. Explanations might prove difficult. But, on the other hand, there was something spooky about Jenny Grant's complete lack of interest.

The house was exactly what a successful property developer would have built for himself. Every feature was immaculately finished, but there were a few too many of them. Did the building need both a turret *and* a bell-tower? Did every upstairs window need a balcony? Wouldn't the front garden have looked better paved with one kind of stone rather than four? And did the Tudor beams over the double garage match the panels of neat flint facing either side of the front door? Come to that, wouldn't the heavy oak front door itself have looked sufficiently monastic without the semicircle of stained glass above it?

Carole anticipated much toing and froing with the Village Committee of Weldisham over the architectural details of Harry Grant's barn conversion.

Jenny Grant was dressed rather like her house. She clearly frequented one of those boutiques which doesn't like plain colours or plain surfaces. Her black skirt was decorated with random pieces of shiny leather and gold buttons; her fluffy pale blue jumper had quilted panels of scarlet silk and some gold braid at the neck. The house looked like a display unit for building effects; its owner a display unit for haberdashery. Her pallor accentuated the fussiness of her garments. Jenny Grant looked literally washed out, as though she had been put too many times through the laundry cycle.

She still expressed no curiosity at Carole's arrival, but ushered her into a sitting room that looked like a display unit for upholstery. Tea things were already on a tray, with a plate of sugared biscuits.

'It's very good of you to see me,' said Carole.

'No problem.'

After she had poured the tea, Jenny Grant sat back, her faded blue eyes blinking, waiting for whatever should come next. She didn't volunteer anything. Maybe she never took any initiative, was eternally reactive. That was perhaps the way to survive as wife of someone as noisily energetic as Harry Grant.

'As I said on the phone, I want to talk about Pauline Helling. Terrible tragedy that was.'

'Terrible,' Jenny Grant agreed, as though commenting on a minor deterioration in the weather.

'Harry said you were actually related to her in some way . . .'

'Distantly. My maiden name was Helling and there are lots of branches of the family round the area. I think possibly our grandmothers were cousins, something like that.'

'So you didn't know Pauline well?'

'I don't think anyone knew her well, except possibly Brian. She kept herself very much to herself.'

'I heard that there was more to it than that.'

'How do you mean?'

'That the village actually ostracized her.' From Jenny Grant's expression, she had never heard the word. 'That she wasn't made to feel very welcome in Weldisham.'

Jenny shrugged. 'There are a lot of very snobbish people up there.'

'And you're about to go and join them, I gather. I heard from Harry that you'd got your planning permission on the barn.'

If Carole had hoped to prompt Jenny's views on whether she and her husband would be accepted socially in Weldisham, she was disappointed. All she got was a 'Yes'.

'You must be delighted about that.'

'It's what Harry wants.'

And Carole had a feeling that in that sentence lay the

secret of the success of the Grants' marriage. 'Anyway, as I gather,' she went on, 'let me get this right . . . Pauline Helling wasn't brought up the village . . .'

'No. She lived not far from here. The Downside Estate . . . Do you know it?'

'Yes. I live in Fethering.'

Downside was the poor end of town.

'And did Pauline marry a Helling?'

'No, she was born a Helling. She never married.'

'So you don't know who Brian's father was?'

A shake of the head. 'No idea. I don't know anyone who knew. It was a long time ago. Brian must be nearly forty now.'

'Do you know him?'

'I know who he is. I've never had a conversation with him.' Jenny Grant didn't sound as though that was a situation she was in any hurry to change.

'And Pauline used to work as a cleaner in Weldisham. For Graham Forbes and his first wife.'

'That's right.'

Still there was no curiosity as to how Carole had got this information or why it was of any relevance to her.

'His first wife was also a Helling, I believe?'

'Yes. Sheila.'

'Did you know her?'

'Oh yes. I went to the same school as she did. Many years afterwards, of course.'

Suddenly Carole realized what kind of school it had been that the two attended. An upmarket girl's private school. Jenny Grant's manner of speech was so lacking in animation that its vowels had been ironed out, but now she concentrated, Carole could detect the upper-class languor underneath. Harry Grant had married a few grades above himself. Maybe Jenny's social status had made up for her lack of more obvious attractions.

So those who had borne the Helling name went through the strata of class, Sheila Forbes and Jenny Grant aiming at the top, Pauline Helling and Lennie Baylis's mother down at the bottom, with no doubt many social nuances in between.

'Did you know Sheila Forbes well?'

'Quite well.'

'Were you surprised when you heard she'd gone off with another man?'

'It did seem odd, certainly.' But nothing seemed to have the power to surprise Jenny Grant for long. She shrugged. 'Still, that's what she did. Maybe a romantic heart beat beneath that forbidding exterior.'

'Was she forbidding?'

'Perhaps the wrong word. She was very correct, though. Always did the right thing. British, in the old-fashioned sense. You know, didn't let her emotions show on the surface. I'm sure that's why she and Graham went down so well abroad.'

'The archetypal British couple.'

'That's it, yes.'

'And would you say their marriage was a happy one . . . You know, before the split?'

Jenny Grant's hands lifted and flopped ineffectually back on to her lap. 'Who can say? A marriage may look fine on the surface, but nobody except the two inside know what it's really like.'

There was a slight change in her tone as she said this. Carole wondered if a comment was being made on the Grants' own marriage. But Jenny didn't seem about to expand on the hint and, intriguing though the subject might be, it wasn't what Carole was there to find out about.

'Graham and Sheila Forbes were quite well heeled, I gather. Someone said he had private money.'

'"Had" being the operative word. I don't think he's got much now.'

'Oh?'

'Well, presumably he's got a British Council pension. Not much else, though.'

'You know that for a fact?'

'Harry told me. I don't know where he got it from, but he's usually pretty reliable. There aren't many secrets round here.'

'So where did Graham Forbes's money go? Has he got a secret vice or something?'

'Don't think so. But I would imagine he's like the others.'

Carole looked quizzical.

'Most people round here who've lost a lot of money – I don't mean from firms going to the wall, I mean investment income . . . Well, it doesn't do to talk about it, but with most of them it was Lloyd's.'

'Ah.'

The crash of many Lloyd's syndicates had hit a lot of 'names', as the major investors were called. In a well-cushioned area like the part of West Sussex around Weldisham, there had probably been many casualties.

'Moving on, Jenny . . . do you remember when exactly Pauline Helling had her pools win?'

'Well, let me think . . .' Jenny's brow wrinkled, and the effect was to make her look younger, suggesting that she might once have had more spark and vivacity. Maybe it wasn't just her social position that had drawn Harry Grant to her. 'She moved into Weldisham round... I don't know... I should think about 1988... so presumably some time round then.'

'Did she put all the money into buying Heron Cottage?'

'I don't know. I've no idea how much she actually won. I don't think anyone knew. I'm sure Pauline would have put a cross in the box for "No Publicity".'

'But you don't know whether she celebrated by taking a trip abroad or anything like that?'

'I don't think so. I didn't know her that well. She could have done all kinds of things I never knew about.'

'Of course. So, as far as you know, she never did travel abroad?'

'No, I don't think... She wasn't the kind to..' Something came through the fogs of memory. 'Oh, just a minute, though... Yes, she did. I remember being surprised when Harry told me. He'd bumped into Brian, who said his mother had suddenly got herself a passport and was going off on a jaunt somewhere. It seemed so out of character, that's why I've remembered it.'

'You don't remember where she went?'

Jenny Grant shook her head. 'I don't think I ever knew. I don't even know if she actually did go. I just remember Harry mentioning about the passport.'

'And when did this happen... presumably after the pools win?'

'I suppose it must have been... except..' Again Jenny Grant screwed up her face with the effort of recollection. 'No, because Harry was out working on a development in Spain for most of 1988 and '89, so it must've been before that. End of '87, I suppose.'

'Really?' said Carole, suppressing the excitement that spurted inside her.

They talked a little longer, but nothing else emerged that was relevant. Not that Carole minded. She'd already got more than she'd dared hope for.

Jenny Grant seemed as unsurprised when Carole said she must go as she had been by her arrival.

'Very good of you to see me, Jenny.'

'No problem. Lucky you called today, though.'

'Oh?'

'Harry and I are off to Portugal tomorrow. For a week. To celebrate the planning permission on the barn.' She made it sound like a death sentence.

Beneath the stained glass of the open front door, Carole shook her hostess's hand, and it was then that she saw something in the woman's eyes that maybe explained her unquestioning passivity.

Jenny Grant was on tranquillizers, Carole felt sure. A hefty dose of Librium or something similar was needed to maintain that placid equilibrium. Maybe that was the only way this rather quiet woman could survive being married to a social climber like Harry Grant.

Chapter Thirty-eight

She desperately wanted to talk to Jude, but Jude was up at Sandalls Manor and Carole couldn't wait. The speed with which her ideas were moving and conjoining and producing new ideas meant she had to talk to someone. And, in a sense, there was only one right person to talk to.

Lennie Baylis answered his mobile straight away. He was up at Weldisham, doing some interviews with local people about the Heron Cottage fire. But when he heard that was what Carole wanted to talk about, he suggested she came up as soon as possible. He was once again ensconced in the Snug of the Hare and Hounds. If she was quick, they could talk before the pub opened at six.

Carole drove to the village as fast as she could, but was impeded by the local rush-hour traffic. That was probably just as well, because her excitement would have made her careless of speed limits.

She was no longer suspicious of Detective Sergeant Baylis and was therefore unperturbed by the readiness with which he'd agreed to see her. Now she reckoned she knew the full scenario, and it didn't involve him. The detective was no longer a suspect, just a useful professional contact.

Carole parked in the Hare and Hounds car park and, when she arrived in the pub at twenty to six, Baylis was in the Snug, chatting to Will Maples. Their behaviour definitely looked more like 'chatting' than 'interviewing'. The sergeant had a very large Grouse in front of him, and the manager was sipping a cup of coffee, in anticipation of a busy evening ahead.

Carole didn't find out what they were chatting about, though. They stopped as soon as she came in. On a little flick from Lennie Baylis's eyebrows, Will Maples rose from his seat.

'Better sort things out in the kitchen,' he said.

'Maybe our lady friend would like a drink . . .'

'No, thank you, Sergeant.'

'Right. And you're OK for the moment, Lennie?'

The whisky glass was raised in acknowledgement. 'Fine, thanks.'

Will Maples left the bar. Detective Sergeant Baylis looked at the eternally repeating flame pattern of the log-effect fire. 'Not so wet as you were last time we met here, are you, Mrs Seddon?'

'No. No, I'm not.'

'But I gather it's still something to do with the same subject you want to talk about. The bones.'

'Yes.'

'Well, fire away.'

Carole nodded, and then a caution struck her. 'What I'm going to say may be tantamount to an accusation . . .' He looked alarmed. 'Of someone we both know.' He relaxed. 'I wouldn't like to think that kind of thing would become public knowledge.'

'Mrs Seddon . . .' Detective Sergeant Baylis spread his hands disingenuously. 'It is my job to listen to wild accusations . . . often a lot wilder than anything I'm sure you're going to come up with . . . and it's also my job to keep the source of such accusations secret. Goodness, if all the murder theories I've heard in Weldisham the last few weeks ever became public, nobody in the village would ever speak to anyone else again. I can't think of a single person who hasn't been accused by someone. It's amazing how the discovery of an unidentified body brings out all kinds of old resentments that have been bubbling under the surface for years.'

'And it still is an unidentified body?'

He smiled cannily. 'Very clever, Mrs Seddon. Worth putting the question in. You might just catch me off my guard, and I might just let slip some classified information to you . . . but don't count on it.'

She coloured at what was unmistakably a reproof. 'I'm sorry.'

A grin. 'OK, let's hear your theory . . .'

Carole took a deep breath, and as she embarked on her theory she became aware that, beneath his laid-back exterior, Detective Sergeant Baylis was tense. He still thought what she was about to say concerned him at a personal level. He was waiting to hear what she had unearthed about his family history.

'I think,' she began slowly, 'that what's happened recently has roots that go back a long way into the past . . .'

He nodded assent. Nothing controversial so far. But he remained taut, waiting to see what would follow.

'I think the bones I found had lain undisturbed for more than twelve years, and might have lain undisturbed for a lot longer, but for certain recent developments.'

Baylis couldn't keep quiet any longer. Still trying to sound casual, he said, 'I assume this means you reckon you know who the bones belonged to?'

'Yes. I think they belonged to Sheila Forbes, Graham Forbes's first wife.'

He gave no obvious reaction, but Carole thought a little of the tension had left his body.

'I think Graham Forbes murdered her over the weekend of the Great Storm, in October 1987, and buried her body in the floor of the old barn behind his house.'

The sergeant gave her a smile that was half congratulatory, half sceptical. 'Nice idea. And I may say you're not the only person to have had that thought.'

Carole felt a pang of disappointment.

'It's a line of enquiry, I can tell you, that we in the police have pursued as well. But I'm afraid, persuasive though the theory might be, it doesn't stand up to the facts.'

'No?'

'Sorry. One of the facts we know is that on the Monday morning after the Great Storm, 19 October 1987, Graham Forbes was witnessed travelling on a British Airways flight from Heathrow to Kuala Lumpur, *in the company of his wife, Sheila*. There's no question about it. Her passport was checked and stamped. It's on the records at Heathrow.'

Carole was a little shaken to find out how closely the official enquiries must have mirrored her own, but she kept her cool. 'I'm sure Sheila Forbes's passport was checked, but I don't believe the person travelling on that passport was Sheila Forbes.'

She had the sergeant's interest now. With mounting confidence, Carole continued, 'I think the woman who travelled to Kuala Lumpur with Graham Forbes that Monday morning was Pauline Helling.'

'What?'

'There was sufficient family likeness for Pauline to pass herself off as her distant cousin, certainly among people who didn't know her well, like passport officials.'

'But what about people who did know her well . . . like the British Council staff in Kuala Lumpur? They were never going to believe that Pauline Helling was the woman they'd seen around the house and office for three years.'

'I don't think they saw her.'

'What do you mean?'

'When the Forbeses arrived at Kuala Lumpur airport in October 1987, Mrs Forbes was taken off in a taxi. Graham Forbes and the writer Sebastian Trent were taken off in a British Council car, but it wasn't driven by Graham's regular driver – in spite of the fact that the driver Shiva had worked with the Forbeses for years and was exceptionally loyal. I think Graham Forbes made that arrangement deliberately, so that the supposed Mrs Forbes wouldn't be seen by anyone who could recognize her as an impostor.'

There was still scepticism around Baylis's mouth, but he hadn't yet rejected her theory out of hand. 'So where did "the supposed Mrs Forbes" go then? Some member of staff must have seen her when she finally got to their residence.'

'I don't think Pauline Helling ever did get to the residence. I think Graham Forbes arranged for her to stay put in a hotel and then, after a suitable interval, she flew back to England on her own passport.'

'But why on earth would Pauline Helling do all that?'

'Money. Graham Forbes had done a deal with her. Don't you think it's a coincidence that, late in 1987, Pauline Helling suddenly has a pools win . . . suddenly finds herself in a position to buy Heron Cottage . . . and hopefully to live in the style in which her distant cousin had lived? A big step from being a cleaner in Weldisham to being a house owner in Weldisham.'

'Hmm . . .' Detective Sergeant Baylis's head was shaking slowly.

Carole pressed home her advantage. 'And don't you think it's another coincidence that round that time, Graham Forbes suddenly loses a lot of money. Nobody knows why he's lost it – and being nice middle-class English people, the good folk of Weldisham would be far too polite to ask – but Lloyd's is mentioned and that seems to make sense. Possibly Graham started the rumour himself . . . that he'd caught a cold in the Lloyd's crash. It's happened to a lot of other people, so no one questions the idea.'

Baylis still wasn't convinced about the whole picture, but some of Carole's ideas intrigued him. 'Let's just go along with your theory for a moment. If it were true, how do you explain more recent developments? If the bones did belong to Sheila Forbes, why do they suddenly turn up where you found them, in South Welling Barn?'

'All right.' Carole took another deep breath. 'There are things that happened in Malaysia which I'm guessing about, but which could be checked. I think Graham Forbes had met Irene before 1987 and fallen in love with her, which was why he did away with Sheila. He reckoned the body would be safe in the old barn behind his house, because it was only used as a village dumping ground and people very rarely went in there. When he retired, and felt able to introduce his new bride to Weldisham, he quickly got a position of power on the Village Committee. A man of his administrative skills, with time on his hands, would be welcomed with open arms. And thereafter, every time an application came up for planning permission to develop the old barn, Graham Forbes marshalled the Weldisham opposition against the idea. Everyone thought his motivation was to protect the village environment, but in fact he was protecting something else that was much more significant to him.'

'So why were the bones moved?'

'I'm getting there, Sergeant. Harry Grant had bought the barn and he, like others before him, kept trying to get permission to turn it into a dwelling. He was always turned down . . . until last week. I don't know how it happened . . . local back-scratching perhaps, maybe a few palms greased . . . that's not important. What was important, from Graham Forbes's point of view, was that the barn was about to be developed, its floor was going to be dug up to build foundations. His guilty secret was about to be uncovered. So, as soon as he got wind of the Planning Committee's likely decision, Graham Forbes knew he had to move his wife's remains.'

'But why would he only move them as far as South Welling Barn?'

'I don't know. Maybe it was a temporary measure. Maybe he was going to take them to a more permanent hiding place and got interrupted.'

Baylis pursed his lips thoughtfully. 'Anything else?'

'Yes.'

'What?'

Carole hadn't really worked out the next part of her allegations. The first bit had been conjecture supported by some facts and a good ration of logic; this bit was pure conjecture. 'I think something . . . my finding the bones perhaps . . . had an effect on Pauline Helling. Maybe she had a guilty conscience about the crime of which she'd been part, but for whatever reason she decided that she was going to tell someone the truth of what happened.'

'Tell who?'

'I don't know. You perhaps. But I think she let Graham Forbes know about her change of heart . . . or he found out about it somehow . . . and, for that reason, he decided that he had to keep her quiet.'

Baylis looked shocked now. 'So you're saying Graham Forbes torched Heron Cottage?'

Stated like that, the theory sounded rather bald. Carole backtracked. 'I'm saying it's a possibility. I'm not certain about that yet. It'll need a bit of investigation.'

'Yes,' the sergeant agreed, slightly mocking. 'That kind of thing often does.'

'All I am certain of, though,' said Carole, reasserting her authority, 'is the fact that the bones I found belonged to Sheila Forbes, who was murdered by her husband.'

The door behind the bar opened. Will Maples stood there. 'Sorry, have to open up to the thirsty public now.'

His manner was full of apology, but of something else as well. Carole wondered how much of their conversation the manager had overheard.

Chapter Thirty-nine

Charles Hilton led Jude up the heavy mahogany staircase to the second floor of Sandalls Manor. The landings off which the bedrooms opened showed no signs of the building's New Age make-over. They were opulently decorated with rich carpets and curtains, as in any other luxury country house hotel. Again Jude got the impression that the minimum amount of change would be required to convert from psychotherapeutic to clay-pigeon-shooting weekends.

Tamsin Lutteridge's bedroom was at the end of the corridor on the top floor. Charles tapped on the door. Jude didn't hear a voice granting admission, but he pushed in regardless.

The room, like the landings, was expensively upholstered. Pine dressing table, chairs, bedhead and wardrobe gave a rustic impression, as did the chintzy curtains and bedcovers. The tall windows behind the closed curtains must in daytime have commanded wonderful views across the Downs and down to the glinting line of the sea. Jude wondered how much Gillie Lutteridge was paying for accommodation, before she even started on her daughter's medical treatment.

The mess around the room was more characteristic of a teenager than a girl in her early twenties. Underwear,

T-shirts and trainers lay on the floor. Make-up and perfume bottles, some open, spread in confusion on the dressing table. Open magazines and paperbacks littered the bedside table. Minidiscs and their boxes clustered at the foot of an expensive stack system.

And, front down on the bed, watching an American high school soap, lay Tamsin Lutteridge.

She looked up without much interest at their arrival, and Jude's first impression was how ill the girl looked. Four months of Charles Hilton's regimen seemed to have made no difference to her health at all. If anything, she looked worse than when Jude had last seen her.

Tamsin Lutteridge was blonde, like her mother, with blue eyes which, at their best, could sparkle and entrance, but were now as dull as pebbles. The hair hung lank, not unwashed but lifeless. Her long, slight body was swamped in a grey sweatshirt and elasticated trousers of the same material. They were probably her normal day clothes, but gave the impression of pyjamas.

The most striking feature of the girl, though, was her pallor. Perhaps aggravated by reflection from the television screen, the face looked actually grey, a kind of papier-mâché colour.

Tamsin recognized Jude and nodded a greeting. It wasn't unwelcoming, but the effort of making the gesture positively affable seemed too great.

Charles Hilton either didn't see the moment of recognition or – more likely – wanted to assert his control over the situation by making the introductions. 'Tamsin, this is Jude, whom I've agreed can come and talk to you.'

'OK.'

The girl's attention was now back on the television screen. Jude had anticipated a reaction of alarm, or even fear, to her arrival, but all she encountered was indifference.

Charles Hilton gestured to a pine armchair and Jude sat down. Then he perched himself neatly on the stool in front of the dressing table.

'Charles . . . I want to talk to Tamsin on her own.'

His eyes grew darker. 'I'm sorry, Jude. I can't allow that. Tamsin is my patient. We're going through a long therapeutic process and I can't risk her getting upset.'

'I have no intention of upsetting her. What I want to talk about is nothing to do with her illness. And, as I believe I mentioned, nothing to do with you.'

Charles Hilton shook his head slowly, as if dealing with someone unschooled in the arcana of his profession. 'I'm afraid, as her therapist, I can't allow Tamsin to be alone with you.'

'Why? Are you afraid she might have some critical things to say about you and the way you're treating her?'

'No, of course I'm not.' He was piqued by that.

Tamsin Lutteridge showed no reaction to the tension in the room. What little concentration she had was focused on her soap.

'It's just that Tamsin is in a very fragile and vulnerable state. I have to monitor all her dealings with the outside world. I can't risk her delicate mental equilibrium being threatened.'

'Charles,' said Jude languidly, 'if you don't leave the room, I'm going to have a word with Anne . . . about what happened on that course where you and I first met . . .'

He didn't like the idea of leaving Jude alone with Tamsin. But even less did he like the idea of his wife finding out about his groping her. Charles Hilton left the room.

Tamsin Lutteridge continued to watch the television.

No customers had come into the Hare and Hounds at six, but Carole and Detective Sergeant Baylis couldn't continue their conversation with Will Maples ostentatiously busy polishing glasses behind the bar.

The sergeant looked at his watch. 'I'd better be off. Got a few more calls to make.'

'Yes. We need to talk about this further.'

'We certainly do.' Suddenly he leaned in close and whispered fiercely into her face. 'Whatever you do, don't mention anything we've talked about to anyone else.'

'Of course I won't,' said Carole, bewildered.

And suddenly Baylis had straightened up, downed his whisky and, with a 'See you, Will', left the pub.

The manager looked across at her, entertained by her discomfort. 'Would you care to have a drink now, madam?'

'Yes. Please. I'll have dry white wine.'

Just one. Then straight back home. Jude must be back soon. They had so much to talk about.

As regulars trickled into the pub, Carole sipped her wine, stared at the unchanging flames on the ceramic logs and felt mounting frustration. If only Baylis had given some response, some reaction to everything she'd just spilled out . . . Did he think of her as a perceptive sleuth or a hysterical menopausal woman? Had anything she'd said struck a chord with him? Had she provided him with any ideas he hadn't already got?

And, above all, how much did the police know? They must've run DNA tests on the bones by now. Had they been looking for a match with the Helling family? Baylis had said Carole wasn't the first person to suggest the remains belonged to Sheila Forbes. Had they made a positive identification yet? What had Detective Sergeant Baylis said to Graham Forbes when he visited him the previous week? And what was the 'everything' that he was afraid might be ruined by her talking?

'Well, hello. This is an unexpected pleasure. Very interesting that you should be here.'

Carole looked up to find herself confronted by Barry Stillwell. He was wearing yet another pinstriped suit and a charcoal overcoat. His blue tie had a repeated gold logo on it. Some golf club perhaps . . . Yes, he probably would play golf. Carole thanked God they hadn't got on to the subject when they'd last met. Golf would have added agonizing new refinements to the torture imposed by Barry Stillwell's conversation.

'Can I get you another glass of wine? The Bordeaux Blanc that Will has as a house white is not unacceptable.'

Carole's first instinct was to refuse the offer, but on consideration she accepted. Barry Stillwell might be an embarrassing creep, but he did know some of the principals involved in the case. Most significantly, he knew Graham Forbes. Barry could be a useful source of information.

He bought her wine and sat down with a half of bitter for himself. 'Just the half. Have to watch it when I'm driving.'

Carole had said exactly the same words many times herself. Why, on Barry Stillwell's lips, did they sound so impossibly prissy? And why was he suddenly talking like that anyway? On their 'date' he had boasted about his immunity to the attentions of the breathalyser police.

He took a sip from his glass and grunted with satisfaction. 'Ah, that hits the spot all right.'

Why is it, Carole wondered, that all men – particularly those who patently aren't – have to pretend they're part of some blokish beer-swilling pub culture?

Barry Stillwell looked at her in a manner that he imagined to be winsome. 'If I didn't know you better,' he said, 'I'd think you'd been trying to avoid me.'

You don't know me at all. And I have been trying to avoid you. But all Carole said was, 'I'm sorry not to have returned your calls. I've just been so busy the last few days.'

'Oh, don't worry,' said Barry archly. 'I'm sure we can make up for lost time.'

Carole let out a thin smile, before asking, 'So what brings you up here – business or pleasure?'

'I was about to ask you the same thing.'

'I got my question in first.' Carole realized that she sounded impossibly girlish. Oh dear, was she actually using her 'feminine wiles'?

Never mind. It was in a good cause. She might get something out of Barry to corroborate part of her theory of the crime. Because, though she was convinced by its general outline, Carole was aware that more than a few details needed filling in.

'So have you been visiting a client?'

'I have indeed, Carole.'

'Graham Forbes?'

'Yes. My oh my, you've got a good memory.'

'Not that good. We did actually meet at the Forbeses—'

'As if you imagine I could forget it, Carole.'

'And you were introduced to me by Graham as his solicitor.'

'So I was. Right. So you didn't need such a good memory after all . . . though, mind you, I'm sure your memory is as excellent as everything else about you.'

Carole couldn't think what on earth he was talking about, until she realized that this was another of Barry Stillwell's ponderous compliments.

'Oh, that's sweet of you.' She giggled coquettishly, then moved firmly on. 'So what have you been seeing Graham about today?'

But he didn't succumb to the direct question quite as readily as she'd hoped.

'Ah, now, Carole, I'm sure you're aware that there is such a thing as client confidentiality.'

'Of course.' Damn. Her 'feminine wiles' were going to need a little more fine-tuning. She backed off and started a more roundabout approach. 'Was Graham very upset when he heard about the planning permission for the barn?'

'I'm sorry?' asked Barry, confused by the sudden change of direction.

'The barn behind his house. You know, the one that Harry Grant's been wanting to turn into a house for so long.'

'Well, we haven't actually discussed it, but I can't imagine Graham's best pleased. It's something he's fought vigorously for many years.'

Yes, and I know why, thought Carole.

'Of course, I could see it coming,' Barry went on, moving into his 'I know everything that goes on around this area' mode. 'Get a few new faces on the Planning Committee and it's amazing how quickly things can change.'

'Presumably you know most of the major players,' Carole suggested sycophantically.

It had been the right approach. Barry Stillwell almost glowed as he said, 'Oh yes indeed. Not many movers and shakers round here I don't know.'

'So you'd probably also know how all the planning decisions get made, Barry . . .'

He chuckled knowingly.

'Who scratches whose back . . . and what with? How much with?'

He raised an admonitory finger. 'Now, Carole, there's no actual corruption in West Sussex . . .' Another informed chuckle. 'Mind you, certain builders who got the decisions they wanted might well . . . find themselves issuing surprisingly reasonable estimates for jobs for certain individuals . . . Or they might build the odd road or do some public maintenance work at a very competitive price . . .'

'And that's not corruption?' she asked ingenuously.

'No, no, no, Carole, my dear. That is simply shrewd business practice . . . Been going on as long as business itself . . . and it'll continue for the foreseeable future . . .'

'Mm. So how far ahead of the Planning Committee meetings will people know who's likely to get their plans given the green light?'

'Oh, I don't think anyone knows *ahead* of the meeting.'

They must sometimes, thought Carole. Otherwise bang goes my motivation for Graham Forbes's moving of the bones.

Meanwhile Barry Stillwell continued his vindication of local business practice. 'There's nothing illegal in any of this, you know. It's just a friendly way of doing business. Everyone likes to work with people they know.'

'As you do. I mean, I dare say, in your case, a lot of your clients have become friends?'

'I like to think that, Carole, yes. And I'm also delighted when it works the other way round.'

'The other way round?'

'When friends become clients. So if there's ever any help you need of a legal nature – if *you* need help with your will or something – please don't hesitate to pick up the phone . . .'

'That's very kind of you, Barry.'

'Though . . .' Carole was aware of the effort as another cumbersome compliment was cranked up into position. 'When we're talking about someone as lovely as you, I hope you won't wait till you need my professional advice before you pick up the phone to me.'

Another girlish giggle seemed appropriate to the situation and, from Barry Stillwell's reaction, it had been the right choice. But, even as she giggled, Carole wondered how she was ever going to get round to the questions she wanted to ask. Unfortunately, she didn't think it was going to work to say, 'Barry, have you been seeing Graham Forbes because he's been charged with murder?'

Still, she had got as far as mentioning his clients being also his friends. Build on that. 'And it was as a client you first met Graham, of course?'

'Oh yes.'

'You did the conveyancing when he first bought the house here in Weldisham?'

'That's right.'

'And did you do his divorce?'

'Divorce?'

The solicitor looked puzzled, and Carole knew she

was on to something. 'Yes, when he divorced his first wife, so that he could marry Irene.'

'Oh.' Puzzlement had given way to confusion, which was now giving way to a cover-up. 'Ah. *That* divorce. I didn't have anything to do with that. I suppose it must have been arranged out in Malaysia . . . You know, that's where Sheila was when she . . . when she went off with this other chap . . . I suppose . . .'

Carole had him now. Triumphantly, she said, 'You mean Graham and Irene aren't actually married?'

'Well, they are in everything but name. I mean, it's difficult to get a divorce if you've completely lost touch with the person you're trying to divorce.'

Or if you've murdered them.

Suddenly Carole realized something else. She'd thought Barry's intonation had been slightly odd when he said to her, 'If *you* need help with your will or something', but now it made sense. 'You've been to see Graham Forbes to sort out his will, haven't you?'

He looked at her in amazement. 'How on earth did you know that?'

'You virtually told me, Barry.'

'Did I?'

It all made sense. Graham Forbes had felt the net tightening around him, and realized he had to put his affairs in order. He'd never been able to marry Irene. Sheila Forbes hadn't been around to give her permission, and for proof to be found that she was dead . . . although it might have freed him for remarriage . . . that was the one thing that Graham couldn't risk happening. As his wife, Irene would have inherited everything by law. Since they weren't married, he needed to make a will if she was to benefit when he died.

Carole smiled triumphantly at Barry, who looked perplexed and a little guilty. He knew he'd said something he shouldn't have done, but hadn't quite worked out what it was. 'And I know,' she announced, 'why he suddenly needs to make a will in a hurry.'

'Well, obviously, because of the stroke.'

'Stroke?'

'Didn't you know? Graham had a minor stroke on Friday afternoon.'

Friday afternoon. When Lennie Baylis had gone to visit him. The sergeant had confronted him with his crimes and the shock had brought on a stroke.

But she needed more information. 'Was Graham taken to hospital?'

'Yes. Only brought back this morning. That's why I came up this afternoon. First opportunity there was.'

'Right.'

Carole was thoughtful. In one way the stroke fitted perfectly into her theory. But in another way it didn't. If Graham Forbes had been hospitalized until that morning, there was no way he could have started the fire in Heron Cottage which killed Pauline Helling.

Her mind raced as she tried to accommodate these new facts into her scenario. She was aware that Barry Stillwell was saying something, but she wasn't listening.

It was only when she felt his hand on her upper thigh that Carole stopped and looked at him. His thin lips were moving towards hers, puckering like a drawstring purse.

'What the hell do you think you're doing?'

She'd spoken louder than she intended and conversations around them stopped. Barry Stillwell looked uncomfortable, but tried an ingratiating grin. 'Come on, Carole,' he urged quietly, 'you know we both feel the same about each other. You know we're going to get it together one day soon, aren't we?'

'When hell freezes over!' shouted Carole Seddon, and, marching out through silenced customers, left the pub.

Outside, the weather had turned suddenly cold, but Carole didn't notice. Nor did she have any reaction to her flare-up with Barry. She'd forgotten it almost as soon as she was through the door, because her mind was full of other thoughts.

One thought dominated the rest. Maybe Graham Forbes couldn't have done the deed, but Irene Forbes could easily have torched Heron Cottage.

She looked across at the gutted building, roped off by police tapes. She remembered the little Chinaman pin-cushion that had stood on the window sill, and would have put money on the fact that Pauline Helling had brought it back from her one trip abroad. A souvenir of Kuala Lumpur.

Carole hurried through the dark car park to her Renault. She needed to get back to Fethering as quickly as possible. She must talk to Jude. They must pool their ideas. Then they must talk again to Detective Sergeant Baylis. Soon they'd have all the loose ends tied up in neat little bows.

She had her key in the car door before she was aware of the noise behind her.

'I think you'd better come with me, Carole,' said a voice she recognized.

She turned. Thin moonlight caught the outline of a long knife in a gloved hand.

Chapter Forty

Tamsin had been persuaded to turn off the television. She lay on the crumpled cover, propped on a pile of pillows against the pine bedhead. Her manner wasn't adversarial, just exhausted and apathetic. Defeated.

'How's it been?' asked Jude.

'I have good days and bad days. Sometimes I have some energy, sometimes I don't have any. I find it terribly difficult to concentrate on anything. Even a half-hour television soap leaves me mentally exhausted.'

'And are you managing to read much?'

A shake of the head. 'That's too much concentration as well. I flick through the odd magazine, but . . .' Tamsin gestured helplessly to the mess around her.

'How about the physical symptoms?'

The girl grimaced. 'Bad. Like having flu a lot of the time. Some days my joints just ache so much that . . . Oh, I don't know.'

'And do you think what Charles is doing is making things better?'

Tamsin seemed to contemplate a quick fiery response and reject the idea. There was a silence. 'I don't know. Sometimes I think it's helping. I mean, I know this . . . what I've got . . . this illness . . . it's partly to do with the mind. I don't mean it's in the mind,' she added sharply.

'I know what you mean,' said Jude gently. 'You don't have to convince me it's a real illness.'

'No. That's a good thing about Charles too. He never questions that it's a real illness.'

Jude felt the uncharitable thought forming in her head: at the prices he's charging, why should he? She wished she could curb the distrust that the thought of Charles Hilton always prompted in her.

'And he's good,' Tamsin went on, 'about showing how the mind works. Some of what he says is garbage, but a lot of it makes sense. So if I can understand my mind . . . see how that ties in with what's happening to my body . . . maybe I'll get closer to getting better . . .' With an unexpected surge of animation, she echoed her mother's words. 'I mean, we've tried everything else! I've had endless tests in hospital. I've been prescribed vitamin supplements, tonics, antidepressants. None of them've worked. Maybe what Charles is doing will help . . .' She shrugged and repeated a despairing, 'I don't know.'

The long speech seemed to have drained her. There was now no colour in her face at all; she was in monochrome, pale, pale grey. And her eyes a darker grey.

'So you're staying here because you think he may be able to cure you?'

An almost imperceptible nod.

'But that's not the only reason, is it, Tamsin?'

A wariness came into the dull eyes. 'I don't know what you mean.'

Jude didn't beat about the bush. 'I talked to your mother. She said you were staying here because nobody knows where you are. She said you were afraid if you were out in the world, someone might kill you.'

The girl was too washed out to argue. 'Yes,' she said,

and tears spilled slowly down her cheeks, as if they too were exhausted.

'Don't bother to say anything, Tamsin. I'll tell you what I think happened. You stop me when I've got something wrong.' Jude took the silence as assent. 'Let's start that night at the beginning of February when you went back to Weldisham. You went to see your mother because your father was away on business. I think that night you couldn't sleep and you wanted a cigarette. You knew your mother didn't like smoking in the house . . . Anyway, there was the danger your father might smell the smoke when he came back and start asking questions . . .

'So, as you often had done before, you went out into the garden to light up. But it was a cold night. Maybe you'd only got a dressing gown on over your nightie. You knew you'd be more sheltered in the old barn at the bottom of your garden.

'I think it's what you saw when you got into the barn that terrified you, Tamsin.'

The haggard girl on the bed nodded and almost smiled. Jude's words seemed to bring relief to her. She no longer had to bear her secret on her own.

'What was it you saw in the barn?'

'There was a light set up, fixed on a pole . . .' The voice was very thin, but quite audible in the intense silence of the room. 'There was someone there, digging . . .'

'Digging like in a grave?'

'Yes. But it wasn't digging to put something in a grave . . .'

'It was digging to get something out? Or someone out?'

Flattened against the pillows the girl's head could only just manage a nod.

'It was a skeleton, wasn't it, Tamsin? The remains of a human body?'

'Yes.' The word was no more than a breath. -

'And the person saw you, didn't they? And they knew who you were.'

'Yes. And he said he'd kill me.'

'Did he come chasing after you?'

'Mm. But he had to . . . put the bones down and . . . I managed to get back into the house and lock the back door . . . and he didn't follow then.' Jude could see the energy demanded by every word, but she could not come to the girl's rescue until Tamsin had finished what she had to say.

'The next morning . . . I just knew . . . I had to get back here . . . I had to stay here . . . It's the only place I'm safe. So long as he's around . . . there's no way I can ever go back to Weldisham . . .'

'Who was it?' asked Jude. 'Who was the man you saw digging up the bones?'

Chapter Forty-one

The vehicle clattered to a halt and its lights were switched off. The darkness around them was thick, almost tangible. They had left the village on the track that led towards South Welling Barn, but soon veered off cross-country, over bumpy fields, through woodland. Carole had quickly lost her bearings. Apart from the fear, all she felt was a desperate desire to pee.

She had tried talking to him at first, but got no response and soon gave up.

Carole had no idea where they were. Just before the lights had been switched off, she'd had an impression of something rising up ahead of them, some barrier, but she hadn't had long enough to identify it.

She felt a solid point pressing against her side. Not pressed hard enough to pierce her layers of clothes, just enough to remind her that he still had the knife. And wasn't afraid to use it.

'We get out here.' He reached to a shelf under the steering column and produced a large rubber torch, which he switched on. He flashed it across into Carole's face, probably just to blind and disorient her while he got out of the vehicle. Then he opened the door her side.

'Out. Don't try anything.'

'What do you think I'm going to try?' demanded

Carole, glad at last of the opportunity for some kind of dialogue. 'I don't make a habit of carrying hidden weapons. I've no idea where we are, so I'm hardly going to make a run for it, am I?'

'I'm sure you're not. But, in spite of that, I'm afraid I'm going to have to tie you up.'

A coil of rope was lifted into the cone of light. He must have picked it up at the same time as the torch. Nylon rope, stridently orange. The bright colour brought to Carole's mind the piercing blue of the fertilizer sacks that she'd found in South Welling Barn. She shivered as she stepped out into the torch-beam.

But other priorities were more pressing than her fear. 'You're not going to tie me up before I've had a pee. Otherwise it could be extremely messy.'

He hesitated for a moment. Then, 'All right.'

The torch was still focused on her. 'I wouldn't mind a bit of privacy,' Carole snapped. 'But I suppose, if you imagine that I'm about to run away with my tights around my ankles, then you'd better keep me fully illuminated . . .'

She reached down through the folds of her Burberry to lift her skirt. The torch-beam stayed put, then faltered and moved discreetly away. At least he had some decency.

The pee was a merciful release, but Carole felt the coldness of the night on her bare flesh. How long was he planning to keep her there? She wondered again where they were, and what he planned to do once she was tied up.

Her eyes were adjusting to the darkness and, as she straightened her clothes, Carole managed to get some impression of her surroundings.

There was a cliff ahead of her. Though mostly

obscured by scrubby vegetation and dangling tendrils of ivy, here and there a dull white glowed through. They were in an old chalk pit. She knew there were many such workings on the Downs. Some, like the one at Amberley, were even tourist attractions.

But it was a long time since anyone had visited the forsaken spot where Carole Seddon found herself. Thick woodland had grown right up to the foot of the chalk cliff.

'Done?'

'Yes.'

The torch-beam swung round to frame her as she finished straightening her Burberry.

'Right. Don't try anything. I've still got the knife. Put your arms behind your back.'

She could do nothing but what she was told. She felt the rope tightening around first one wrist and then the other as he strapped them together. He wasn't gratuitously sadistic. He tied the rope over the cushion of her jumper and raincoat, and not so tight as to wrench her shoulder blades.

But tight enough. There was no way she could free herself.

He stopped when her wrists were secure.

'Aren't you going to do my feet too?' asked Carole, managing to find a note of insolence from somewhere.

'Not yet,' he replied ominously. 'Come on, walk ahead of me. I'll show you where to go.'

The beam of the torch marked out the route. They seemed to be heading through a tangle of snagging undergrowth straight towards the cliff face.

Carole stopped. 'I can't go any further.'

'Yes, you can. Down on your knees. Push that lot aside.'

Once again, the torch-beam showed her the way. Pushing through the natural barbed wire of roots and creepers, she saw a narrow horizontal crevice in the chalk. Its lips were stained green with the slime of old vegetation.

'Inside.'

A cold recollection came to Carole. She was sitting in the Forbeses' dining room and Harry Grant was talking to her. 'There are some nasty places out on the Downs . . . Marshy bits . . . Chalk pits . . . Caves . . . We used to scare ourselves witless, some of the games we played. Tying each other up, that kind of stuff. Not very nice to each other, kids . . . Certainly we lot weren't.'

She started to object. 'But I—'

'Inside!'

Once again, obedience was Carole's only option. She kneeled, crouched and slid, awkwardly crabwise, into the gap.

Inside she found herself slipping down, and would have rolled, but for the tension of the rope securing her wrists.

She didn't slide far. The cave was bigger than it appeared from outside, but not very big. She felt a sepulchral chill. There was a smell of death, of trapped air, stagnant water, rotted vegetation.

The space filled with flickering light as he came in after her.

'Now we do your feet.'

Again, he wasn't vindictive as he trussed her ankles together. But he was efficient. There was no way she'd be able to free herself unaided from those knots.

But Carole's panicked mind was still circling on thoughts of escape. Though the floor of the chalk cave was lower than its entrance, she still reckoned, if she were left alone, even tied up as she was, she'd be able to work her way back up and out.

He put paid to the thought even before it had taken proper shape. The low curved ceiling of the natural vault was broken here and there by gnarled rafters of tree roots. And round one of these thick loops of wood he tied the loose end of the orange rope.

He left enough slack so that Carole's legs weren't actually lifted off the ground, but not enough for her to be able to stand up. She was stuck where she lay until someone decided to untie her.

'Why're you doing this?' she demanded. 'What do you hope to get out of it? This is only going to make things worse for you.'

He didn't answer, just let out a little dry laugh.

Then he flashed the torch over his handiwork to check the knots were solid and rolled back out of the cave. Leaving total darkness. And the smell of death.

Carole felt her body trembling uncontrollably.

It trembled more when she heard the engine spark into life. The noise of the motor receded until it was lost in the silence of the dark.

Chapter Forty-two

Jude thought it odd that she hadn't heard from Carole after she got back from Sandalls Manor on the Wednesday evening. There was so much she wanted to discuss. But she knew her neighbour was sometimes spikily unpredictable and assumed that an early night had seemed a more attractive option than staying up late over a bottle of wine spinning theories of murder.

Jude had been mildly surprised, but unfazed. It was not in her nature to be judgemental about other people's behaviour. If Carole didn't want to talk that evening, her decision should be respected.

Still, perhaps she should make an official report about what she'd heard. Carole had given her Detective Sergeant Baylis's number. Jude tried it. He didn't answer. She was invited to leave a message. She asked him to ring her. Nothing else she could do at that point.

So, although Jude's mind was seething with the implications of what she had heard from Tamsin Lutteridge, she put those thoughts away and spent the late evening dealing with a much more difficult problem. She'd had a letter that morning from the man she'd met in London the weekend before. He claimed to have seen the error of his ways and claimed to want her back. Though she knew the idea was insane, Jude could not pretend that she wasn't tempted.

Couching her reply to his letter in words that were neither dishonest nor misleading took a long time and a lot of concentration.

She woke the next morning, tired and a little wistful. But she was still convinced that she'd made the right decision. Her long-term sanity demanded that the relationship should be over for good.

She knew she must post the letter before any hairline cracks appeared in her resolve.

It was on her slightly melancholy way back from the postbox that Jude decided she would shift her mood by talking to Carole.

No reply when she rang the doorbell of High Tor. Probably out taking Gulliver for a walk on Fethering Beach.

Jude had turned back down the path to return to Woodside Cottage when she heard the whimpering. It was the sad sound of a dog who not only hadn't been fed, but had also, deprived of his morning walk, done what he knew he shouldn't on the kitchen floor.

Jude went straight across the front garden to open Carole's garage. There was no sign of the Renault.

She wasn't prone to panic, but she knew this was serious. Before even sorting out Gulliver's needs, Jude rang Ted Crisp.

They stood by the Renault in the car park behind the Hare and Hounds.

'Doesn't look good.' Ted Crisp bent down to pick

something up off the ground. He held it out. Jude recognized the bunch of keys immediately.

'She'd never just have dropped them. Carole's far too organized for that. Someone must've surprised her by the car and . . .'

'And what?'

'I don't know. Taken her off somewhere.'

'Did she tell you she was going to come up here yesterday evening?'

'No. I guessed. I knew she'd been doing a lot of thinking about what's been happening in Weldisham. It seemed a reasonable assumption that she'd come up here to continue her investigations . . . You know, to meet someone.'

'Who? Her boyfriend?'

The hurt in Ted Crisp's voice was so overt that Jude looked at him curiously. 'Boyfriend? Carole hasn't got a boyfriend.'

'Yes, she has. Don't pretend you don't know. She's been going round with some local solicitor.'

'No, she hasn't.'

'She has. His name's Barry Stillwell. Look, Jude, I know Mario, guy who works as a waiter in an Italian restaurant in Worthing. This Barry bloke took Carole out for dinner there last week.'

'Yes, he did, but . . .' A thought struck Jude. 'Is that why you were so standoffish to Carole last time we were in the Crown and Anchor?'

'I don't know what you're talking about,' Ted Crisp mumbled. He had his pride.

'Ted, we haven't got time to go into all this now, but I can assure you Carole thinks Barry Stillwell is the most boring man on God's earth.'

'Oh. Oh, does she?' And he couldn't help a little grin appearing through the foliage of his beard.

'Anyway, time enough for that. What we've got to do now is to find her. Better check whether she actually was in the pub last night.'

They couldn't avoid seeing the blackened shell of Heron Cottage, separated from the road by the police plastic tapes. Neither said anything, but the same dark thoughts were in both their minds as they rang the bell of the Hare and Hounds opposite.

Though the pub wouldn't open for another half-hour, Will Maples was already there. He opened the door, but didn't invite them in. 'Don't open till eleven,' was all he said.

'I know.' Jude turned on her full charm, which few men could resist. 'But a friend of ours has left her car in your car park and we just wonder where she might be.'

'Usually, when a car gets left overnight in the car park, it's because someone's had a skinful and been sensible enough to order a cab. I expect your friend'll be back later in the morning to collect the car.'

'I don't think so in this case.'

Ted Crisp held out the bunch of keys. 'She dropped these by the car.'

'Are you asking me to look after them until she comes in?'

'No,' said Jude. 'We just want you to confirm that she was in the pub last night.'

'Well, since I don't know who you're talking about, that could be a bit difficult.' Will Maples wasn't being exactly uncooperative; but equally he wasn't making things easy for them.

'Her name's Carole Seddon . . .'

He shrugged. 'Not a name I know. Not one of my regulars.'

'Thin. Glasses. Grey hair. Light blue eyes. Wears a Burberry raincoat. My sort of age.'

'Oh right, I think I know the one you mean. Yes, she came in before we opened yesterday evening. To talk to Lennie Baylis.'

'The detective?'

'Mm.'

'Do you know what she talked to him about?'

He was affronted. 'What do you take me for? I don't eavesdrop on other people's conversations!'

The response was so vehement that Jude wondered whether the manager was protesting a little too much.

'And did she leave with Sergeant Baylis?'

'No. She stayed and had a drink.'

'On her own?'

'At first, yes. Then a man joined her.'

'Who was that? Did you recognize him?' asked Ted.

'Yes. Name's Barry Stillwell. Comes into the pub quite often. He's a solicitor . . . in Worthing, I think.'

'Ah,' said Ted Crisp, deflated. Then, unwillingly, he asked, 'Did they leave together?'

'I didn't notice,' Will Maples replied smugly.

'But they didn't stay in the pub all evening?' asked Jude.

'No. I remember they were sitting in the Snug, and when I looked a bit later, there were some other people in there.'

'What time are you talking about?'

'They must've both been gone by seven, seven-fifteen.'

'Well, thank you.' Jude got out a piece of paper and

wrote on it. 'That's my mobile number. Could you give me a call if Carole comes back to collect her car?'

'Yes, all right,' Will said grudgingly. 'But I probably won't get a chance to look till after three. We tend to be pretty busy at lunchtime.' He smiled at Ted Crisp in a way that must have meant he knew who his visitor was. 'I'm running a very successful pub here, you know.'

The landlord of the Crown and Anchor nearly snapped something back, but was quelled by an urgent look from Jude's brown eyes.

'If that's all,' said the manager of the Hare and Hounds briskly, 'I've got a lot to get on with.'

'Yes, of course. Thank you so much for your help,' said Jude charmingly to the closing door.

They stood for a moment in front of the pub, both still avoiding looking at the wreckage of Heron Cottage.

'So what do we do now?' asked Ted Crisp.

'I think you try to contact Detective Sergeant Baylis. Tell him we're worried about Carole. Try and find out what she talked to him about last night.'

'I'll track him down. And what do you do meanwhile?'

'I talk to some people here in Weldisham,' Jude replied mysteriously.

Behind the bar of the Hare and Hounds, Will Maples punched in the number of a mobile phone. 'Hi,' he said. 'Two people came looking for her.'

Chapter Forty-three

Carole had passed a night of misery, probably as close to despair as she'd even been. Immobilized in her cold prison, she envisaged the slow death that she must suffer. Would hunger get to her first, or would the hypothermia win? Either way, it wouldn't be an easy passage out of life.

After the departure of her captor's vehicle, the total silence had begun to be broken. Not by human sounds, but by the rustling and scuttering of small animals, to whom the night belonged. In their world, Carole was an intruder, an alien presence. At first they would keep a proper distance from her, but then, when they realized she was incapable of movement, they would become bolder. As the strength drained from her body, they might not wait till death to obey their scavenging instincts. It was not a cheering thought.

She didn't think she slept at all, but the suddenness with which she was aware of the light outside meant that maybe she had dozed fitfully towards the end of the night. Her body felt bruised, aching from the hardness of the floor and the constrictions of her bonds. In spite of the cold, she had managed to control her bladder through the night, but she knew that couldn't last for ever.

Carole Seddon was a fastidious woman; she didn't want to die in a mess of her own making.

She didn't want to die full stop. Now that death was a realistically imminent possibility, she realized how enormously she wanted to live. She wanted to see Jude again. She wanted to see Ted Crisp. She wanted to experience another bone-headedly enthusiastic welcome from Gulliver. She wanted to walk again on Fethering Beach with the dog scampering manically around her.

But none of that looked very likely, as thin sunlight, reflected in pools of stagnant water, began to play on the slimy dome of the cave. The day had started for the rest of the world. In her prison that was irrelevant. However hard they searched, no one would ever find her here. She had been left to die in her own time. She found herself praying for a big freeze-up so that that time would be as short as possible.

She had reached the point where she could deny the imperative of her bladder no longer, when she heard the sound of an approaching vehicle. Even though she felt certain that it was her captor returning, the fact that he had come back gave a disproportionate lift to her spirits.

His return changed the nature of her incarceration. All through the night she'd thought he'd left her there to die. Now it was clear he had some other agenda. Carole Seddon wasn't about to be murdered; she had merely been kidnapped.

She shut her mind to the other reasons why he might have come back to her.

His body blocked the light as he rolled in through the narrow aperture. Carole wasn't feeling light-hearted, but she thought a light-hearted approach might be worth trying.

'If you've come to give me another loo-break,' she said, 'you're only just in time.'

He didn't speak, but untied the end of the rope from its root and helped her out into the open. The air was cold outside, but didn't have the deathly chill of the cave.

'You're going to have to untie me or I'll wet myself.'

He obliged, releasing her legs. But he only freed one hand, keeping her like a child on a parental lead in a shopping precinct. For a moment Carole thought she'd fall over, but she stamped some consciousness into her legs and arms, before giving in to the urgency of her bladder and squatting down. Again he averted his eyes.

Once she'd rearranged her clothing, Carole sat down facing her captor. 'How long are you planning to keep me here?'

'That depends,' he said, the first words he'd spoken to her that morning. 'Depends on how much you know.'

'About what?'

'Don't play games!' He snatched at the rope that still held her wrist and gave it a vicious tug.

Carole realized that, up until that point, she'd just been lucky. He wasn't afraid to hurt her; he just hadn't hurt her so far.

'I know some of what you know,' he went on. 'Will Maples keeps his ears open in the Hare and Hounds.'

'And he tells you everything, does he?'

'Will Maples owes me a few favours.' He grinned complacently.

'Why? Is it something to do with drugs?'

'Oh, well done. Not just a pretty face, are you?' His grin turned cruel. 'Not even a pretty face. Still, you're right. Will Maples has been dealing drugs from the Hare and Hounds ever since he's been there. I've known that for a long time, and so for a long time he's done exactly what I tell him.'

'Otherwise you'll shop him to his bosses?'

'Exactly.'

'Is he involved with the Brighton dealers?'

'Yes.'

'Strange life yours, isn't it?' Carole felt defiant now. Since nothing she said was likely to do her much good, she might as well say what she thought. 'A counterbalance of threats and blackmail. You've got information on someone, they've got information on you.'

'Exactly, Carole. And so long as the people concerned agree to keep that information to themselves, everything in the garden's lovely.'

'And, if they don't agree to keep that information to themselves?'

'Ah, then . . .' He shook his head regretfully. 'Then, I'm afraid, they have to die.'

Suddenly he was alert to a sound that Carole had not heard. 'Get in the cave!' he hissed. 'There's someone coming!'

Chapter Forty-four

Irene Forbes ushered Jude into the sitting room. She seemed unfazed to have a visitor, but then it was hard to tell what emotions lay behind that smooth Chinese face. Jude was moved by the woman's beauty, and also by her appearance of youth. From what Carole had said of her history, Irene Forbes must have been at least in her late forties, but she could have been twenty years younger. Her skin, the colour of Rich Tea biscuits, was unlined, and there was no touch of grey in the black bell of her hair.

She was simply dressed in white trousers and brown jumper, but somehow contrived to look exotic, a hothouse flower in the Englishness of a Weldisham sitting room.

Jude refused the offer of tea or coffee and said, 'I was very sorry to hear about your husband's illness.'

Irene Forbes bowed acknowledgement of the sentiment. 'I'm pleased to say he's a lot better than he was at the weekend.'

'Good. People seem to make complete recoveries from strokes these days.'

It was unlike Jude to get caught up in this cycle of civilities, but there was something about her hostess's serenity that unnerved her. Jude, a woman with her own inner strengths, could sense in Irene a matching or even stronger power.

'Look,' she went on, trying to be more assertive, 'it's very kind of you to invite me in when you have no idea who I am. We have a mutual friend, actually. Her name is Carole Seddon and she came to dinner a week or two back.'

'A charming woman,' said Irene. 'She comes from Fethering, I believe. Graham very much enjoyed her company. I believe they have a mutual interest in the *Times* crossword . . . Something, I fear, that I could never master.'

'Nor me.' Jude found the woman's stillness seductive. She felt the urgency within her seep away and it was with an effort that she continued, 'Look, Carole's gone missing, and I'm very worried about what may have happened to her.'

'I am sorry she's gone missing. And if I could do anything to help you find her, of course I would. But I'm afraid I do not know your friend well. I only met her that one evening.'

Jude took a deep breath. 'I'm sorry, this is difficult to say, but I'm afraid Carole's disappearance may have something to do with the bones.'

'Ah.' The monosyllable was one of acceptance.

'The bones that she found at South Welling Barn. Carole had managed to discover a lot more about where those bones came from and, in doing so, she may have upset someone.'

'I would think that was very possible.'

'Mrs Forbes, I haven't got time to beat about the bush. Carole thought the bones belonged to your husband's first wife, Sheila.'

There was a silence. Then Irene Forbes slowly

lowered her face, so that she was looking at the floor. 'They always say it is impossible to keep anything secret in an English village.' She sighed and looked up again, with a trace of a smile around her lips. 'Graham and I have had thirteen years together, three in Kuala Lumpur and ten here. We have been lucky. Many people do not have so much in their lifetime.'

'But how long have you known about . . . what happened?'

'About Sheila? Not long. Only a matter of weeks.'

'It must have been a terrible shock for you.'

'A shock certainly. But more a sadness.'

A detail fell into place. 'My friend Carole told me she first saw you in the church. St Michael and All Angels. She said you were crying. Was that because of what you'd heard?'

The helmet of black hair hardly moved as the woman nodded. 'Yes. Religion can sometimes help. Faith is so much more forgiving than morality. No, it was very sad. That for Graham and me to be happy, someone else had to suffer so much.'

'Did it affect how you felt about him . . . when you knew?'

Irene Forbes shook her head slowly, but very firmly. 'No. You love what a person is, not what they've done.'

'And the police know about it, do they? About the murder?'

'They suspect. Soon they will know for sure. A policeman – Detective Sergeant Baylis – came to see Graham last Friday. He had phoned in the morning to say he was coming.'

'Which was why Graham didn't go for his usual pre-lunch drink that day?'

A graceful inclination of the head acknowledged this. 'I don't think Sergeant Baylis had to come. I think he was just giving a warning, giving Graham time to prepare himself. He said there were suspicions about the bones belonging to Sheila, and that DNA tests would be conducted to try and make a match with other Helling relatives.'

'So, from that moment, your husband knew that his time was limited?'

'Yes.'

'Hadn't he known before?'

'No. I tried to keep it from him. But when the police came, I could keep quiet no longer. That was the shock that brought on his stroke.' With sudden passion, Irene Forbes said, 'I hope he will not live long. Graham has always hated the idea of being impaired, of doing anything at less than his best. He would make a bad invalid. And he would not enjoy court proceedings.'

'No.' Jude let a moment of silence hang between them, before going on, 'I'm sorry to keep interrogating you, Mrs Forbes . . .'

'I am not really Mrs Forbes. Only in my soul.'

'Yes. But, look, I'm very worried about Carole. I'm sure she's been abducted by someone because of what she'd worked out about the bones.'

Irene Forbes let out a humourless laugh. 'Well, I can assure you it wasn't Graham. He's lying upstairs in bed, with only one side of his body working. He's not capable of abducting anyone.'

'I wasn't suggesting he was. I was thinking of Brian Helling.'

'Ah.'

'He was the one who dug up the bones in the old barn, wasn't he?'

'Yes. And he was the one who came and told me about his discovery. He took pleasure in it. He liked the idea of having power over Graham. He liked the idea of having power over anyone.'

'Irene, I've got to find him!'

'I don't know where he is.'

'I know you don't, but I just wondered . . . when he came to see you . . . presumably he talked of blackmail . . .'

'Of course. That's the only reason he'd dug up the bones in the first place.'

'But presumably he also gave you a promise that, if you coughed up the money, he'd hide the bones somewhere safe . . . somewhere nobody else except for him could find them.'

'Yes. He said he'd do that. I asked him to hand them over for us to dispose of, but he wouldn't. He wanted to keep them, so that if he ever needed to raise his ransom demands . . . So that he would always have a hold over Graham . . .'

'Mrs Forbes . . . Irene . . . did Brian Helling say anything about where he might hide the bones?'

'No. Well, he didn't say anything that meant anything to me.'

'What were his exact words?'

'He said, "Don't worry about anyone finding the bones. Nobody ever goes to Fort Pittsburgh."'

Chapter Forty-five

Though flickers of unhealthy light intermittently penetrated her prison, Carole could see nothing of the outside world. Nor could she draw attention to herself. She had been securely gagged. But she could hear the two men talking.

At first she was full of a wild, crazy hope. This was a rescue. Why else would he have come? He was her saviour.

But they weren't far into their conversation before that hope was crushed. More than crushed – stifled, strangled till no breath of life remained.

'It's an impasse,' she heard Brian Helling's voice say. 'A Mexican stand-off with no weapons.'

'No weapons?' Lennie Baylis's voice echoed.

'Well, no guns. One knife between the two of us.'

'But I hold all the cards,' said Baylis. 'I've got the authority of the West Sussex Constabulary behind me.'

'Hardly.' There was triumph and derision in Brian Helling's tone. 'You shop me, I tell them about your deals with the boys in Brighton. How long have you been taking a percentage for turning a blind eye to their transactions? Nice little pay-offs from all the pubs and clubs. You must've salted away quite a bit by now, Lennie.'

'The police look after their own. Nobody'd in the force'd believe you, Brian.'

'No? All right, maybe not me on my own, but I could get Will Maples to back me up.'

'He won't say anything. He'll keep quiet to save his own skin.'

'You can't be certain of that. I still know too much for you to turn me in, Lennie. You can't afford the risk.'

'Maybe not.' There was a silence. 'Of course, it needn't be the police. I could just alert the Brighton boys to where you are.'

An intake of breath. Brian Helling was frightened, but he disguised his fear as well as he could. 'Another risk too far. I might still be able to get information to the police.'

Baylis seemed to accept this and changed tack. 'I've got plenty on you, though, Brian. I know about you digging up the bones in the barn behind the Forbeses' place. I can get you on blackmail – and on torching your mother's place.'

'You've got no proof of that. The fire could have been an accident.'

'No way. There was petrol on the dog's fur.'

'The dog? Wasn't that little bugger burnt to a cinder?'

'No, it got out of the cottage. Forced its way through a half-open window, we reckon.'

'Damn.'

'Yes. Bad luck, Brian. Always enjoyed hurting animals, didn't you?'

'Better than enjoying hurting people, Lennie.' The line was spoken with deep viciousness. 'You remember what you did to me here, don't you?'

Baylis laughed, and in her prison Carole shivered. The sound was pure cruelty.

Then he asked, 'Why did you kill your mother, Brian?'

'She'd lost her nerve. After Carole Seddon went to see her and then you went to see her the same day, she was all set to turn me in. I couldn't allow that.'

'I see.'

'And with the insurance on Heron Cottage, I'll be able to pay off what I owe in Brighton.'

'What? No way you're ever going to get the insurance. You're mad, Brian, do you know that? Always have been, from when you were a kid.'

'I'm not! But if I were, what you did to me here might help explain why!'

There was another callous laugh from Baylis.

With an effort, Brian Helling calmed himself. 'So, like I said, it's a Mexican stand-off. We know too much about each other. Each one of us has the power to destroy the other. And that's what's going to keep us both quiet.'

There was a long silence while Lennie Baylis took this in. At the end he asked flatly, 'So what about her?'

'We both know the answer to that. Carole Seddon's got rather a lot of information, hasn't she? You know exactly how much. That's why you've been taking such a personal interest in her investigations – to find out if she's got anything incriminating on you.'

'Hm.'

'And you know she has, or you wouldn't have come out to this godforsaken place. Carole Seddon knows enough to shop both of us – particularly if she's overheard what we've just been saying.'

'Yes.'

To Carole the ensuing silence felt very long. Agonizingly long.

'So we have to kill her?'

'Needn't be as proactive as that.'

'You mean we just leave her here?'

'That's right. We just leave her here.'

Chapter Forty-six

'No sign of Baylis,' said Ted Crisp gloomily. 'I've phoned his office. They don't know where he is. Or if they do, they're not saying.'

He and Jude were sitting in his car by the village green in Weldisham. Her brow wrinkled with effort as she tried to make sense of what she'd heard. 'Fort Pittsburgh . . . Fort Pittsburgh . . . I'm sure Carole said something about forts. Someone had talked to her about forts. I've heard someone talking about forts. Oh, damn, who was it?'

There was a long silence, finally broken by Ted. 'If anything happens to her, I'll never forgive myself.'

'Don't worry, Ted. Carole will survive,' said Jude with a confidence she didn't feel. Suddenly she slapped her hands to the side of her face. 'Forts – yes! Harry Grant said something about him and Lennie Baylis playing with forts when they were kids. Maybe Fort Pittsburgh fits in with that!' She reached for her mobile. 'I must get Harry Grant's number.'

Directory Enquiries obliged, but when she called, the phone rang and rang. Jude wasn't to know that Harry and Jenny Grant were at that moment getting off a plane in Portugal.

She and Ted Crisp exchanged looks of total despair.

There was nothing they could do. Both felt sure that Carole was somewhere close, but they had no means of tracing her.

Jude put her hands over her eyes and tried to focus on the scene in the Hare and Hounds when Harry Grant had mentioned forts. Her brow scrunched up with the effort. Then it cleared. She snapped her fingers.

'Nick! Harry mentioned someone else called Nick. He'd played their games with them.'

'But where are we going to find him?'

'He works on one of the farms. I'll ask Irene Forbes. She may know.'

When Ted's car drew up beside him, Nick was on a tractor with a fork-lift attachment, lowering a huge cylinder of hay over a fence to a circling herd of hungry cows. He was aware of Jude and Ted's presence, but ignored them till the bale was grounded. Then he climbed over the fence and used a knife to cut the string around the hay, forcing the eager animals back as he did so. Only after he had methodically coiled up the string round his hand and crossed back over the fence did he look full on at his visitors.

He folded the arms of his plaid working shirt and said nothing. His eyes, buried in weather-beaten folds of skin, were cautious.

'Nick?' A curt nod acknowledged that that's who he was. 'My name's Jude and this is Ted. Look, I'm sorry to interrupt you like this, but I want to know if you've ever heard of Fort Pittsburgh.'

There was an aching silence. Jude was beginning to be afraid he was never going to say anything, when finally he spoke. 'Long time since I've heard Fort Pittsburgh mentioned.'

'But do you know what it is, where it is?'

Again he left a silence before he said, 'Chalk pit. Out on the Downs.'

'Could you tell us how to get there?'

'Why?' he asked, with a suspicion of strangers that went back through generations.

'Because I believe a friend of mine is being imprisoned in Fort Pittsburgh.'

The words sounded melodramatic, but Nick took them seriously. 'Who's imprisoned her then?'

'Either Lennie Baylis or Brian Helling.'

The effect of the names was instantaneous. 'We'd better get out there!'

Ted Crisp began, 'If you show me the way—'

'We'll go in the tractor. It's cross-country.'

The March sky was already darkening as the tractor lumbered off the track and started across fields. On the higher parts of the Downs the ground, though wet, was fairly firm. When they got into the dips, the going would be stickier. But the tractor's high wheels rode steadily over the terrain.

In the enclosed cab, conditions for the three of them were cramped and stuffy.

'It's a kids' name – Fort Pittsburgh,' said Nick, suddenly loquacious. 'If you were brought up in Weldisham, you used to go a long way out of the village to play. Lots of secret places you could find. All our kids' games were kind of military . . . lots of building camps, having pitched battles, stalking your friends, trapping them. It wasn't like

in a city. We didn't have many toys and stuff, so we . . .
as the expression goes . . . made our own entertainment.
Just a few of us . . . and some of the games we invented
were pretty rough.'

Neither Jude nor Ted Crisp said anything. They were
too anxious for words, and so they let Nick's monologue
roll.

'Anyway, all around the Downs we had our camps,
forts we called them, and we invented names for them.
Well, I didn't do much of the inventing. Lennie and Harry
did that. They were in charge. Lennie had heard of Pittsburgh and he thought it sounded American and flashy, so
when we found this old disused chalk pit, it became Fort
Pittsburgh.'

'A chalk pit?' said Jude.

'Yes. In the middle of some woods. Very overgrown.
Great place to play and . . .' He seemed to lose impetus.
'That kind of thing.'

'What kind of thing?'

'Well, we . . . As I say, our games were pretty rough . . .
cruel, you could say. I'm sure they'd be called cruel nowadays, but then . . . that's how kids were . . . Like I said,
Harry and Lennie were the leaders . . . And Brian Helling
always wanted to play with us . . . and we didn't want him
to . . . you know, because he wasn't from the village . . .
he only spent time up there when his mum was working.
His mum was a cleaner . . . and Brian was a mummy's
boy . . . and he was a bastard . . . and . . . Like I said, kids
can be very cruel . . .

'So one day Lennie said we'd play this trick on Brian.
I wasn't keen, because I knew what Lennie's tricks were
like, but you didn't argue with him, nor with Harry. You
just went along with them. So, anyway, Lennie told Brian

yes, he could come and play with us. He could come to this special place we'd found which we called Fort Pittsburgh. So Brian came along with us, all innocent and, like, very cheery because he thought now he was part of our gang, and we . .'

There was a silence. 'What, Nick?'

'We tied him up and left him in a cave overnight. In what we called the Prison. The Fort Pittsburgh Prison.'

'How old was he then?'

'Seven . . . eight . . . I don't know. It's not something I'm proud to have been involved in, but Lennie had a very strong personality and, like I said, kids are cruel. So anything that happens between Lennie and Brian goes back a long way. They both got a really cruel streak and if they've captured someone, they—'

But the farm worker's narrative got no further. The tractor had reached the edge of a thick tangled wood. He brought it to a halt.

'We walk the last bit,' said Nick.

Chapter Forty-seven

'You can't just leave me here,' said Carole, as she felt the nylon rope being tied around both her wrists. After the other man had departed, he'd let her out of the cave again and kept her tethered by the one arm. She'd tried to engage him in conversation, but without success. He'd given her permission to relieve herself and even given her some food.

Why did he bother? She knew they'd agreed to leave her there to die.

'Back in the cave now.' Brian Helling jerked the rope taut, less gentle than he'd been the day before. He pulled her face round to face his. 'I'm going to write about you, you know, Carole Seddon.'

Panic snatched away her breath. 'Write about me?' she managed to say. 'What on earth do you mean? There's nothing to write about me.'

His answer made her feel even bleaker.

'Oh, there will be. *A Diary of Decay*. That'll be the breakthrough book for me. A minute dissection of how someone actually dies . . . How long it takes them to die . . . What actually happens to their body . . . and to their mind.'

Carole fought off terror with cold logic. 'If you're going

to make that kind of detailed observation, you'll have to come out here. You'll draw attention to my hiding place.'

'No way. I know this area. I grew up round here. I know every copse and fold of the Downs. I'm a good tracker, a good countryman. Nobody'll find me out here.'

'They will if you keep coming out in a Land Rover.'

'I won't use the Land Rover after today.'

'Somebody must know where you are.'

Brian Helling shook his head complacently. 'Only Lennie Baylis. And he'll keep quiet.'

Carole clutched at a straw. 'Will Maples! He tipped you off and told you where to find me. He knows where you are.'

'As you know,' said Brian quietly, 'if you were listening to what Lennie and I said, we've both got something of a hold over Will Maples. Incidentally,' Brian went on, aware of the cruelty of what he was about to say, 'Will rang through on the mobile earlier. He told me two friends of yours had arrived at the Hare and Hounds looking for you.'

'What did they look like?'

'Chubby woman with blonde hair, big fat chap with a beard. Needless to say, Will didn't tell them anything.'

A shadow of despair engulfed Carole.

Brian Helling tugged on the rope. 'Better get you back in your little niche, hadn't we? I've got to be off.'

'When will you be coming back?' asked Carole, trying to make it sound like the most casual question in the world.

He let out a dry chuckle. 'Oh, I don't think I should tell you that. It'd spoil the fun.'

'So what is going to be the fun for you? Killing me? Watching me die?'

'I suppose so, yes. But,' he said rather primly, 'it's not just random cruelty. There's a practical side as well. Writers need experience. There are some things you can't make up. You have to live through them. All my other books were rejected, not because they weren't horrifying enough, but because they weren't authentic enough. They lacked that little bit extra that can only be given by first-hand experience.'

'And you didn't get that first-hand experience when you set fire to Heron Cottage?'

'No.' He spoke with genuine regret and a frightening objectivity. 'I wasn't able to watch my mother die. Pity, I'd been looking forward to that for a long time.'

'So she couldn't give you the authentic material you were looking for?'

'No.'

'So . . . you couldn't get what you wanted when you killed your mother . . . Whereas I, on the other hand, can go to my death with the great satisfaction of knowing I've helped you, for the first time in your life, to write a publishable book?'

He didn't like the scorn in her voice. He lashed out and slapped her face hard, hissing, 'Yes.'

'Well, don't bother putting me back in that smelly cave. Why don't you just kill me with your knife?' Carole demanded defiantly. 'Get it over with. Watch me die here and now. Sit with your notebook and describe every last twitch of my body. I'm sure that would add the necessary "authenticity" to your precious book.'

'Oh no,' said Brian Helling, with an icicle of a smile. 'That wouldn't do. That wouldn't fit. I've been thinking about this for a long time. I have to watch someone die in the Prison of Fort Pittsburgh.'

'Why?'

His face clouded with painful memories. But the only explanation he could give was, 'I have to do it.'

He tugged on the rope, again with unnecessary harshness. 'Come on, it'll be dark soon. Time to settle you in for the night, Carole. Though in fact what we're talking about is nights and days, and more nights and days . . . You won't be coming out of there again.'

'But you'll be coming in to watch me?'

'I must make sure my *Diary of Decay* is authentic.'

'Well, may I at least have another pee before—'

'No!'

This time the tug on the rope was so hard that Carole fell to the ground. Brian Helling dragged her upright and pushed her towards the undergrowth-hidden entrance to the cave.

When she tried to resist, he hit her hard around the head. He had lost the restraint that previously curbed his violence. He was very dangerous.

Cowed, Carole could do nothing but what he wanted. She dropped to her knees and then rolled sideways into the rank darkness.

She could still feel the tension on the rope, and waited for him to follow her in and truss her up again. He'd tie her legs, and shackle her once again to the tree root. And that was the position in which she would stay, for the rest of her life. Which wouldn't be very long.

Then one day perhaps another walker, wandering off the beaten track across the Downs, would stumble on her catacomb. And another set of female bones would be found to feed the mills of gossip and conjecture that ground endlessly in the village of Weldisham.

Carole Seddon had often thought her life was unimportant. Never till that moment had it felt so essential. She dreamed of being back in a hot bath at High Tor, and she knew how unlikely that dream was ever to be realized.

She lay on the slimy floor, breathing the chill, dank air, waiting for her murderer to come into the cave after her.

There was a moment of stillness, then a shout, and a yank on the rope that almost pulled her arms from their sockets. She was aware of herself screaming.

Chapter Forty-eight

Suddenly, mercifully, the rope was released.

There were sounds of confusion, shouting, possibly fighting, from outside. Then the entrance to the cave was once again darkened by a human body.

And Carole heard the most welcome sound of her life. It was the anxious voice of Ted Crisp asking, 'Are you all right, Carole? I'll kill the bastard if he's hurt you.'

She felt Ted's strong arms helping her out and, once she was upright, fell into them. His body felt huge and wonderfully solid.

It was still just light at the foot of the chalk cliff. Carole took in Nick, holding a tyre iron, guarding the Land Rover to prevent Brian Helling's escape by that route. Beside him was a sight almost as welcome as Ted Crisp – Jude.

But Jude was looking upwards with fear in her eyes and there was shouting from above them.

Carole, still holding Ted Crisp's hand, moved backwards to see what was going on at the top of the cliff.

Brian Helling had scurried up a narrow diagonal ridge across the chalk face. An escape route from Fort Pittsburgh that they'd found in their childhood games. But, at the top of the cliff, knowing the way Brian would come, stood Lennie Baylis.

The sergeant was much heavier in build than his opponent, who looked effete and slightly ridiculous in his trademark beret and black coat. The leather was scored with white chalk marks where Brian had scrambled against the cliff.

They faced each other for a moment in silence, then Brian Helling's escape was cut short as Lennie Baylis's heavy body slammed into him. For a moment it looked as though the lighter man had lost his balance and would fall back down the chalk. But somehow he managed to grab hold of his assailant and, watched with appalled fascination by the four below, the two bodies grappled together on the cliff top, re-creating a long-remembered childhood conflict.

There was a sound like a gasp and, gradually, the bodies separated. As in slow motion, one slipped away from the other. Then, gathering momentum, the body slithered down the face of the cliff, leaving a livid smear of red on the discoloured chalk.

At the top, with bloodied knife in hand and an expression of triumph on his face, stood Brian Helling.

Chapter Forty-nine

Jude had rung the police on her mobile. Brian Helling offered no resistance when Ted Crisp tied him up with the orange nylon rope. The murder of Lennie Baylis seemed to have calmed him down, perhaps provided a resolution to emotions that had tortured him throughout his life.

The police arrived in a convoy of Range Rovers. They were very solicitous, and a female officer looked after Carole. Respectful of the state she was in, they kept their questioning to a minimum and, once reassured that Brian Helling hadn't touched her sexually and that she really did feel all right, allowed her to fulfil her fantasy of ending up that night in a hot bath back at High Tor.

There would be more questions later, but, they implied, not until Carole felt ready to answer them.

Jude went back with Carole, but neither felt like talking. Carole promised Jude she'd ring through if she woke in the night feeling bad, but she didn't think it'd happen. The emotions of the previous twenty-four hours had left her so drained she didn't feel anything, except extraordinarily tired. She could sleep for a week.

The police were back to Carole earlier than she'd expected. The very next morning, in fact. But her visitors weren't from the teams investigating the three Weldisham murders. They comprised an assistant chief constable, resplendent in his uniform, and a female detective constable in designer plain clothes.

They were polite, but went straight to the purpose of their visit. 'Mrs Seddon,' said the assistant chief constable, 'we're here in connection with the late Detective Sergeant Baylis.'

'Yes. It must be dreadful for his family.'

'Of course.' He dismissed the family with a perfunctory wave of his hand. 'I need to understand, Mrs Seddon, how much you knew about Detective Sergeant Baylis.'

'Not a lot. I met him first a few weeks back. He was called out to Weldisham when I reported my discovery of the bones in South Welling Barn.'

'And you saw him after that occasion?'

'Yes, once or twice. He encouraged me to let him know how my thoughts were going about the . . . well, I suppose I have to call it the "case". He seemed very concerned that I should keep him up to date with anything I'd observed round the village.'

'Didn't you think that was odd?'

'Well, I suppose a bit . . . He did seem to take a very personal interest in the case.'

A look passed between the assistant chief constable and his sergeant. It seemed to confirm some conjecture that they'd shared before the meeting.

'Did Detective Sergeant Baylis say anything to you about drugs, Mrs Seddon?'

Some instinctive caution made Carole decide to forget the conversation that she had overheard at Fort Pittsburgh. 'Well . . . He did say that Brian Helling had got involved with drugs . . . that Brian owed a lot of money to some men in Brighton.'

'Nothing else?'

'No.'

Her answer seemed to satisfy the assistant chief constable. 'Mrs Seddon, I must request your complete confidentiality in this matter. Please don't talk about it to anyone, least of all the press. The fact is that Detective Sergeant Baylis had been under internal police investigation for some time . . .'

'About drugs?'

'Yes. Baylis used to be based in Brighton and there were allegations that he . . . got rather more friendly than he should with certain club owners . . . That he from time to time turned a blind eye to deals that . . . As I say, these were only allegations, which were in the process of being investigated when he died . . .'

'Yesterday.'

'Precisely. Now what will happen to that investigation in these new circumstances . . . Well, who can say at this point? Obviously, if the investigation is wound up, that will save Sergeant Baylis's family a good deal of suffering . . .'

Might also save you a good deal of adverse publicity, thought Carole.

'As yet, as I say, no decisions have been taken about the inquiry, but, because of its sensitive nature, I hope I can rely on your . . . absolute discretion.'

'Of course.' Carole's cases were solved. She had no interest in the unsavoury past deeds of the late Detective Sergeant Baylis.

One thing she did wonder, though . . . Had Lennie Baylis been tempted to supplement his income so that he could one day afford a property in Weldisham? Was he another wistful local boy, like Harry Grant, who wanted to demonstrate his success by moving back into the village where he had grown up?

'Thank you very much, Mrs Seddon. We appreciate your cooperation. Now there's someone else we have to see nearby . . . What was the address, Sergeant?'

A rustle of papers consulted. 'Woodside Cottage.'

'It's right next door.'

So Jude was going to get the same request to keep her mouth shut.

Chapter Fifty

The news that Graham Forbes had had a second stroke came to Jude via Gillie Lutteridge. As soon as she heard, she told Carole and they agreed she should ring his wife.

On the phone Irene Forbes sounded as poised and serene as ever. She gracefully accepted Carole's commiserations and hopes for her husband's speedy recovery. Graham was in a private hospital in Chichester. There hadn't been much change in his condition since the second stroke, but the consultant was optimistic about his chances for at least a partial recovery.

Irene was taken aback and seemed poised to say no when Carole asked if she could go to the hospital to visit. 'I would like to go with my friend Jude.'

'Jude . . .'

'The blonde woman who—'

'Yes. I know who you mean.' There was a silence, during which perhaps Irene Forbes was reliving her conversation with Jude. 'Very well, you'd better visit him. But go on your own. Graham hasn't met Jude. He can't cope with anyone new at the moment. Go before three o'clock today. I will be going to the hospital at three. He will be busy then.'

*

It was not easy to hear what Graham Forbes said. The stroke had pulled his face sideways, like a poster misapplied to a wall. Saliva dripped from the useless edge of his mouth.

But if Carole concentrated, she could understand him.

His thin body looked too long for the hospital bed in which it was coiled. He'd been prepared for her arrival, however. Presumably Irene had rung through and told him the visitor was on her way. Even in his debilitated state, Graham Forbes managed a courteous greeting.

Then he gasped out the words, 'Have you come to ask me if I'm sorry? Do you want me to say I regret what I did?'

'No,' said Carole.

'Just as well. Because I'll never say it. I can't say what I don't mean. I had twenty-eight years of misery married to Sheila, thirteen years of bliss living with Irene. I'm afraid, for me, those facts answer all the moral arguments.'

'"Thou shalt not kill"?'

His thin shoulders managed a shrug. 'That one too. Even in the days when I went along with the observances of organized religion, I never believed any of it. We have to make our own moral values, according to the circumstances in which we find ourselves. There's no absolute right or wrong. And we're only here once.' There was a cough that could have been a chuckle. 'Not that I'm here for a lot longer.'

'Can you just . . . would you mind . . . for my personal satisfaction . . . telling me if what I've worked out about what happened is actually right?'

'Oh, Carole, you been playing amateur detectives, have you?'

'Well . . .'

'All right, you spell out how you think the master criminal wove his evil schemes, and I'll tell you where you go wrong.'

So Carole did as she was told. Occasionally, Graham Forbes nodded, though she couldn't tell whether it was in appreciation of her cleverness or his own.

When she got to the events of Thursday 15 October, the night of the Great Storm, he couldn't help himself from taking up the narrative. 'I remember how miserable I'd been that evening, stuck in the house with a woman I had hated through most of our marriage, knowing that – if I didn't put my plan into action – in a few days I'd be back in KL and I'd see Irene again, and I wouldn't be bringing what I'd promised her.'

'What was that?'

'Myself. Free. I'd met Irene two years before. We both knew what we felt for each other, but she was very . . . proper. Had been brought up to do the right thing. Strange, really, Chinese girl, raised as an Anglican in Malaysia. Anyway, she made her rules clear. I was married. Nothing could happen to our relationship while I remained married. She didn't deny she loved me, but . . . Rather quaint and old-fashioned in these cynical days, isn't it?

'Anyway, before I left KL for that leave, I promised Irene I'd talk to Sheila about getting a divorce. And I did. Nothing. She wouldn't give an inch. Sheila wasn't going to give up her status as the memsahib out East, or as the Lady Bountiful back in Sussex. Since passion had never played any part in her life, she had no sympathy for what I was going through. So . . .'

He paused, exhausted by his confession.

'But you'd planned it,' Carole prompted gently. 'To

have time for Pauline to get her passport, you must have planned it.'

'Yes, I planned it, but I still didn't know whether I could carry it out. That was why I was so depressed the evening before the storm . . . because I thought I didn't have the guts . . . or I was too decent . . . too British . . . that I'd just accept my lot in life . . . and lose Irene.'

'When had you worked out your plan?'

'Soon after we came back for the beginning of that leave. Pauline was cleaning here one morning, and Sheila was being her usual hyper-critical self, bawling the woman out for not dusting on top of the picture rails or something, and they had a row. Suddenly, as the two of them stood toe to toe, shouting at each other, I realized how incredibly alike they looked. Once that seed was planted, the rest of the details fell into place.'

'But you still didn't think you'd summon up the nerve to carry it out?'

'No. I have the storm to thank for the fact that I did.'

'Oh?'

'The Great Storm started late the Thursday evening and got worse in the small hours. I remember, you could hear the wind getting louder and louder. And then gates began banging, windows rattling, dustbins being blown over, branches torn off trees. Well, all this noise . . .' He smiled a lopsided smile. 'It had the nerve to wake Sheila up. Never a good idea, as I'd discovered very early in our married life.

'And, of course, being Sheila, when something she didn't want to happen happened, she had to find someone to blame for it. And there, as ever, in the single bed beside hers, was me.

'So she starts in at me. Why hadn't I fixed the gates

more securely? Any husband worth his salt would have
had Warren Lodge's loose windows replaced. Why was I
so incompetent? It was all my fault.

'And that was it. I didn't mind being blamed for things
that I might possibly have done or failed to do, but to be
blamed for freaks in the weather . . .

'In one movement I rolled out of bed, put my hands
around her throat and squeezed harder than I'd ever
squeezed anything in my entire life . . .

Carole let the silence ride, till he broke it with a little
choke of laughter.

'Funny. The killing wasn't premeditated. But unavoidable. At the moment I did it, I couldn't have done
anything else to save my life.' He became aware of what
he'd said. 'Or indeed to save hers.

'I stayed still in the bedroom for a some time, while
the storm roared and crashed around outside the house.
And then, slowly, I realized it had all been meant. My
plan had been set up. I'd only lacked the nerve for the
vital moment of murder. The storm had given me that
nerve.

'Unlike Irene, I don't have any religious faith. But I
believe that moment was orchestrated for me by some
kind of higher power.'

'Be a strange kind of higher power that facilitates
murder.'

'Don't you believe it, Carole. Read some history. Start
counting up the number of wars that have been started
for reasons of religion.'

'Maybe. What happened then, Graham?'

'I was very organized. I wrapped Sheila's body in a
sheet, carried it down to the barn. With the way the storm
was still raging, I was in no danger of anyone seeing me.'

'But weren't you in danger of people going into the barn and finding the grave? Everyone in the village seems to use the place as a rubbish tip.'

'They do now. But it's only been happening the last five years or so. One person chucked in a fridge and . . . suddenly everyone was doing it. A nasty *element* has moved into the village recently, you know.' The was a slight edge of parody in his voice, sending up some of the crustier members of the Village Committee. He shrugged and turned his faded brown eyes on to Carole. 'And do you know, very soon after Sheila had died, I forgot about it. I could put it from my mind. My life was so much better, so much more fulfilling, that her death was something that was clearly meant to happen.'

'You weren't worried?'

'Not after the first few days, no.'

'And you didn't tell Irene what you'd done?'

'No. That was bad of me perhaps. When I got back to KL after . . .' He seemed amused as he thought of the word. 'After the murder . . . I didn't contact her for a week or so. Then, when I did, I gave her the story about Sheila having gone off with another man. Irene was so delighted to hear I was finally unencumbered that she didn't question me about the details.'

'So your life together has been based on a lie?'

'Don't go all po-faced on me, Carole. It doesn't suit you.'

She was appropriately contrite, before continuing, 'But when you heard I'd found the bones in South Welling Barn, didn't that worry you?'

'No. Never occurred to me they might be Sheila's.'

'Hadn't Brian Helling already made an approach to blackmail you?'

'No. I'd been out when he called. He spoke to Irene and she . . . kept it to herself.' He chuckled. 'Proverbially inscrutable, the Chinese.'

A lot of contradictory details explained themselves in Carole's mind – why Graham had seemed so insouciant when she first saw him in the Hare and Hounds, why Irene had been weeping in St Michael and All Angels. But another detail still needed clarification. 'So you didn't know they were Sheila's bones when you invited me to dinner?'

'Good lord, no.'

'Then why did you invite me?'

'I told you. Someone had dropped out. You seemed intelligent, literate . . . you did the *Times* crossword . . .'

So there had been nothing sinister about the invitation. Carole thought ruefully of the time she had wasted trying to work out the hidden agenda in Graham's gesture.

'And also,' he continued sheepishly, 'we did need someone to pair up with Barry Stillwell.'

The expression she turned on him didn't need words.

'Sorry about that, Carole. So there you have it. I may be guilty of many crimes, but inviting you to dinner was not among them . . . Unless of course you're of the – quite legitimate – view that inviting anyone to meet Barry Stillwell constitutes a crime.'

The old man's angular body made an attempt at a shrug. 'And that's it. You know the rest. You worked it all out. Well done.'

'Thank you.'

'What put you on to the fact that it was Pauline who went with me to KL?'

'You weren't met at the airport by your favourite driver. You'd talked about Shiva, how he always drove you everywhere in Malaysia, and yet you organized a new

317

driver at the airport, one who'd never seen your wife and who wouldn't realize that Pauline was an impostor.'

He nodded appreciation for her logic. Then a thought struck him. 'But who on earth did you get that information from?'

'Sebastian Trent.'

Graham Forbes winced with distaste. 'Him.'

'Doesn't he conform to your rule about all writers being *enormous fun*?'

'God, no. Sebastian Trent is a complete arsehole.'

There was a warm, mutual chuckle. Then Carole asked, 'Have you told all this to the police?'

'Oh yes. Told them everything. Made a clean breast of it. Confession eases the guilty soul, eh? And it brings other benefits too.'

'Like what?'

'After thirteen years of living a lie, poor old Sheila is now officially dead.' This time the cough was definitely a chuckle.

'And, for those who demand retribution, I'm being punished. It's no fun lying here like this, let me tell you. Had the first stroke when Lennie Baylis told me they'd be checking whether the bones belonged to Sheila, second when some other policeman came to charge me with her murder. I'd say that's my punishment . . . and a very big disincentive ever to leave this place.

'I want to die now,' he went on, but there was no unhappiness in his tone. 'And when I do die, I dare say you'll look back on my life as a crime story. I wouldn't. Nor will Irene. So far as we're concerned, my life has been a love story. But not any more . . .

'While I could do the things I wanted to do, I wanted to live. While I could be with Irene, love Irene, while I could use my mind, I wanted life to go on for ever. Now . . . I don't want to continue if I'm *impaired.*'

His choice of the exact word Irene had used to Jude made Carole realize how the two lovers must have discussed this eventuality, and prepared their reactions to it. Maybe that was the explanation for Irene Forbes's serenity in the face of tragedy.

'Even if they let me smoke in here, I couldn't keep the pipe in my mouth, so there's one of my pleasures gone. Can't even do the *Times* crossword either,' Graham Forbes went on wistfully. 'What's the point of being alive if you can't do the *Times* crossword?'

Carole noticed there was a copy of the paper at his bedside. The first section was folded back in the familiar way to frame the crossword. But the grid was blank.

'Come on, Graham,' she said softly. 'I'm sure you can fill in one answer . . .'

He grunted. 'Make it a very easy one.'

Her eyes were nowhere near the paper as Carole invented her clue. 'Pope's versified magistrate. Six and seven.'

'Good. Very good.' The side of his face that could smile smiled. 'Poetic Justice,' said Graham Forbes.

In the entrance hall of the hospital, Carole found Jude chatting to Irene Forbes. The latter was dressed in white and very animated. Girlish, almost giggly.

On the dot of three she was joined by a priest. Irene asked Carole and Jude if they'd be witnesses.

And, as the four of them went through to the private rooms, Carole realized what Graham Forbes had meant about the benefits of his first wife being officially dead.

Chapter Fifty-one

Brian Helling was charged with two murders – those of his mother and Lennie Baylis. He was also charged with the abduction of Carole Seddon. There was discussion in the Hare and Hounds as to whether his counsel would put up a defence of insanity, though the general view was that he was not mentally ill, just a bad lot. And, now the murder had happened, everyone was suddenly full of recollections of bad blood between Brian Helling and Lennie Baylis, the antagonism that went all the way back to their childhood.

But the British justice system ensured that the trial lay a long way off yet.

The Hare and Hounds got a new manager, and, so far as the residents of Weldisham were concerned, Will Maples slipped off the face of the earth. Whether he'd been sacked by Home Hostelries, whether he'd ever been charged with drugs-related offences, no one knew.

Harry Grant got his own builders started on the barn conversion. The plans had been approved, but members of the Village Committee watched night and day for any evidence of extraneous features sprouting on the building. The first sign of a turret or solarium and they'd be on to the local authority straight away. In Weldisham the

Neighbourhood Watch was generally more concerned about builders than burglars.

Meanwhile Jenny Grant increased her dosage of Librium and waited with mounting terror for the day when they'd have to move. Harry wouldn't be aware of it, but she knew they'd never be accepted in Weldisham. She anticipated spending the rest of her life in an isolation as total as that of Pauline Helling.

The old woman's spaniel, incidentally, was never seen again in the village after Heron Cottage burnt down. The police initially put the dog into their kennels, but soon arranged to have it adopted by a nice family with three young children in the adjacent village of Blundon. Nobody in Weldisham knew of the spaniel's fate. Blundon was three miles distant, and that was a long way away.

Graham Forbes didn't die immediately. He stayed in hospital, too ill to be moved to prison, too ill to appear in court, and his adoring second wife went to visit him every day. Sometimes he could do a few clues of the *Times* crossword; other days he looked at it as though it were in a foreign language.

Like Graham's, the health of Tamsin Lutteridge hovered between the positive and the negative. After Brian Helling's arrest, when his threat to her life no longer posed a danger, the girl had been visited at Sandalls Manor by her mother and Jude. They had gone in the full expectation of bringing Tamsin home to Weldisham with them. But they found her unwilling. She really thought that Charles Hilton's treatment was beginning to work.

And some days it was. Then she felt optimistic and positive. Other days she was listless and ached all over. But, until a real cure for her debilitating illness was found, what Charles Hilton did seemed neither better nor worse than any other treatment on offer.

He meanwhile continued to offer therapy, understanding and personal attention to his patients. The young, pretty female patients continued to get more personal attention than the others, and Anne Hilton continued to have suspicions but no proof.

Within two months of Brian Helling's arrest, Gillie and Miles Lutteridge had quietly separated and set divorce proceedings in motion. Gillie lived alone in Weldisham for a few months more and then their showhouse was sold to another Londoner who'd 'always wanted to live in the country'.

When he met this newcomer in the Hare and Hounds, Freddie Pointon put him at his ease, asserting what a wonderful place Weldisham was, and when he got out of the train at Barnham how really uplifted he felt by that first breath of country air.

Meanwhile, in their weekend cottage, Pam Pointon continued to get noisily pissed.

At a Ladies' Night of the local Rotary Club, Barry Stillwell met the widow of another past president. Since they both found life very interesting, they decided to get married.

It was a couple of weeks after her abduction, and Carole was sitting in the Crown and Anchor having an early evening drink with Jude. Carole had noticed her friend seemed a little subdued recently and deduced that the change of mood had something to do with the man Jude had spent the weekend with in London. But when she tried to find out more about the situation, the conversation kept doing its old trick of moving on to other subjects.

'You going to be all right this evening?'

'Yes, sure,' said Jude. 'I'll probably grab something to eat here, and then go back for a really long soak in the bath.'

'With all your aromatherapy oils?'

'You bet. My idea of bliss.' Jude didn't say that, before her bath, she planned to look through some estate agent's details for houses in Ireland. The break-up with that man had really unsettled her and she'd never stayed anywhere for long. She hadn't made any firm decision about moving yet, but it was a thought . . .

As usual, Carole had no idea what was going through her friend's mind. Her own was happily full, particularly of the new blouse she was wearing that night. Marks & Spencer's were getting in some quite designery things these days. Carole wouldn't have thought she could wear red, if she hadn't been so firmly told that it made her look great.

The door from the kitchen clattered open and Ted Crisp appeared. He was wearing a suit. Not only that, it was a suit he had had cleaned. And he was wearing the tie Carole had given him.

His hair and beard remained as unkempt as ever, which caused her a momentary pang of annoyance. But she quickly reassured herself. Rome wasn't built in a day. Time enough to get his hair – and a few other things – sorted.

Jude let out a low whistle. 'My God, it's Rudolph Valentino!'

'Rudolph the Red-nosed Reindeer more like,' said Ted.

Then he stepped round the bar and crooked out his arm in a self-consciously gallant manner.

'Mrs Seddon . . . are you ready to accompany me? And may I say how well you look in the red? Positively in the pink, if you'll pardon the expression.'

'Thank you,' said Carole, dropping a mock-curtsy before she took his arm.

'Where is it you're off to tonight?' asked Jude.

'New Mexican place just opened in Worthing,' Ted replied. 'Won't be able to move in there for sombreros and zimmer frames. Are we set then, Carole?'

'Certainly are.'

'Right. Good luck,' he called out to his bar staff. 'Don't drink all the profits. See you, Jude.'

'Yes, sure,' she said, and looked down into her drink.

Carole Seddon liked the bulk of Ted Crisp's arm against hers. And she looked forward to the evening ahead. She didn't have much to thank Barry Stillwell for, but at least he'd reminded her what a date was.

THE TORSO IN THE TOWN

Grant and Kim Roxby had hoped that their first dinner party at Pelling House would make an impression with their new neighbours. And the next day it's certainly the talk of the town of Fedborough. For their guests – including the couple's old friend Jude – had been enjoying a pleasant meal before they were rudely interrupted by a gruesome discovery. A human torso hidden in the cellar.

Jude races home to Fethering and her friend Carole with the news. And soon the pair are back in Fedborough, questioning the locals. But why is a town so notoriously distrustful of outsiders proving so terribly amenable to their enquiries? . . .

'A crime novel in the traditional style, with delightful little touches of humour and vignettes of a small town and its bitchy inhabitants'
Sunday Telegraph

The Torso in the Town, the third novel in the Fethering Mysteries series, is published by Pan Books. The opening scenes follow here.

Chapter One

'The other thing about Fedborough,' said Grant Roxby that evening before the torso was discovered, 'is that everybody mixes together. There are no social divisions.'

What? thought Jude. He's got to be talking about somewhere else.

Fedborough was a country town some eight miles inland from where the River Fether reached the sea at Fethering. The town's considerable architectural splendours attracted tourists throughout the year, in the summer its streets were clotted with the elderly contents of coaches and adolescent foreign language students, wandering around looking for something to do. Most ended up in the antique dealers, tearooms and gift shops. Fedborough was the perfect venue for someone trying to buy an antique brass bedpan, a cream tea or a china figurine of a ballet dancer, less suitable perhaps for those in search of basic groceries.

The assertion by her host that the town had no social divisions suggested to Jude the truth – that Grant Roxby hadn't lived in Fedborough very long. Her own life had more important priorities than where she stood in any social hierarchy – she judged people by their inner qualities rather than their backgrounds – but she could still recognize that Fedborough was riddled with class-consciousness.

The town's inhabitants, mostly well-heeled, cosseted by sensible pension arrangements and private health insurance, knew to a nicety where they stood in the middle-class pecking order. The people up the road had public school education and inherited money, so they were upper-middle-class. The people opposite had money from retail trade and no taste, so they were lower-middle-class. The couple in the next road, who seemed to have no money, but dressed in worn well-cut tweeds and spoke in patrician accents of relatives in the House of Lords, must be lower-upper-middle-class. And the people on the council estate were common.

What made these rules of Fedborough society even more complicated was that no two residents of the town saw them in exactly the same way. People whom the neighbours on one side would condemn as lower-upper-middle-class might be seen by their neighbours on the other side as upper-lower-middle-class. In England at the beginning of the twenty-first century the much-vaunted ideal of a classless society remained as far off as ever.

The permutations became more intricate still if you factored in the self-images of the individuals involved. As always in life, how the individual people of Fedborough saw themselves and how the world saw them were very different. The void between those two views led to much of the town's humour (from the viewpoint of an outside observer). And also to much of its tragedy.

Jude had often found herself in the role of an outside observer, particularly since she had moved to Fethering. A comfortably rounded woman in her fifties, she had blonde hair piled up in a random coil on her head, and a predilection for layers of floaty garments in a haphazard mix of colours and patterns. The resulting image should have been a mess, but somehow contrived to be stylish.

Jude had done many things in her life, but in conversation didn't volunteer much detail about any of them. She rarely got the chance. People found her easy to talk to, there was a warmth about her that invited confidences; on very brief acquaintance, total strangers frequently found themselves telling her their life stories. So they never got round to asking about hers. Which suited Jude very well.

She had met Roxby and his wife Kim on a holistic holiday in Spain. He had made an indecent amount of money in computers, and the Roxbys had at the time been 'looking for some dimension in our lives beyond the material'. The couple – particularly Grant – had embraced the various therapies, counselling and soul journeys available on the holiday with enormous butterfly enthusiasm. He had the ability – which must have been invaluable in his business career – to get completely caught up in the moment. His self-belief was total, and so was his belief in a new idea. The fact that the next day he could believe in an opposing idea with equal conviction never dented the self-belief. He liked to think that he went as deeply into everything as the very soul of his being, in fact, he went as deeply into everything as the sole of his shoe.

Grant Roxby's enthusiasms were infectious. His past was scattered with the husks of lifestyle options he had snatched up and discarded without recrimination or rancour. Jude wondered whether moving out of London to the country was just the latest in this series.

Certainly their relocation had had nothing to do with

her. She hadn't even lived in Fethering when she'd met Grant and Kim, but they'd quickly followed up on her change of address card when they moved into the area.

The Roxbys had, as ever, done the thing in style. Pelling House, the Fedborough mansion they had instantly settled on after one viewing, was a tall, late Georgian oblong, red-brick in the best sense, with three storeys and a cellar. The frontage boasted a classical white portico, and stone steps led down to Pelling Street, one of the town's most exclusive residential addresses. The rooms were high, with tall windows, which had folding shutters on the inside. There were two staircases, a rather grand one in the hall, and another at the back of the house, used in the past for invisible domestic stage management by the servants. The previous owners of Pelling House had made a start on renovating the property, but there was no doubt that Grant Roxby's computer-generated millions would soon be employed to complete the job to an even more exacting standard.

On the evening of the dinner party, any suggestion that moving to Fedborough had been a mere whim would have been condemned as sacrilege. Grant and his wife were totally caught up in their new dream. 'It's going to be so great for the children,' Kim enthused. She was a thin, blonde woman in her early forties, dressed down in designer-hippy, expensively cut jeans and mock-snakeskin cowboy boots. Grant, sleek with success, his hair an unlikely chestnut, wore Levi's, a blue fleece and leather moccasins. Their clothes struck a more casual note than those of their guests, except for Jude.

The two couples who'd been invited demonstrated the extremes of Fedborough fashions, and the resolution of the dilemma which must have faced them earlier in the evening: what level of dress do you think these new people expect? Donald and Joan Durrington had opted for the traditional. It wasn't difficult for him. As one of the local doctors he wore the uniform of a double-breasted pin-striped suit. If his bleeper summoned him he would look appropriate at a patient's bedside – or even deathbed. Because he was potentially on duty, Donald Durrington was drinking only mineral water, but his wistful air as he watched others' wine glasses being filled suggested he'd rather not be on duty.

His wife, who was also on the mineral water, had perhaps overdressed for the occasion, but only by comparison with the host and hostess's jeans. She was wearing a little black cocktail number, decorated round the top with spangly black beads. The chest revealed by the décolletage was freckled and slack; its depth suggested greater confidence than did her uneasy blue eyes. Her hair had been recently and neatly cut; also recently blonded. Given the thinness of her frame, her face was surprisingly broad, puffy under heavy make-up. Though she hadn't contributed much to the general conversation, earlier in the evening Joan Durrington had spoken with trepidation of her approaching sixtieth birthday. Trepidation, indeed, seemed to be her dominant emotion. She kept looking nervously at her husband, as though fearful she might in some way let him down.

The Burnethorpes, Alan and Joke, were at the more casual end of the clothes spectrum. He, trying to look younger than his late forties, wore a collarless black shirt and black jeans, with a rough-knit grey sloppy cardigan on top. She, fabulously toned and twenty-eight, wore what looked like a track suit in a burgundy crushed velvet. Her English was excellent, her Dutch origins betrayed only by a tendency to say 'dat' and 'dere' for 'that' and 'there'. On introduction, Jude had been told that the name was pronounced 'Yo-kah', though, as Alan said with practised ease, 'the spelling's a joke'. Then, in case she hadn't got it, he'd spelled out, 'J-O-K-E.'

It had been established early in the evening that he was an architect whose office was a converted houseboat near Fedborough Bridge, and that this was his second marriage. Joke had been working in Fedborough, they had met and fallen in love, so the first Mrs Burnethorpe and two children had been put out to grass. Joke, in her turn, had quickly produced two children; her conversation was dominated by their skills and charms. Alan, having been through the process before, seemed less ecstatic about their growing family. But he was clearly still obsessed by his young wife. His eyes hardly left her during the evening. He looked capable of deep jealousy.

On the other hand, he still had an eye for other women. On being introduced to Jude, he had repeated her name and looked deeply into her brown eyes. His hand had held hers that moment too long and too tightly, immediately identifying him as one of those men who believe themselves to be irresistible to the opposite sex.

The eighth member of the party, matching Jude's single state, was the local vicar, the Rev Philip Trigwell. Of thinning hair and blotchy complexion, he'd reached the stage of unattractiveness that comes with age, and gave the impression that he'd never gone through the stage of attractiveness that can come with youth. Being of the school of clergy that doesn't believe in thrusting religion down people's throats, he wore an ordinary collar and tie, and spent the entire evening avoiding mention of his profession. He also seemed deeply aware of potential flashpoints in Fedborough society, and on any subject expressed no opinion which was not immediately counter-balanced by the opposite opinion. If the Roxbys are matchmaking and have lined up the Rev Philip Trigwell for me, thought Jude, they have seriously wasted their time.

The dinner party could not have been described as 'sticky', but then again nor was it particularly relaxed. Dinner parties were not Jude's favourite social events under any circumstances and, with the Roxbys having only just moved, they had assembled an *ad hoc* guest list for the occasion.

The mix was, she reflected, pretty standard for new-comers to a town. She was the one old – though not close – friend, met somewhere else. The Roxbys would have encountered the local vicar and the local doctor in the natural course of events – being visited by the one as part of his parochial duties, registering with the other. And she'd put money on the fact that Alan Burnethorpe was the architect Grant and Kim had consulted about the extensive alteration plans they had for the old house that was new to them.

So the Roxbys had made their first social foray in Fedborough predictable enough, while the long-estab-lished principle of reciprocal entertainment would ensure that they soon met other locals and, presumably in time, came across some they got on really well with.

The established Fedborough residents – the Durring-tons, the Burnethorpes and the Rev Trigwell – all knew each other, and most of their conversation revolved around mutual acquaintances whose foibles and back-ground they kept having to explain to the newcomers. For the Roxbys, characteristically enthusiastic to immerse themselves in the new community, presumably these explanations were relevant, but they failed to hold Jude's attention. There is something stultifying in being constantly told 'he's a character' about people one is unlikely ever to meet, particularly when the accompanying illustrative anecdote suggests that the person in question has very little character at all. Jude was beginning to get the impression that not a lot happened in Fedborough.

'Yes,' Kim Roxby was saying now, 'kids can breathe when they get out into the country.'

'I'd hardly call Fedborough "country",' objected Alan Burnethorpe. 'I was brought up here and it's very definitely a town.' Lacking the professional restraint imposed on Donald Durrington, he was letting himself go with Grant Roxby's excellent choice of Chilean and New Zealand wines.

'But country's so readily accessible from here. All of the South Downs to walk on, and you can follow the Fether for miles, you know. And then all those beaches to wander over. Still, I don't know why I'm telling you all this. You know. You must spend all your spare time taking walks like that.'

Kim's pronouncement prompted a slightly embarrassed concert of throat-clearing. It had marked her out irredeemably as a 'townie'. Few people who actually live in the country ever walk further than they have to, and then only if they've got dogs.

'But also the health factors,' she persevered. 'London – all big cities – are so choked with pollution these days. I feel happier knowing my children will be out breathing healthy country air. There are so many less allergies in the country.'

'I wish that were true,' said Donald Durrington with

professional gloom. 'The number of kids I see through my surgery with asthma and similar complaints . . . you wouldn't believe. It's partly the pesticides and other pollutants out in the country. Then, of course, living in centrally heated houses and being ferried around in cars all the time doesn't help. Compared to ours, the next generation are incredibly vulnerable to infections.'

'Oh.'

Kim was cast down for a moment, and Joke Burnethorpe muscled in to shift the conversation. 'How many children do you have, Kim?'

'Three.'

'For our sins,' Grant threw in meaninglessly.

'What ages?'

'Harry's fifteen . . .'

'With all that that entails,' Grant added darkly.

'Tina's thirteen . . .'

'Going on twenty-five.'

'And Grace is eleven . . .'

'And she can twist all of us round her little finger.' Grant chuckled.

Joke Burnethorpe looked across the empty laid-up place at the dinner table. 'I thought you said Harry was going to join us.'

'Ye-es.' Grant Roxby looked flustered.

Kim came to his rescue. 'You've just got the two kids?' Her question was completely gratuitous. Since she'd arrived, Joke Burnethorpe had talked about nothing else.

'That's right. Caspar and Linus.'

'Ah.'

Donald Durrington cleared his throat. His wife watched him nervously, as if afraid he was about to reveal some deeply protected secret.

But he didn't. All he said was, 'Have you thought about schools at all yet?'

Oh dear, thought Jude, is it going to be one of *those* dinner parties?

But it didn't develop that way. Joke Burnethorpe, who Jude had already assessed as a very strong-willed young woman, persisted with her line of questioning. 'So where *is* Harry?'

Grant again seemed embarrassed by the question, and a moment of marital semaphore passed between husband and wife. 'He must've got caught up in . . . you know what they're like at that age . . . some computer game . . . something on the internet—'

'Or just exploring the house,' Kim cut in; and then, as though such a pursuit were somehow more respectable than computer games or the internet, she went on, 'All the children are fascinated by history, you know, and this house is full of history.'

'So's all of Fedborough,' said the Rev Trigwell, pausing for a moment to check that this statement had not been controversial. Reassured, he continued, 'You must get James Lister to take you on one of his Town Walks. He's a real character, James . . . though of course in the nicest possible way,' he concluded weakly.

'Oh, yes, a great character,' Donald Durrington agreed. 'I tell you, it was very amusing during the Fedborough Festival a couple of years back when . . . well, let's say the drink had flowed liberally in the Sponsors' Tent and Jimmy had indulged rather more than his wife Fiona would have approved of and—'

But the anecdote which was to detail James Lister's qualification as 'a character' would have to be wheeled out some other time. A child's scream was heard from downstairs. Seconds later, Harry Roxby burst in through the dining-room door. He carried a large rubber-covered torch, which was switched on. His face was so red Jude could hardly see the spots which had been prominent earlier, and his eyes were staring.

'Dad!' he shouted in sheer childish terror. 'We've found a dead body in the cellar!'

Visit **www.panmacmillan.com** to read more about all our books and to buy them. You will also find features, author interviews and news of any author events, and you can sign up for e-newsletters so that you're always first to hear about our new releases.

www.panmacmillan.com

GIFT SELECTOR
YOUR ACCOUNT
WISH LIST
WAITING LIST

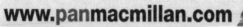
HOME | ABOUT US | IMPRINTS | TRADE/MEDIA | CONTACT US | ADVANCED SEARCH | SEARCH | GO

BOOK CATEGORIES | WHAT'S NEW | AUTHORS/ILLUSTRATORS | BESTSELLERS | READING GROUPS

Coming Soon...

Reading Groups

Competitions
Feeling Lucky?

Extracts
Sneak Previews

Interviews

Events
Meet Our Stars

Reviews
What The Critics Say

News & Awards

Editor's Choice
What We're Reading